SMILODON

ROBERT M. KERNS

KFP

Published by Knightsfall Press
PO Box 280
Mineral Wells, WV 26150

ABOUT THIS BOOK

A hapless hiker. A rogue cougar. An outcome no one expected.

Wyatt took a dead-end job in his hometown for two reasons: hiking, and being close to his family. When trekking over the trails he loves, he comes face to face with a cougar he cannot avoid.

As the pre-eminent hunter for the Shifter Nations of North America, Gabrielle isn't surprised when the Shifter Council calls her. A rogue cougar has been killing hikers. The job: put the beast down, and do it fast. She has never failed a hunt.

The trail leads her to the site of a fierce, bloody battle. She finds a wounded hiker, a dead cougar, and one inescapable conclusion.

There's a new cat in town.

A cool breeze rustled the leaves of the surrounding trees, tugged at my clothes and brushed my face to say hello as it made its way on down the valley. The breeze smelled of pine, spruce, and a fresh rain. I always loved the smell of a forest after a good rainstorm. That's why I took the day off from work to go hiking.

I stepped out of the partial shade created by the tree cover and stood on the rock shelf I knew so well. It overlooked the valley sprawling below me, and like so many times before, the sheer magnificence of nature lightened my soul. I eased my backpack's straps off my shoulders and removed the belt carrying my grandfather's knife, because the knife's length was such that it jabbed its pommel into my ribs when I sat on the ground. In form, it resembled the Bowie knife, but the strange markings engraved into the blade gave it an almost sinister character. Grandpa always told me those engravings were magic runes, but I'd seen nothing to make me believe that, of course. Magic—like Santa Claus—didn't exist. I slid the sheathed knife through the carry handle of my backpack and returned my attention to the vista before me.

There was no explaining the complete and total peace this place inspired in me, and it was because of this very trail —more than any other reason—that I refused to leave the dead-end tech job at a company that forgot to pay me as often as not. This valley was home. It was where I belonged.

I don't know how long I sat there. Well... not precisely. The sun warmed my back when I sat, and it glared in my eyes and heated my chest when I stood. So several hours at least. I would have stayed, but I still wanted to reach the small lake at the end of the trail and make it back to my car by nightfall. As much as I loved this trail and the surrounding woods, there was a reason it didn't have any campsites. Weird stuff happened in this stretch of the national forest. The stories dated back beyond when my grandfather had been a little boy. He said those stories were why he gave me the knife and made me promise to carry it whenever I hiked this trail.

I stretched one more time, rolling my shoulders and twisting from side to side. I wasn't as young as I used to be, and my body was stiff from sitting on the rock shelf for so long. I guess the human body really was made to move.

A rustle in the underbrush behind me drew my attention as I leaned over to grab my backpack. I could tell something stalked just out of sight, but there wasn't enough of a gap in the foliage to see what. Unfortunately, I didn't have to wonder long. A massive mountain lion stepped onto the edge of the rock shelf, looking right at me. Both of us froze. Well... I froze. The mountain lion just stopped. What struck me most were its eyes. In all my years volunteering at nearby zoos and animal hospitals or rescues, I had never seen a mountain lion that carried such intelligence in its gaze. I tried to angle myself to put my back toward the trail I'd just hiked and took a half-step backward, giving the big cat a little more space. It complemented my movement with a

2

half-step of its own, and what's more, it bared its teeth in a silent snarl.

I bit back a sigh. This would not end well.

$$\sim$$

GABRIELLE BARELY SWALLOWED a snarl as she led her team through the national forest. They were tracking a rogue cougar, and he'd already killed ten people so far. She was the best hunter for the job—the best hunter period full stop—and a part of her seethed that the Shifter Council hadn't given her this task when the toxicology report came back on the first person mauled to death. The rogue cougar stalking the national forest was a shifter, and no human hunting party from the Forest Service had any hope of finding him, let alone dealing with him. Not unless they fielded the better part of a battalion to get the job done.

The sole bright spot in the cougar's rampage was that he killed his victims. Shifters—like vampires—could turn humans into shifters. A turned shifter was never as powerful as a born shifter, with a few exceptions so rare they were almost fables, but they still made humans seem like weak, undeveloped children in comparison. If life had existed in any of the victims—even the minutest sliver of life—they'd now have ten new cougars on their hands... and if whatever drove the rogue in its slaughter was a sickness, he could pass that sickness to anyone he turned.

She spied tracks in a stretch of mud that was still damp from the recent rain, and Gabrielle stopped and knelt. The stride here was closer to a walk, and by the far end of the mud, the stride looked closer to a stalk. Gabrielle glared at the tracks for just a moment. Then, she closed her eyes and reached out to the part of her that wasn't human... and never had been.

The wind had shifted at some point. It no longer drifted down the valley. Now, it blew into their faces, and there was... something. She identified the normal scents of the forest and set them aside. There was something there, but she was too limited in human form to identify it. A very feline-like huff escaped her.

So be it. There was more than one way to chase a cat.

"Hey," Gabrielle said, as she pushed herself back to her feet. The other members of her team all turned to her. "I'm going over behind that big oak to shift. There's something on the wind. Bring my pack, please, and try to keep up."

Nods and affirmative vocalizations came back to her, and she nodded once. She turned and made her way to the large oak tree that was more than sufficient to grant her some privacy. She never understood why all the humans writing shifter fiction just seemed to assume shifters would take a casual approach to nudity. Sure, sometimes one didn't have other options, but no shifter she'd ever met liked to walk around naked as the day they were born.

It was a quick task to strip and stuff her clothes into her pack, tying her boots to a convenient carabiner she kept for such an occasion. Then it was a simple matter to touch the part of her mind that had never been human, for unlike a couple of people in her party, Gabrielle was a born shifter.

The change was also unlike most shifter fiction depicted. Everyone seemed to think it would hurt... or the human would just wink out and the animal would appear. But for Gabrielle it was neither uncomfortable nor immediate, and every born shifter she asked described an experience like hers. The change was as normal as standing up, sitting down, or walking across a room. Yes, she felt her physical form shifting. Her limbs shortened. Her muzzle elongated. But there was no pain. There was no discomfort. In fact, there were times it felt like she was coming home, becoming the truest version of herself.

The change complete, Gabrielle enjoyed a moment to luxuriate in her form. Stretch all four legs. Flex her claws. Lash her tail. She only took a couple of heartbeats, though. She had an important task.

Cats did not have the same quality of olfactory sense that canines do, but cats weren't exactly nose-blind, either. She opened her mouth and took a slow, deep breath, drawing the air across the roof of her mouth. She closed her eyes and concentrated. A second breath. The forest was normal, not important. She didn't care about the scent of pine or mint or spruce. The cougar's scent was faint, hours old but still recent enough to identify. And there it was. Human. The cougar had new prey.

Gabrielle hoped she would be in time as she darted out from behind the oak.

IT WAS ALWAYS an experience hunting with Gabrielle. Almost every predator shifter was a natural hunter, but Gabrielle was in a class by herself. She held several medals and titles from various shifter hunting games or contests. Several of her hunting party turned toward the tree as a four-legged shadow shot across the track they'd been following and disappeared into the forest's undergrowth.

A melanistic jaguar. One type of the so-called black panther. Gabrielle.

One of the veteran hunters stared at the patch of foliage where the jaguar vanished and sighed. He muttered, "Keep up, my ass," even though every shifter around him heard it with ease. Then, at a normal volume, "Well, gang… we just became the clean-up crew."

~

My ARMS ACHED. I just finished the third run-through of all the ways they say to drive away a mountain lion. On the bright side, it wasn't snarling at me anymore, but I'd swear the thing was smiling at me. Like I was funny. Like it knew what I was doing and why... but didn't care. I took a half-step backward while waving my arms. I knew my backpack was behind me somewhere, and Grandpa's knife could mean the difference between being a survivor or cat chow.

Then, the scariest thing yet occurred. I watched the mountain lion shift its gaze from me to something behind me. Its eyes seemed to narrow, almost like it glared at the object of its focus, and then it shifted its eyes back up to mine. In that moment, I knew it wasn't just looking toward me. It stared directly into my eyes. The snarl came back with more force, and it made a standing lunge.

Oh shit.

The cat's forepaws hit my chest, and its weight and momentum drove me to the ground. My head struck the butt of my grandpa's knife and continued down to slam into the rock shelf. The mountain lion screamed and came in to rip out my throat, but I jammed my left forearm between its jaws. Yeah, I know... stupid move, but I could survive a broken or amputated arm. I haven't known the human yet that could survive a ripped-out throat.

Not content with gnawing on my arm, the mountain lion shredded my jacket and shirt with its claws. It wasn't long until those claws found my torso, and I let out a scream of my own. Panic tried to set in, and I struck the mountain lion's neck with my right fist while it continued to maul me. I felt the claws rake across my bones, and I knew I wasn't leaving this rock shelf alive. But that didn't mean this cat wouldn't earn it.

Beating the thing's neck wasn't making any headway, and as I tried controlling the cat's head with my forearm it was gnawing on, I figured why not? With all the panicked force I could muster, I drove the toe of my hiking boot between the cat's hind legs. It rewarded me with a pain-fueled scream and jumped back. Yeah... I don't care what species of mammal you are, no male enjoys getting kicked in the balls.

The pause in the fight gave me the few necessary heartbeats to grab my grandpa's knife, open the retaining strap, and flick the sheath into the underbrush. Since I still figured I wasn't living through this fight, I didn't really care what happened to the knife's sheath... as long as I had the knife.

I brought the blade around, and the movement drew the cat's focus. It snarled at the sight of the knife. I glanced at it myself and gaped. Those engraved runes on the knife's blade glowed with an eerie silver radiance. Well, damn... I guess the runes were magic after all.

For what felt like the longest time, the big cat just stared at me, its eyes shifting from me to the knife and back again. I would've sworn it recognized the knife and was gauging its chances. As I grew weaker with blood loss, it must've decided its chances were still good, because it returned its eyes to mine and lunged at me.

The pain of wedging my savaged left forearm between its jaws again drowned out any remnant of the agony I felt merely lifting my arm into position. But I didn't care. If I was going down, I wanted to do everything I could to take this cat with me.

I thrust the knife toward the cat's side, expecting I'd have to force it through its hide and muscles and tissue. The moment the tip of the blade touched the cat, that eerie radiance flared, and the knife slipped inside with almost no resistance at all. The cat screamed around my forearm, much louder and much more anguished than when I'd kicked it, and it redoubled its efforts to kill me just as I redoubled my own.

Stab after stab. Claw swipe after claw swipe. Our reason for existing came down to ending this fight and taking the other with us. I regretted not taking Biology now. Several stabs in, and I still hadn't found the damn cat's heart. It breathed heavy and labored, though, so I hoped I'd at least punctured a lung. But still, it wouldn't let go.

It wasn't long before my strength waned. Darkness rimmed my vision. I was dying. I could feel it. The oddest part was the sudden clarity. The lack of panic. Well, damn. I had a knife, and the cat had a throat. I picked a point as close to halfway between the cat's jaws and its shoulders as I could and raked my blade across its throat. Blood erupted from the gash and threatened to drown me in the deluge.

Now, the fight left the mountain lion. Finally. I used its collapse as its own strength waned to push it to my side. If I had to die, I didn't want to die buried under a massive cat corpse. Something about that just seemed like adding insult to injury.

My last thought as the world faded around me was that, at least, the mountain lion would harm no one else. I heard my knife striking the rock shelf, and then there was nothing.

GABRIELLE RAN at a pace she could maintain for miles; she didn't want to face the rogue fatigued after a long sprint. She heard the cougar's screams, and she smelled the blood in the air. She wanted to believe she might still arrive in time, but in her heart, she knew she was too late.

She broke through the foliage onto a rock shelf and almost skidded to a stop. The scene was gruesome. A cougar with multiple stab wounds to its torso and a vicious slash across its throat lay beside a man with a shredded chest and mangled arm. Blood drenched the man, and a smaller pool formed around the cougar's corpse.

Something about the scene felt wrong. No shifter would die of the wounds she could see on the cougar. Yes, a throat slash would take a shifter out of the fight, but unless you followed up with a beheading or used a shifter-bane weapon, the shifter would heal. The cougar's wounds showed no sign of healing, and the man... oh, shit. The man's wounds were closing. He was still alive.

Her eyes fell on the knife laying just outside the man's right hand, and she padded closer for a better view. When she saw the runes in the blade, she hissed and almost jumped back. It was a shifter-bane blade. But the man couldn't be Magi. Shifters couldn't turn Magi; they were not technically human.

She moved closer, low and slow. Stalking the blade as if it were alive. Reaching a vantage point for the crossguard, she saw what she sought. The blade's artisan stamped the family mark into the blade just below the crossguard, and for the first time in a long while, Gabrielle felt true terror. That family mark was the Magnusson Glyph. The Magnusson clan was old, old power... ancient, even. No one really knew how far back their family went. This man—whoever else he might be—was Connor Magnusson's family.

Shit. This would not end well.

A listair Cooper sat at his desk. He savored the French vanilla wafting through the space; it was just strong enough to enjoy without overpowering his wolf-shifter senses. He never waded into the mind-numbing drudgery the Shifter Council called reports without putting a fresh candle in the warmer. Only a small sliver of the stack remained when the sound of voices raised in heated exchange overpowered the crackling of the paper in his hands. He recognized Gabrielle's voice almost at once and returned the form that had been his focus to its stack. Then, he cleared his desk of anything throw-able or flammable or otherwise spoilable and leaned back against his chair to wait.

"I don't care what family the kid's from," a man's voice said, muffled slightly by the thick oak door. "We should have killed him."

"Dammit, Jack! How stupid are you? Do you honestly think Connor Magnusson would just accept that his family-member disappeared in the national forest?" Gabrielle shot back.

Wham! Wham! The impact of what sounded like a

clenched fist on the outside of his office door seemed just high enough for Gabrielle's shoulder. Jack Hastings, the other veteran hunter he'd sent with the team, was almost a full foot taller.

"Welcome back, Gabrielle," Alistair said, loud enough for her to hear him. "Do come in."

The oaken door swung open on silent hinges, and Gabrielle strode inside. Her steady, relentless gait brought back memories of Patton's forced march to Bastogne. Jack closed the door behind him and followed her, stopping at her side.

"All right, you two," Alistair said. "Let's take a moment to step back and regain our calm."

Jack bowed his head and closed his eyes, while Alistair watched Gabrielle continue to glare at Jack. Once or twice, he saw her pupils shift to vertical slits, a testament to her fury if she needed so much effort to keep her human form. After a few seconds of Gabrielle not calming at all, Alistair swallowed a sigh.

"Very well. One of you, tell me what this is all about," Alistair said. "I heard you a few seconds before you... ahem... knocked."

Jack's head shot up, and he said, "We weren't able to catch the cougar before he claimed another victim, but this victim killed the cougar without dying. Gabrielle insisted on bringing him back here to the infirmary when we should have just finished him."

Alistair nodded. "I see. And how does Connor Magnusson fit into this?"

"I'm as certain as I can be that the victim is Magnusson's family," Gabrielle answered. "He used a shifter-bane blade with the Magnusson glyph to kill the rogue."

Alistair gave a few slow nods, then pierced Jack with his gaze. "And why were you advocating killing him, Jack?"

"We don't need another crazy mountain lion, Alistair. I don't care what family he's from. I don't see how we can take the chance the rogue's madness wasn't a sickness."

Alistair worked his lower lip between his teeth, bringing his eyes back to his desk. No matter how he turned the matter over in his mind, there didn't seem to be a 'right' answer. Yes, there was a truce between the Magi and the shifters, but that truce was uneasy. Very uneasy. It was only a dozen years old, plus or minus, and that didn't even equate to a blink of the eye for either side.

"And you're certain the cougar turned the boy, and it wasn't just a regeneration charm or something like it?" Alistair asked, looking to Gabrielle.

She shook her head. "The cougar turned him, Alistair. By the time we made it back here, he already smelled like a shifter."

"Another mountain lion in our ranks," Alistair grunted.

"No, sir," Gabrielle countered. "I don't think so. His scent isn't like any mountain lion I've ever tracked."

Alistair's eyebrows quirked upward. "It isn't?"

Gabrielle shook her head. "He's definitely a feline shifter. I just can't tell what breed. I've never encountered a feline shifter with his scent before."

Alistair felt a pit forming in his gut. If Gabrielle couldn't recognize his scent, the scent was still in flux, or... no. There was no way—no way at all—that he could be a primogenitor. Primogenitor shifters were beyond rare, and they most often occurred in the more prevalent shifter lines... like the wolves. Alistair could think of only two dire wolf shifters in the world, but he'd never heard of the cats producing a primogenitor.

"Yes... well, I'm sure his scent is still in flux," Alistair remarked. "We have that sometimes with turned shifters. I've also come to agree with your decision, Gabrielle. I see no outcome from us killing Connor Magnusson's family that isn't bad, whereas allowing him to live just might prove beneficial in the long run."

"Okay, fine. Junior gets to live," Jack growled, "but that still doesn't excuse Gabrielle from securing that vile blade with the possessions we recovered. We should destroy that blade now... while we have the chance."

Gabrielle resumed her glare at Jack. "For all your skills as a hunter, you're still an idiot, Jack. Just how do you think it would play out when he goes to visit Connor and tells him that he lost the blade? Or better yet, that his new shifter friends destroyed it before he woke up? Are you trying to get us killed? And beyond that, just how do you propose we touch the thing to destroy it, anyway? Sure... bane weapons should only harm their targets when used, not simply carried, but do you really want to risk it?"

Alistair fought to maintain his non-expression. He found Gabrielle's passionate assault on Jack's statement far too enjoyable. He cleared his throat and said, "We'll leave what to do with the blade up to the young man. I can't imagine he'd want to keep it, but he might want to return it to his grandfather once he understands both its nature and his. Is there anything else?"

Jack looked like he still wanted to argue his case, but he clenched his jaw and shook his head.

Gabrielle shook her head, saying, "No, sir. Thank you."

"Thank you both," Alistair said, nodding once to signal his dismissal.

Both Jack and Gabrielle returned his nod, then pivoted and left his office. Alistair waited until he heard the door latch to heave a sigh, and his thoughts drifted to an ancient Chinese curse: May you live in interesting times. There was no doubt in his mind the coming weeks—perhaps even the coming months—would be very interesting.

~

Damn, I'm sore. When I woke up, the first thought in my mind was how my entire body ached. Wait… I thought I was dying. Aw, damn. There's no way I'm dead; I cannot believe the afterlife smells like that nasty hospital disinfectant when it's not diluted enough. Holy cow… did they dunk me in a tub of the stuff?

I tried opening my eyes, and for the first moment or so, all I could do was blink. It was all so bright… and white. The ceiling tiles, the curtain surrounding my bed. Everything I could see was a bright white. I felt like I'd been lying down too long, and I wanted to sit up at least. I didn't feel like I had an IV or anything like that, but I still checked myself just to be sure. Nope. Nothing.

I pushed back the covers and swung my feet over the side of the bed. The world spun around me when I rolled myself into a sitting position. It settled down after a few moments of light-headed weaving, and I looked around my space. My backpack leaned against the wall beside the head of my bed. Ah, ha. There we go.

Even though I should probably have waited to speak with a doctor, I didn't feel bad per se, beyond the world spinning like a top for a heartbeat or three. And since I'd never been one for hospitals, it was time to expedite my departure. I had to get back to my sucky job, if nothing else.

I moved from sitting on the edge of the bed to standing without the world spinning again, and I took the couple steps necessary to reach my backpack. I felt a wave of unsteadiness pass through me as I leaned over to pick up my pack, but I pressed my hand against the wall for support. I lifted my pack to the bed and withdrew the extra set of clothes I always carried when hiking. Because you know, life happens. I thought it odd that my grandpa's knife was inside

14

my pack, in its sheath with the belt wrapped around it, but I already had enough weird things to think about. I'd save that one for later.

In short order, I whisked off the awful hospital gown and started getting dressed. By the time I finished buttoning up my shirt, I couldn't shake the feeling that my clothes didn't feel right. It was odd, and I couldn't really explain it. I pushed it to the back of my mind to be something else I'd examine later.

My hiking boots awaited me on the floor by the foot of the bed, and flecks of dried blood now dotted them. I lifted them to my nose and took a quick sniff. Yep... that's blood, all right. Well, nothing for it. I needed shoes, and the insides of the boots didn't look bad. I'd wear them out of here—wherever here is—and replace them later.

I was lacing up the second boot when I heard a woman's voice.

"Hiya, doc! How's your newest patient?"

"Hello, Gabrielle," a man replied, his voice carrying the hint of a New England accent and sounding resigned. "He was still sleeping, the last I checked, but you're welcome to see for yourself."

Before I could react, a shadow approached the curtains surrounding my bed, and I watched two arms reach up and pull the curtains back. The woman had a dark complexion, and she gaped at me sitting on the bed and lacing up my boot. Maybe eastern Mediterranean or Middle Eastern?

"Uh, doc? He's not sleeping anymore," she said.

"He isn't?" The man replied, and footfalls preceded a middle-aged man arriving at the woman's side. Wavy, snow white hair covered his head, and he wore the classic white lab coat. I watched his eyes take in the whole of me, moving from my head to my feet and back before he remarked, "No, it seems he isn't. How do you feel, young man?"

I shrugged. I couldn't help it. "Okay, I guess. I mean, I feel sore all over, but it's no worse than after a long hike. Except it seems like everything aches, not just my muscles. My head swam a little when I first sat up, but that only happened the one time."

The HVAC system kicked on and delivered faint food smells within seconds. I realized I was starving as my stomach rumbled so loud it sounded like a kitchen disposal. Both the woman—Gabrielle, apparently—and the doctor looked at my stomach. Gabrielle grinned.

"I believe it would be good to get our patient some food," the doctor remarked.

Gabrielle turned to the doctor, lifting an eyebrow. "Our patient?"

The doctor looked at Gabrielle and smiled. "Excellent. I knew I could count on you." He turned back to me, saying, "If you develop any new symptoms, come back. Gabrielle can explain everything else."

"Now, wait a minute, Doc!" Gabrielle protested. "Since when did I become the orientation staff?"

The doctor smiled again and added a shrug. "Eh... why not?"

Then he turned and ambled over to his desk.

Gabrielle glared at the man for a moment before turning back to her newest charge. She held out her hand. "Hi, I'm Gabrielle, though you probably caught that."

I smiled and accepted her hand. Our handshake was firm. It wasn't a crush contest, but it wasn't a limp-wristed affair, either. "It's nice to meet you, Gabrielle. I'm Wyatt Magnusson."

Gabrielle nodded. We ended our handshake by unspoken mutual assent. She turned and started walking toward the door, asking, "You any relation to Connor Magnusson?"

"He's my grandfather," I said, adding a nod as I picked up my pack by its carry handle. "Have you met him?"

Gabrielle shook her head. "No. I only know of him, but 'Magnusson' isn't such a common name."

I grinned. "No, it isn't."

Gabrielle led me down a short hallway, around a corner, and through a door. We left the building, and I found myself on what looked like the main street of a small country town. Moving from inside to outdoors gave the sun a splendid opportunity to assault my eyes, and the food smells were stronger than ever. My stomach growled again. A general store stood straight across the street from us, and just to the left of it, I saw a diner.

"Welcome to Precious," Gabrielle said as we crossed the street. Even at mid-morning—judging by the sun—the street wasn't too busy.

I blinked. "I've heard of this town. We're about an hour from where I live."

Gabrielle nodded. "I led a hunting party tasked with locating and eliminating the rogue cougar, and when we found you, we brought you back here."

That brought it all back to me in a rush. Sitting on the rock shelf. The attack. The desperate fight just to take the big cat with me into death.

"So, Gabrielle... how am I alive? That mountain lion shredded my chest and possibly broke my arm. I don't understand how I'm up and walking around. I don't even know what day it is."

Gabrielle stepped onto the sidewalk and stopped. She turned to face me, and her expression informed me there was a serious and potentially unpleasant topic awaiting me.

"Look, Wyatt... there's some stuff we need to discuss. It won't be easy, and I don't want to discuss it with you on an empty stomach. As long as your stomach growls like it has been, you won't be able to focus on anything else. It's not horrible or anything, really; it's... it's just a life-changing discussion that requires your focus. Okay?"

Well, damn. That wasn't ominous or anything. But she was right; the main thing on my mind was food. I nodded. "Good call. Let's eat, then talk."

Gabrielle led me into the diner, and I almost couldn't believe my eyes. The dining area was immense. It was like someone took a military mess hall or large high school cafeteria and built a bar and kitchen onto one side of it. People occupied many tables, and as we stepped through the door, the buzz of conversation faded to silence as everyone stared at us. Or rather... me.

The silence extended, became awkward. A great hulking brute of a man stood from a table about halfway into the room and approached us. He had to be six and a half feet tall if he was an inch, and he was one of those guys whose muscles had muscles. The underlying arrogance of his expression and swagger reminded me of all those asshole jocks in school that loved to push around anyone weaker than they were.

"What do you think you're doing in here?" He stopped about ten feet away. "You don't belong here."

It sounded like Gabrielle growled as she stepped forward. "Not now, Buddy. He needs food, and we don't—"

"Stow it, Gabby," the brute shot back, adding a growl of his own. He reached out, planted his right hand on Gabrielle's right shoulder, and casually threw her aside.

I watched Gabrielle stagger a half-step and go down. She scattered a couple tables. Her head struck the edge of one before cracking off the floor. The scent of blood hit me.

3

B eing shoved aside pissed off Gabrielle more than anything else. Yeah, the edge of a table drew a little blood, but with shifter healing, her 'injuries' didn't even reach the level of paper cuts. She wanted nothing more than to jump to her feet and drag Buddy Carrington outside for a proper ass-kicking, and she pushed herself back to her feet. But no matter how fast she might have been, she was already too late.

In an explosion of fabric and other materials, Wyatt Magnusson experienced his first shift, and Gabrielle's mind locked at what she saw. Four thick legs the size of tree stumps ended in paws the size of dinner plates, if not larger. A stubby tail reaching not quite half the length of his hind legs. Sandy blond fur like a lion with darker tawny stripes. A massive muscled body standing four feet tall at the shoulder. And long curved canine teeth that descended at least four inches from his upper jaw and tapered to needle-sharp points. Wyatt Magnusson was the first feline primogenitor Gabrielle had ever heard of... and he was a Smilodon.

Before Gabrielle could even begin diffusing the situation,

Wyatt lunged at Buddy and took him down to the floor, placing a massive paw on Buddy's sternum. The crashing clatter of tables and chairs scattering like bowling pins filled the diner. Wyatt's muzzle was less than eight inches from Buddy's face when he roared his rage, rattling windows and dinnerware as he flooded the diner with a suffocating burst of alpha dominance.

Buddy pissed himself on the spot... and not just a tiny leak. Buddy Carrington—one of the most dominant non-alpha shifters in town—full-on fear-peed. Scents from around the room told Gabrielle he wasn't the only one.

For one moment of weakness, Gabrielle wanted to remain where she was and watch how the situation unfolded. Buddy was an over-muscled bully, and only the other over-muscled bullies in town liked him. But they needed every shifter... even the assholes. She rolled to a crouch and stood, approaching Wyatt from his left side. He still stood over Buddy with his right forepaw on the man's chest, and once she had a better vantage point, she saw Wyatt flexed his claws just enough to pierce Buddy's skin like five large-gauge needles.

Wyatt didn't react to her arrival at his side, so Gabrielle reached out to his shoulder. She couldn't help smiling at the touch of his fur. It was coarse and bristly, like an Irish wolfhound's coat. At her touch, Wyatt's growl and snarl faded, and he turned his massive head toward her. Gabrielle stepped back to stand in front of Wyatt, but to the right of Buddy.

"Wyatt, it's okay. I'm fine. He didn't hurt me."

Wyatt's jaw worked as if he spoke, but the only sounds that came out were deep-toned mixtures of meows and rawrs. Gabrielle fought the urge to snicker; he sounded like a baritone house cat. But he conveyed questioning concern.

"Wyatt, you can't speak human languages when you're shifted, but yes, I'm fine. I'm not even bleeding anymore."

Wyatt looked at Buddy and growled. It sounded like a massive engine with aggressive glass packs in its exhaust. Buddy paled, and a minor part of Gabrielle enjoyed it.

"Yes, I know," Gabrielle said. "He's an over-muscled asshole with too much testosterone, but as much as I hate to say it, he has his uses. You don't need to hurt him any further."

Wyatt looked up at her again and rawr-ed a question.

Gabrielle nodded. "Yes, I'm sure. So… you ready to shift back?"

Wyatt bobbed a nod.

"Focus on that part of your mind that still feels human. It's just like moving your legs to walk. Just decide you're going to shift."

It took a few seconds—maybe a minute—but soon, a naked man kneeled over Buddy with a hand on Buddy's chest. Wyatt stood, but when Buddy moved to stand, Wyatt placed his bare foot on the man's chest and glared at him.

"If you ever cause harm to another soul that isn't in self-defense or defense of another," Wyatt said, his voice cold and implacable, "I will rip off your head and give it to someone to use as a chamber pot. Do you understand?"

Buddy jerked a choppy nod.

Wyatt's gaze hardened. "I didn't hear you."

"I understand." Buddy's voice carried none of his normal arrogance. In fact, it sounded a little shaky.

Wyatt nodded. "Forget this moment at your peril."

Before the ensuing silence became awkward, Gabrielle touched Wyatt's bicep. "Come on, big guy. Let's go next door and get you some clothes. Buddy needs a shower and a change of clothes, too."

"No," Wyatt replied, shaking his head. "He can shower and change clothes right before bed."

Gabrielle gaped. "But everyone will know…"

Wyatt turned to meet her shocked gaze. "I sort of figured that."

Without another word, Wyatt pivoted on his heel and looked down at the destroyed remains of his clothes. He heaved a small sigh, kneeling to clean up the mess he'd made.

In seconds, a woman Wyatt didn't know arrived at his side. Her voice carried hints of kindness and gratitude as she said, "Oh, don't you worry about that. I have this broom right here. You just get whatever you need and leave the mess to me."

"That's not fair to you," Wyatt replied. "You shouldn't have to clean up after me."

The woman smiled. "Think nothing of it. Buddy and his crowd have a tendency to run roughshod over anyone who can't stand up to them, so consider this my thank you for what you did."

Wyatt slipped his wallet, keys, and phone into the water bottle pocket of his backpack and lifted the pack by its carry handle as he stood. He regarded Buddy, who was only now beginning to stand, and Gabrielle wanted to groan at the look on Wyatt's face.

"So, he makes a habit of being a bully?" Wyatt asked.

It took all of Gabrielle's willpower to keep from wincing. Seriously? She just stopped Wyatt from ripping Buddy a new orifice. Why couldn't Gladys keep her mouth shut?

Buddy was on his feet now, and he lifted his hands up like he was surrendering. His expression made it clear that he knew he was on thin ice with Wyatt.

"Oh, yeah," Gladys replied. Her tone casual, matter of fact. "He's been pushing people around ever since he hit puberty. He doesn't even listen to Sheriff Clyde, and those idiots that hang around him—acting like they all want to hump his leg—aren't any better."

Wyatt's eyes flicked to Buddy's table and the five or six people still seated there, and in the silence that descended on the diner, it seemed like even the physical building wanted to gasp, "Oh, shit… this will hurt."

Wyatt shifted his pack to his left hand and held out his right to the woman. "I'm Wyatt."

"Gladys," she replied, shaking his hand.

"Gladys, I figure I'll be around for a few days, getting a handle on how I've changed," Wyatt said. "I'd appreciate you finding me if you hear that any of them are acting out."

The high-pitched squeal of tables and chairs sliding across the tile floor filled the diner as everyone around Buddy's table put some distance between themselves and Buddy's crew.

Gladys beamed. "Well, I surely will, Wyatt. Thank you."

Wyatt looked to Gabrielle. "So, we're going to the general store?"

Gabrielle nodded.

"Okay," Wyatt said and pivoted, walking out the door.

I HELD it together long enough to walk beyond the diner's windows, but when I reached the building's corner, I stepped into the space between it and the general store, dropped my pack, leaned against the wall, and put my face in my hands.

What the hell happened to me? I have never been someone to force submission like that. I made that guy pee himself out of fear, like he was some tiny lapdog.

I heard footfalls on my right just before Gabrielle said, "Hey, there. You all right?"

I pulled my hands away from my face. Something inside

me tried to make myself stand straight, present a commanding presence even in the buff, but I pushed whatever it was aside.

"Yeah, I guess so... but no, I'm not. I mean, I'm not hurt. I'm not in pain or discomfort or anything like that, but my mind is spinning right now. Where the hell did that come from in there? I almost didn't recognize myself when I faced down that guy, because that wasn't me. I'm the quiet, geeky kid."

"I told you we needed to talk," Gabrielle replied, "but I don't feel so bad about not recognizing your scent anymore. You're the first Smilodon shifter I've ever met. Come on. Let's at least get you some clothes, so nothing's swinging in the breeze."

Her eyes and the slight curve of her mouth told me she aimed for a joke. It was a little funny, and I couldn't keep from chuckling. I leaned far enough to grab the carry handle for my backpack and fell in beside Gabrielle. The thought occurred to me I could use the pack to cover myself, for the time being, and by the time we entered the store, I was kind of calm.

A bell jingled as Gabrielle opened the door, and I smiled at the sight of an honest-to-goodness, small-town general store. There was a clothing section, a hardware section... pretty much anything you'd expect in a dry goods store.

"Afternoon, Hank," Gabrielle said. "Wyatt, here, just experienced his first shift and destroyed his clothes. We hoped you could help him."

Hank looked somewhere around early middle age. The hair over his ears had a few wisps of gray, and the top of his head was bald. He wore a checkered shirt with suspenders and what looked like garters to keep his sleeves away from his hands and wrists.

"I sure can, Miss Gabrielle," Hank replied. "I just need

your sizes, sir. You don't look like you'll need something in a size I don't carry, but proper sizes will ensure a suitable fit."

Wyatt wanted to shrug. "Uhm... the clothes I shredded pretty much fit, but they felt off a little. Any chance we could do some measurements? I don't think the sizes I know are a hundred percent correct anymore."

Hank gave a reassuring nod. "Of course, young man. It's very common for a person's measurements to change after they've become shifters. The changes a person's body undergoes takes what's there and optimizes it."

"You still hungry?" Gabrielle asked.

I nodded. "I feel like I could eat ten or twelve triple cheeseburgers."

"While Hank's getting you set up, I'll go back to the diner and get them started on our food. How do you like your steak?"

I meant to say 'well done' out of reflex, because I ate no meat that wasn't. But I didn't say that. "Make sure it's not mooing" came out of my mouth instead.

Gabrielle grinned. "Sorta figured, but I wanted to be sure. Meet you back there when you're finished here?"

"Sounds good, and thanks."

Gabrielle waved and left me in Hank's expert care.

WE SPENT MAYBE thirty minutes taking measurements and selecting three sets of clothes. What I didn't wear, I folded and stuffed in my hiking pack. I couldn't remember the exact amount left in my checking account, so I used a card my grandpa gave me for emergencies. I figured I'd pay him back across a few paychecks. When Hank handed me the receipt, he also gave me a small card that had my new measurements written on it. Talk about customer service.

"Thank you for the measurements and the card, sir," I said, hefting my now-heavy pack. "I appreciate it."

"It's been a pleasure doing business, and I always take care of my customers, sir."

I smiled. "Please, call me Wyatt."

He extended his hand to me. "Only if you call me Hank."

"Thanks again, Hank. I hope you have an excellent day." I gave him a proper handshake and left the store.

THE FIRST THING Gabrielle noticed when she returned to the diner was the absence of Buddy and his gang of bullies. It was probably just as well. She didn't think they would have wanted to remain in the diner after Wyatt came back, and she knew they wouldn't have wanted to walk past him to leave. Gabrielle selected a vacant table, and Gladys was at her side before she even had her chair ready.

"So, where did you find him?" Gladys asked.

Gabrielle frowned. "Who? You mean Wyatt?"

"Duh… of course, I mean Wyatt. He's not from around here, is he?"

Gabrielle fought the urge to sigh. She never wanted to hurt anyone's feelings, but nobody wanted to cross Gladys. She ran the best diner for three counties in any direction.

"Yeah, he kind of is. The rogue cougar Alistair sent us to track turned him. He killed it before it killed him."

Gladys gaped. "You mean he's not a born shifter?"

Gabrielle shook her head.

"And he's that strong, plus an alpha?"

Gabrielle shrugged. "Seems so. Most turned shifters even get a little stronger after their first shift, as they grow into their new abilities."

"Oh, lordy," Gladys replied, fanning herself with her order

pad. "Buddy had better walk the straight and narrow, or he won't be living too long."

Gabrielle chuckled. "I wouldn't let Wyatt go that far, and to be honest, I'm concerned about what today's humiliation will mean for Buddy's future behavior. He may double-down on bullying others just to 'prove' his dominance."

Gladys shook her head. "And just what makes you think you could stop Wyatt, Gabrielle? But anyway, what would you like to order?"

Gabrielle ordered their meals, but even after Gladys left to check the other tables, her question echoed in Gabrielle's mind. Would she be able to stop Wyatt if he ended Buddy and his crew?

The bell over the diner's door interrupted her thoughts, and she looked up to see Wyatt enter. He wore a blue-checked green shirt and khaki cargo pants. Wyatt smiled when he saw her and walked straight to her table. His backpack went into an empty chair, and he sat across from her.

"Everything go okay with Hank?" Gabrielle asked.

Wyatt nodded. "I have two more sets of clothes in my pack, beyond what I'm wearing. He even gave me a card with my new sizes on it."

"Hank's good people," Gabrielle remarked. "Have you given much thought to where you go from here?"

Wyatt chuckled. "I don't even know what day it is, Gabrielle."

Gabrielle regarded him for a moment, then said, "Today's the fifth day after the rogue cougar attacked you."

A KNOCK at the study door drew Connor Magnusson's attention. His fingers traced a pattern that was well-established muscle memory, and the door swung open noiselessly. Roger Hennessy entered the study and approached Connor's desk.

"Any word, Roger?"

"Possibly, sir."

Connor's eyebrows arching upward betrayed his surprise.

Roger continued, "We have a hit on the card you gave Wyatt. Someone used it at a general store in Precious."

Connor fought the urge to scowl. Precious—well, its whole county really—was shifter territory. He'd never been one of the more rabid anti-shifters in the Magi community, but if those animals had harmed his grandson, he'd wipe the town off the face of the world.

"Prepare three cars," Connor almost spat. "Split the teams fifty/fifty between security personnel and war-mages, and distribute heavy weapons to one in four of the security personnel. Everyone gets shifter-bane ammunition and be sure the medics have the anti-turning treatments."

Now Roger betrayed surprise. It sounded very much like Connor was going to war.

"Uhm, sir," Roger replied, "are you sure about this?"

"Is Grandpa sure about what, Roger?"

Before Roger could turn, Vicki Magnusson arrived at his side. Wyatt's twin sister, Vicki, already displayed a mastery over several Magi talents, and she was only a couple years into her studies.

"Someone in Precious used the card I gave Wyatt," Connor replied. "I'm taking a team out there."

"I'll come with," Vicki replied, pivoting on her heel. "Just give me five minutes."

"Vicki," Connor said, "I'd much prefer you stay here."

Vicki stopped about halfway to the study's door. She turned, and Connor recognized the determination in her eyes. "Wyatt is my brother, Grandpa. He's always been there for me, even though Mom and Dad shunned him for not being Magi, and I'm not about to stay here when he might need me."

Connor bit back a sigh. "Very well. I've asked Roger to prepare three cars. That'll take over five minutes, so let's say fifteen."

Vicki beamed. "Thank you, Grandpa!"

"Please, see to the cars and the teams," Connor said as he watched his granddaughter leave the study.

4

Gabrielle and I ended up in the town park. It was a pleasant day, and a cool breeze swept through the area. We were the only people in the park at the moment, and we settled at a picnic table under the shade of a massive oak tree.

"Okay," I said, spearing Gabrielle with my eyes. "I'm fed. You're fed. I'm not naked. What on Earth is going on with me?"

Gabrielle sighed. "It's not that complicated, Wyatt. The rogue cougar that attacked you turned you. The scary part is that you're a primogenitor, instead of just a cougar. I've never heard of a turned shifter being an alpha shifter, especially not one as strong as you are, and definitely not a primogenitor. This will ruffle some fur. To be honest, I'm still trying to wrap my head around the idea that the cougar turned you at all."

I blinked. "That cougar shouldn't have been able to turn me? Why?"

Something about Gabrielle's expression made me feel she

was uncomfortable. I watched her eyes scan the area for several moments as she remained silent.

When the silence extended, I said, "Gabrielle, please... I don't understand any of this. I mean, five days ago, I was an entry-level tech at a software and web-design firm that could barely make payroll once a month. That magic and shifters are anything other than fiction is difficult to swallow."

Gabrielle sighed. "I can't believe your grandfather discussed none of this with you."

"Why would he? And what's my grandpa have to do with any of this?"

"Wyatt, the Magnussons are one of the oldest Magi families in the world. Your grandfather is the North American delegate to the Magi Assembly. Beyond that, shifters or vampires can't turn Magi; you're not technically human."

"Not human? Seriously?" I couldn't wrap my mind around that. How could my grandpa not be human? "Wait... do you know whether Grandma is... what did you call it?"

"Magi?" Gabrielle asked.

I nodded.

Gabrielle closed her eyes and sighed. "I should not be the one telling you all this, Wyatt. Your parents—or at least your grandfather—should've told you all this long, long ago." She sighed again. "But yes, your grandmother is also Magi. In fact, she was the daughter of another prominent Magi family; their marriage established one of the most powerful Magi family alliances in existence."

"Okay, wow," I said, still having difficulty wrapping my head around the idea that my grandparents were wizards. "Let's leave the Magi stuff for a moment and get back to me being able to turn into a sabertooth cat. What do I need to know about being what I am now?"

Gabrielle shook her head. "So much. You're an alpha. I

know scientists and behaviorists have debunked the idea of a pack alpha for wolves in the wild and such, but for shifters, alphas are serious. Remember how half the people in the diner pissed themselves when you roared? You burst out such strong alpha dominance with your roar that everyone wanted to prove they were no threat. I think you might even be stronger than the alpha in charge of the town, which might cause some problems once he returns from his business trip to Chicago."

"How would it cause problems? You mean he'd fight me or run me out of town?"

Gabrielle shrugged. "Maybe. I mean, it's common for there to be dominance fights when new shifters move into the area, just to establish where they are in the pack or pride. Wolves have packs, and felines have prides, like a lion pride. I'm not sure how it will sort out, because as strong of an alpha as Jace is, he's never made Buddy piss himself in submission. Buddy's too dominant, which is not such a good thing considering his personality."

I couldn't keep from heaving a heavy sigh. "Will that happen to me? I mean, you say I'm some kind of super-powerful alpha dominant. Am I going to turn into someone like Buddy?"

Gabrielle chuckled. "No, I doubt it. More often than not, getting turned just makes a person… more. If they're already a bullying asshole, they'll be more of one. Likewise, if they spend their days helping elderly cross streets, they'll still do that."

"Okay. You said, 'more often than not.' That implies there are exceptions."

"There are always exceptions, Wyatt," Gabrielle replied. "The cases that are the odd ones out are those people who have survived abuse most of their lives and never felt they could do anything about it. If someone like that gets turned, that's the one you want to watch, because it's close to fifty-fifty that they'll go power-mad and end up in bad straits."

I nodded. "Okay. Is there anything I have to watch out for now? Like my grandma's sterling silver dinner utensils or bags of catnip?"

Gabrielle burst out laughing. "No... you don't need to watch out for catnip. Well, you can if you want to, but for us, it's kind of like good quality weed. Just mellows us out. In our feline forms, anyway. I've never had it affect me at all in my human form. And no, don't worry about silver, either. Like crosses or garlic for vampires, that's just old tales. It probably got started because some hunters back in the Middle Ages had shifter-bane weapons and told everyone they were silver."

"Shifter-bane?"

"This is something else your grandfather should probably explain, but that knife you have in your pack? The blade has a shifter-bane rune; that's why the cougar didn't shrug off your attacks and finish you. Our supernatural healing doesn't work on wounds caused by shifter-bane weapons."

I nodded and leaned my elbows on the picnic table as I tried to think of my next question.

CONNOR DIDN'T WAIT for Roger to open his door when the vehicles rolled to a stop in front of the general store in Precious. It was a quaint little town, reminding him of so many towns he'd visited in his youth. Several pedestrians walking the sidewalks gave him and his people long or weird looks, but he didn't mind.

Before Connor could head into the general store, he heard someone say, "Hello, old wizard."

Connor pivoted on his heel, and he grinned at seeing one

of his oldest friends, Alistair Cooper. "Hello yourself, old wolf. What are you doing west of the Mississippi? I thought you were settled in Boston with no intention of leaving."

Connor walked around the vehicle and approached Alistair with his right hand out. His friend gave a respectable handshake as he shrugged.

"There was a major uptick in the number of rogues coming out of the Western Ranges, so for my crimes of doing such a marvelous job policing young pups in New England, the Council sent me out here to find out what the issue is."

"Then, you may be just the person I need to speak with," Connor replied. "Someone used my grandson's card at this general store this morning. He's been missing for five days." The expression that crossed Alistair's face told Connor his old war buddy knew something. "You've never been a talented poker player. What do you know?"

Alistair sighed. "We should move this into my office, Connor. Wyatt's alive and well, but we should talk."

"If my brother's alive and well, what's there to talk about?" Vicki asked as she arrived at her grandfather's side.

Connor smiled. "This is my granddaughter, Vicki. She's Wyatt's twin sister. All right, old wolf. I'll trust you." Connor turned and made eye contact with Roger. "Vicki and I will speak with Alistair. He said Wyatt's fine, but there's something he wants to discuss. I think we can have everyone stand easy for now. I don't think this will be the situation I expected."

Roger nodded and spoke into a radio as Connor turned back to Alistair.

A SHORT WALK across the street later, Alistair invited his guests to have a seat in his office. He eased into his own chair and steepled his fingers, his elbows resting on the chair's armrests.

"Okay, Connor," Alistair said without preamble. "The short of it is that a rogue cougar turned Wyatt. The hunting party I sent arrived in time to bring Wyatt back for some basic first aid, but not soon enough to keep the cougar from attacking him. Wyatt saw to the rogue himself with that knife you gave him." Alistair chuckled. "Seeing a shifter-bane weapon with the Magnusson crest unsettled my lead hunter, in case you wondered. Wyatt has been unconscious in our infirmary since the attack; he just woke up this morning. There was a—well, let's call it an incident—at the diner across the street that caused a need for clothes."

"His first shift," Connor said, making it a statement instead of a question. "I suppose, if this had to happen, there are worse animals than a mountain lion."

Alistair made something like a half-wince. "About that... Connor, Wyatt isn't a cougar shifter."

"But you said a rogue cougar turned him."

"I did, and that's true. But he didn't become a cougar."

Connor's eyes narrowed as he ran through the possibilities in his mind. The only way Wyatt wouldn't have been a cougar was if... Connor locked gazes with Alistair again. "You mean he's a primogenitor?"

Alistair simply nodded.

"I've never heard of a feline primogenitor," Connor remarked. "You said he's already had his first shift? What's his feline form?"

"Please forgive me," Vicki said, "but I feel like I'm only catching every third word or so. What's a primogenitor?"

Connor and Alistair locked gazes again, and they both ended up shrugging. Connor turned to his granddaughter, saying, "Vicki, please forgive us. I was the Magi liaison to his shifter unit back in the war, and we became good friends. I'm sorry that we fell into old patterns and left you to fend for yourself."

"Yes, my apologies too, dear lady," Alistair agreed. "Primogenitors are rare. So rare in fact that I can only think of two in existence right now across the entire population of shifters… well, before Wyatt, that is. They're both wolves. Primogenitors take the form of ancient versions of their kind. Those two wolves I mentioned are dire wolves; they make even the larger wolf shifters look like puppies, in both size and power."

"You said Wyatt's a feline primogenitor?" Vicki asked. "So, he's what… an American lion?"

"Not quite," Alistair answered. "I didn't see him in the fur myself, mind you, but I have it on very reliable authority that Wyatt is a Smilodon."

Connor blinked. "A what?"

"Holy crap!" Vicki almost squealed. "Are you serious?"

Alistair nodded.

"That is so cool!" Vicki cheered again.

Connor shifted in his seat to regard his beaming granddaughter with a raised eyebrow. "Care to share with the rest of the class?"

"He's a sabertooth cat, Grandpa," Vicki said.

"That's not all he is, either," Alistair added. "He's a more powerful alpha than Jason McCourtney. To tell you the truth, I'm glad Jason and his betas are back east right now; that simplifies matters. Come to think of it, there's something that all of us have been wondering since the hunting party brought him back. Neither shifters nor vampires can turn Magi, so how is Wyatt alive?"

Now Connor winced. "Alistair, I'm sure you know that Elizabeth and I raised Wyatt and Vicki, but what you apparently do not know is why. My son and his wife—in their inestimable wisdom—were going to cast my grandson out when he was born with no trace of Magi talent. You know how I feel about family, Alistair, so I told them they had no right to raise any of their children if they didn't want one of them."

Alistair shook his head. "I'm surprised they didn't fight you."

Connor smiled. It wasn't a cheerful smile. "Oh, they did. It was shaping up to have the potential of being a rather epic feud… until I gave them the option of agreeing to my wishes or being disowned with zero rights to the family name and resources. The only part of it all that I truly regret is costing Vicki her parents. Rather than be civil to their own mundane son under my roof, they haven't spoken to either child or me and Maeve in the better part of fifteen years."

"Wyatt and I have told you before, Grandpa," Vicki spoke up. "Their conduct is on them. It's their fault they're missing out on what an amazing son and daughter they have."

"The thought occurs," Alistair said, "that this is the perfect opportunity to strengthen relations between shifters and Magi… or at least shifters and the Magnusson clan."

Connor nodded his agreement. "The same thought crossed my mind, old wolf. We must navigate matters carefully, though, if we want to ensure that outcome. It will take a deft hand… on both sides."

A somewhat-awkward silence descended on the office until Alistair cleared his throat, saying, "Would you like me to have Wyatt join us? The hunter in charge of the team that brought him back has been easing him into what it means to be a shifter."

"That might be for the best," Connor replied. "Since he wasn't Magi himself, I made the tough decision not to share

37

that part of our lives with him. Vicki didn't like it, but she eventually agreed with me."

Alistair grinned. "Please, excuse me a moment."

The old wolf picked up his phone's handset and dialed a number. Moments later, he said, "Hello, Gabrielle; it's Alistair. Wyatt's grandfather and his sister have arrived, and they're with me in my office. Would you mind bringing Wyatt to us?" He was silent for a few moments, then nodded. "Excellent. Thank you. Bye now." Once he hung up the phone, he turned back to his guests. "They're in the city park right behind the building we're in. It shouldn't be too long."

I WAS a bundle of nerves as I walked with Gabrielle into the city's administration building, and I didn't know why. It was just Grandpa and Vicki. It wasn't like I didn't know them. Still, the closer we came to our destination, the more my stomach roiled. Gabrielle stopped at the door long enough to knock twice before opening it and gesturing for me to enter first. I stepped up to the doorway and saw my sister leap out of her chair and charge me with her arms wide. It wasn't quite a flying hug, but it seemed like she tried.

After a few moments of Vicki trying to compress my ribs to fit into a soup can, she released me and stepped back, then said, "All right. I want to see."

"See what, sis?"

"Grandpa's friend told us you're a kitty cat now, and I want to see."

"Kitty cat? Really, Vicki?"

She grinned, and I recognized the mischievous glint in her eyes. "What? You were always the purr-fect brother, anyway. Now, it's just official."

I sighed and bowed my head. "Sis, I'd better not find a litter box in my room at any point."

Her innocent expression was far too contrived for my taste. "Why, my dear brother... how could you ever think I'd stoop so low? Now, come on; show me. If nothing else, I need to measure your neck for flea collars."

"You're being a brat, and besides, I'm not the only shifter in the room. Don't you think you might insult our hosts with your talk of flea collars?"

Vicki just grinned. "Oh, no... they're fine. They have no need of flea collars. I'm just concerned about you, my dear furry brother. Now, come on; show me... please?"

"I'm not about to strip down right here just to show you my cat, Vicki."

"Strip down? Why...?"

"I destroyed a set of clothes when I shifted earlier today. I'd rather not do that again, if I can keep from it."

"The office next door is vacant," Gabrielle offered.

"Et tu, Gabrielle?"

I watched her shrug. "You're the first Smilodon I've ever seen that wasn't an artist's theoretical depiction. I wouldn't mind a second look, now that I don't have to focus on keeping you from turning Buddy into a chew toy."

"What do you mean by that?" Vicki asked.

"Oh, Wyatt experienced his first shift today when one of the local bullies knocked me into some tables at the diner. I don't think Wyatt understood that I wasn't in any danger and that, in fact, I was getting ready to drag his worthless ass outside for a proper beating. He shifted, put the twerp on the floor, and blasted so much alpha dominance with his roar that half the diner pissed themselves in submission, including the bully."

Vicki swung around to face me and put her secret

weapon into play. I'd never been able to resist her sad puppy face. "Please, Wyatt? I'd love to see your cat form."

"Okay," I said, adding a much-put-upon sigh for flavor. "Gabrielle, do you mind helping me with doors please?"

Gabrielle nodded, and I went to the vacant office. I pulled off all my clothes and tried touching the part of my mind I'd touched to shift earlier... but nothing happened. It took a few moments of concentration before I found a part of my mind that felt like my cat, so I touched that and willed the shift. The next thing I knew, I was on all fours and furry. I padded over to the door and pawed at it before backing up. Gabrielle opened it for me, and I walked beside her to Alistair's office. She opened that door, and I stepped inside far enough for Gabrielle to close the door behind me.

The moment she saw me, Vicki squealed and clapped her hands. She almost bounced over to me.

"Can I pet you?"

I nodded, and Vicki wasted no time.

"I love your fur," she said, as I felt her hand slide down my spine and side. "You have such a pretty pattern, too."

With absolutely no warning, Vicki dropped to her knees and threw her arms around my neck. As she hugged me, she whispered into my right ear, "I love you, Wyatt; I'm so glad you're okay."

My sister and I have always been close. It's almost like we're each half of one whole. Even as I luxuriated in our bond surviving my new status, I knew—knew with no doubt or question—that I would soon find a litter box or flea collar or scratching post or *something* in my room or another personal space. Vicki has been an incorrigible imp cloaked in the guise of an innocent, wide-eyed prom queen since shortly after she could walk.

With that in mind, when Vicki released my neck, I stepped back the minute distance necessary to look her square in the eye… and performed my preemptive strike. I licked her from chin to forehead; my tongue almost covered her entire face.

Vicki slid back from her kneeling position to sit heavily on the floor, giggling. Amid the giggles, "Wyatt, your tongue is scratchy!"

5

I eased into a seat between my grandfather and Vicki, once more human and clothed. Gabrielle sat off to one side; she'd tried to leave, but Alistair had waved her to a side table. Alistair's office smelled like old books, but in a nice way, not the stale smell old libraries sometimes had. I wanted to scan the bookshelf along one wall and see what titles I found, but it seemed like everyone wanted to focus on me.

"Have you given any thought to what comes next, Wyatt?" Alistair asked.

I had. I just wasn't sure I wanted to admit that. "How do you mean?"

"You stand at a crossroads, my boy," Grandpa said. "Yes, you can return to your old life, and once the fervor over you being missing for five days fades, it will be like you knew it."

I nodded at that. Part of me wanted the comfort of what had been my status quo. Yes, I hated the job, but most days, it was enough to let me do what I wanted to do with my life. At least what I *had thought* I wanted to do with my life.

"If I'm at a crossroads, as you say," I replied, "what are my other options?"

Grandpa glanced at Alistair across the desk, then met my eyes with his own. "Explore what it means to be a shifter. To a certain extent, you have little choice about it now. You could *try* to return to your old life as if nothing happened, but the new shifter side of you won't let you stuff it in a closet somewhere in your mind and forget about it. If you try, it's only a matter of time before you shift again without your choice, and if that happens, there's no guarantee you won't expose us all to the world. Besides, an old friend I trust with my life has led me to believe being a shifter can be rather fun. And who knows? You may even find yourself in a leadership position in time. It all depends on what you want out of life."

All I wanted out of life was... what? Until that moment, I'm not sure I ever thought about it. I enjoyed helping people with their computer problems; I would've enjoyed being *paid regularly* for my time, but such is life. But what other options did I have?

Turning it over in my mind, I realized that maybe I had been drifting through life, with little in the way of a plan or intent. That realization carried with it undertones of shame seasoned with a pinch of anger. Okay... that was a little weird. Coasting through life never bothered me before. Why would I feel shame and anger now?

Because I've been wasting my life and *my potential, idiot.* The thought sounded almost like a growl, and it came from that part of my mind I touched to shift into my animal form.

"I'm not leadership material, Grandpa," I replied. Another growl in my mind: *Yes, I am.*

Echoed by Gabrielle not even a moment later, "Yes, you are."

I turned to face her, and I wasn't the only one. I countered with, "No, I'm not. I never have been."

Gabrielle shrugged. "I can't speak to the type of person

43

you were six days ago, but the Wyatt Magnusson *I* know is very much a leader. At least a leadership candidate. Wyatt, you stood up to the strongest shifter in three counties after our alpha... and you *dominated* him to the point that he pissed himself in utter submission along with over half the diner."

I grimaced. "True leaders don't terrorize people into pissing themselves."

"Maybe not among humans, but that's the only type of leader shifters will follow. We're not all sweetness and light, Wyatt. The predator shifters only follow strength, and the prey shifters need a powerful leader to protect them from the predators. Look, I'm not saying you're ready to jump out in front of everyone and lead us all to greatness or whatever. I'm just saying you have more potential than you think, but you won't achieve any of it unless you embrace all of who you are now."

I should listen to her, the growly voice opined.

"The only way I can embrace all of who I am is to move to Precious and learn what it means to be a shifter."

Grandpa and Alistair shared another glance, and Grandpa nodded. "I think that's an excellent idea, Wyatt, and I ask two things. One, don't be a stranger; your grandmother, sister, and I care deeply for you and want to see you occasionally. Two, never forget that we are a family before we are anything else; if we can help you, *tell us*."

I smiled. "I think I can agree to both. So, are there any specific protocols involved in moving to Precious?"

Alistair and Gabrielle looked to each other, and it was Alistair who spoke. "Normally, a shifter needs the permission of the local Alpha to move into a region, and also, it is usually the case that the new shifter will join the local pack, pride, herd, or what have you. We're in something of a gray area, right this moment, because the local Alpha is back east along with most of his betas and enforcers. They're attending a meeting of the North American Shifter Council. If it's a short meeting, they'll return next week. The easiest thing to do would probably be to return with your grandfather and sister, secure any loose ends still out there from your human life, and then return here later this week or next. If the local Alpha hasn't returned by then, rent a room in the hotel and explore the town and surrounding area. Gabrielle, will you continue to act as his orientation advisor?"

Gabrielle nodded. "I can do that. If I have to go on any hunts, I'll even take him along... unless he has no wood-sense about him at all."

I shook my head and chuckled. "I'm not horrible in the woods. I'm sure I'm nowhere close to your level—*yet*—but I do okay."

Gabrielle gave me a predatory smile. "I'll be the judge of that."

AFTER SPENDING a little while longer chatting with Alistair and Gabrielle, Connor decided it was time that he should get back to his responsibilities, and he offered to give Wyatt a ride to the trailhead where his car still waited for him. The trip from Precious to the trailhead took a little over thirty minutes.

AS THE THREE-SUV convoy pulled away from the trailhead, Vicki asked, "Grandpa, why didn't you tell Wyatt of your discussion with Alistair about closer ties between our family and the shifter community?"

Connor regarded his granddaughter and offered her a kind smile. "You saw how he reacted to the idea of being a leader, Vicki. The only way to ensure that Wyatt becomes the ambassador between both cultures is for him to choose that path on his own, which won't happen if we try to push him in that direction. So, we'll step back and give him some time to get used to his new reality. Knowing Wyatt like I do, I think it will only be a matter of time before he ends up in a leadership role whether or not he wants it."

"I suppose you're right," Vicki replied and grimaced. "It just feels wrong keeping Wyatt in the dark about it. I don't like keeping secrets from him. I never have liked it."

Connor nodded his understanding. "I understand, Vicki; I promise you I do. But sometimes, as Magi, we must take a path that challenges us for an overall better result. I believe we've discussed this in the past."

"I remember, Grandpa. I never thought it would bother me this much."

"If it were anyone else," Connor remarked, "it probably wouldn't."

Vicki nodded and turned to gaze out the window at the passing scenery.

I RAN through the list of stuff I needed to do to close out the human portion of my life as I drove back to town from the trailhead. I didn't like that Grandpa called his accountant and told him to transfer a tidy sum to me, but given the lack of regular payment with my old job, it was unfortunately not the first time he'd done that. A part of me rankled a bit at the idea of not giving my employer the standard two weeks' notice, but that part couldn't gain too much traction.

The largest unknown on my mind was my apartment's lease. Even though they'd never said or done anything to make me feel unwelcome, I guess I'd always known there was something that set me apart from my grandparents and Vicki. And I reacted to that by getting my own place when I started the tech support job.

I LOOKED at the car's clock as I entered the town I'd called home for so long. Three-thirty. I had ninety minutes before my soon-to-be-former workplace closed. Might as well get that over with before heading over to my apartment building. I was looking forward to the conversation, and yet, I wasn't... all at the same time.

The company operated out of a suite of offices on the fifth floor of an ancient office building. Aside from a few apartment complexes scattered around town, it was the tallest. The elevator ride was boring as usual, and it still did the little bunny hop as it passed the fourth floor. No one could ever explain to my satisfaction *why* the elevator made that little hop, and it always unnerved me a bit. At least the elevator was hydraulic and not cable-operated, right?

My eyes landed on the reception desk as I entered the office suite, and I was a little disappointed. Becky—not Sal—staffed the desk. Becky was an absolute sweetheart who had the sad puppy face down to an art form; she could make even the most uncaring, hard-hearted person wilt and sniff back a tear. I always wished I could ask her out without being the weirdo at work, but since I could now turn into a gigantic cat, it was probably just as well that I'd never figured it out.

"Well, well..." Becky said, breaking into a smile. "Look what the cat dragged in."

I hoped I managed not to wince at her phrasing. "Hi, Becky. Is Tom in?"

"Yeah, he is. I don't think he's busy, but I can check if you like."

I weighed my options. If I just walked straight back and

invited myself inside his office, there was always the chance he'd take any frustration or displeasure out on Becky for not warning him I was coming. If I asked Becky to call him, I'd lose the element of surprise. Hmmm…

"Say," Becky interjected, pausing my thoughts, "are you okay? Nobody's seen you around since your day off."

"I got nasty sick, and I didn't feel like standing until today. And even when I first stood up earlier, the room still kind of spun for a few moments."

Becky blanched. "You're not contagious, are you?"

Good question…

"Uhm, not exactly. I could probably share it with you if I bit you, but just shaking hands or breathing around you shouldn't do anything. But yeah, call Tom, please. I just need about five minutes of his time."

Not even a professional poker player could've hidden the sheer magnitude of the relief Becky showed. She grabbed the phone's handset and dialed Tom's extension. "Hi, Tom. Wyatt is here, asking for five minutes. What should I tell him?"

Becky jerked the handset away from her ear, and thanks to my new shifter senses, I heard Tom almost shout, "You tell that worthless lay-about to get his ass in here! Right now!"

How dare he speak like that about me? The growly voice whispered from its home in my mind. *I should teach him a lesson.*

Becky's expression started out apologetic, but I guess she saw something in my eyes, because she went from apologetic to uneasy—almost fearful—in an instant.

"It's okay," I said in my best approximation of a soothing tone. "You've had no reason to be afraid of me before, and that hasn't changed. All right?"

Becky mutely nodded before turning back to the phone. "He's on the way, Tom."

I gave her a half-wave and walked away from the reception desk. As I turned the corner into one of the office suite's two hallways, I heard her hang up the phone without even saying goodbye.

Tom's office occupied the far-left corner of the suite, one of only two corner offices the company had. The other one had a door plaque stating it was his wife's office, but the company mainly used it for storage. To my knowledge, she hadn't set foot in the place since before I started working there.

I tapped twice on the door to Tom's office and didn't even wait for him to call me inside. I barely had time to close the door behind me before Tom shot to his feet, his face a storm cloud.

"What the hell do you think you're doing, disappearing for five days? I ought to write you up *and* dock your pay. If you weren't one of the best techs I have, I'd fire you."

I should squash this waste of life like an insect, the growly voice urged.

No. I won't do that, I replied.

Another growl. *Fine, but I should establish dominance before this goes any further.*

How? I sent back.

I felt a pressure building inside my chest, and the part of my mind that was no longer human seemed to push, somewhere between a snort and a roar in strength. At once, I felt *something* burst outward and fill the office.

"Sit down and shut up," I growled, and I'd swear I felt my incisors trying to lengthen. "I'm only going to say this once."

Tom's angry visage vanished. He dropped into his chair, almost missing it completely, as most of the color in his face fled at speed.

"Of course, I'm one of the best techs you have, idiot," still growling. "You only have *two*. Well, you did."

I took the two steps across the office necessary to reach

Tom's printer. I pulled a piece of paper out of its tray and scrawled the words, 'I quit, effective immediately,' on it before signing it and dating it. I threw the paper at his face and pivoted on my heel.

As I walked out the door, I spoke so the rest of the people could hear, "And you can keep the pipe dream you call severance. It's a joke when you can't make payroll half the time, anyway."

BECKY LOOKED up as I passed the reception desk. "Did you really just quit?"

I paused long enough to look her in the eyes and nodded. "Yep. It's the best decision I've made all month."

"What if he comes after you for breach of contract?"

I grinned, and I'm sure it looked absolutely predatory. "I have zero doubt my grandfather's attorneys would enjoy ripping him a new one in court. In fact, I almost hope he does."

"Must be nice," Becky mumbled, but I still heard it.

Letting the suite's outer door close, I walked back to the desk and pulled a piece of paper off a notepad and retrieved a pen. I wrote the email address of my grandfather's right hand in business on it and pushed the note across the desk to her.

"Send your resume to that email address. Use the email for your cover letter, and explicitly state that I said to send it. Odds favor you'll get a call."

Becky looked at the note and frowned. "Chantelle Packenham? Who is that?"

"Grandpa's right hand in his business. If you'd like a better job—or at least a less frustrating one—I'm sure she'll have something."

Without waiting for a response, I turned and left. I hoped

she'd email Chantelle. She was too good of a worker to stay at the messed-up den of chaos Tom called a company.

FROM MY FORMER EMPLOYER, I drove to my apartment building. I hoped the landlady, Sophia Rodriguez, was available. I wasn't looking forward to breaking my lease, but I just didn't need the apartment anymore. Sure, Grandpa would've handled the rent until the lease expired, but I didn't want him to do that. I enjoy standing on my own two feet.

Mrs. Rodriguez's late husband built the apartment building, and while I know many of my fellow tenants view the place as only a shade better than a rathole, I have nothing bad to say about it. Mrs. Rodriguez always fixes problems promptly—usually through hiring someone, but they're still fixed. The building is clean and secure. As far as I know, there's never been a break-in or violent crime in any of the apartments.

I switched off my car after pulling into the assigned spot for my apartment, 302, and eased myself out. Some idiot parked right up against mine in 301's spot, and I almost didn't have enough room to squeeze through the door. The person drove a classic Trans Am waxed to the point I could see my reflection in the body panels. Nice car, but shitty person.

I smiled at the flowerbeds scattered throughout the lawn on either side of the walk up to the building's courtyard. They were beautiful arrangements, and with my newly heightened senses, it seemed like I could almost smell each flower. All of them combined made for an enjoyable bouquet.

Then my ears pricked. It genuinely felt like they stood up and leaned forward, even though I knew they were fixed on the sides of my head.

"Please, sir, you need to leave. Don't make me call the *policía*." That was Mrs. Rodriguez's voice.

"Shut it," a man said. I didn't recognize his voice.

I stepped into the courtyard and found Mrs. Rodriguez with her hands clasped together as if she were pleading. She faced a man in ragged denim shorts and a dirty sports jersey. My neighbor from 301, Amy Courtney, crouched almost to her knees in front of the man I didn't know; he held her wrist in a painful joint lock.

"Sir, please, you're hurting her." Then, Mrs. Rodriguez saw me, and her entire expression lit up. "Mr. Wyatt, can you help, please?"

"I thought I told you to shut it, bitch," the man growled and backhanded Mrs. Rodriguez across the right side of her jaw. The kind landlady who kept from hurting butterflies— let alone higher forms of life—crumpled to the paving stones.

I felt my incisors lengthen as the part of me that wasn't human raged to take control and *end* this deplorable specimen of humanity.

"And if you know what's good for you, sport," the man said, addressing me, "you'll keep right on walking. The little woman and I were just sorting out some... domestic... disagreements."

Anyone who could see the rictus of pain that contorted Amy's face would know it for what it was. Still, she somehow turned my way and give me a pleading look. Pleading for what, I wasn't sure, but I wasn't about to leave her.

"No, I don't think I will."

The man shifted his eyes back to me and affected a look of surprise. "Excuse me?"

"It doesn't take much courage to strike a woman on the cusp of being a senior citizen. You want to try that with me?"

The man looked me over from head to toe, his faked surprise slipping away. "Nah, I'll just use this."

Using the same hand that struck Mrs. Rodriguez, he pulled a snub-nosed revolver from behind his back. As he lifted it to kind of aim at me, I exploded into motion. Covering the twenty feet between us almost in the blink of an eye, I grabbed the man's gun-wrist with my left hand and put every bit of strength I could muster into a savage left twist. I *wanted* to do something to him like what he was doing to Amy, but that's not what happened. It seemed I no longer knew my body, because I snapped his wrist like a dry twig in a drought.

He screamed. No... it wasn't a scream; it was a high-pitched shriek. I didn't know men could reach that octave after puberty. The revolver clattered on the paving stones as he collapsed to his knees.

"You broke my freakin' wrist! I'm gonna kill you!" The rest of his tirade devolved into an unintelligible expression of pain.

Off to my left, I heard, "*911, what is your emergency?*"

I turned and saw Mrs. Rodriguez holding her cell phone. A small trickle of blood ran down toward her jaw from the corner of her mouth.

"I need the *policía* and an ambulance. This is Sophia Rodriguez at Rodriguez Apartments on Hawthorne Court. There's a man here who is violating a restraining order, and he threatened one of my tenants with a gun. He's subdued right now, but please, send help."

"Hang up the—" the man stopped speaking when I placed my foot on his chest.

We made eye contact. I felt the non-human part of me aching to end him in a gory mess of blood, tissue, and bone. The moment his eyes met mine, I said, "Don't make me regret letting you live."

He jerked his head in a nod, the movements small and

slow but obvious. I stepped back, but his eyes never left me. He looked cowed down to his DNA.

In just a few minutes, I heard faint sirens that grew louder and stopped out front. A uniformed police officer led two paramedics with a gurney into the courtyard. The officer had his hand on the grip of his holstered sidearm.

I pointed to the revolver on the paving stones. "The guy's pistol is right there, officer."

The officer pulled on a pair of latex gloves once he saw that there was no immediate danger. He snapped pictures of the scene, focusing on the firearm. Then, he emptied the revolver of its ammunition and put the firearm in one evidence bag and the ammunition in another. While the paramedics moved in, he filled out the chain of custody information on each evidence bag.

After taking Amy's and Mrs. Rodriguez's statements, the officer turned and headed my way. When he came within about six feet, he stopped cold, and I picked up an unfamiliar scent.

Hmmm... elk shifter, the growly voice whispered in my mind.

"Uhm... I don't think we've met, sir," the officer said, his entire demeanor changed from the take-charge person he was mere moments before.

I smiled. "Wyatt Magnusson," and—leaning close—whispered, "turned five days ago."

"The rogue cougar up in the hills?"

I nodded.

The elk shifter nodded, clearing his throat. "Yes, well, I need to take your statement, but I'll try to keep you out of the investigation as much as possible. We have something of an off-the-books agreement with mundane law enforcement to keep us out of the human justice system unless there's no other option. With the evidence and the statements from the victims, I don't see why your involvement will go any further than a simple write-up. I'll put the code for a cougar shifter on it to keep people from hassling you."

"Code?"

"Right, you're new. Each breed of shifter has its own code that we put in any official reports. The mere presence of the code seals the report to a very specific clearance level, so the rank-and-file stay in the dark about what truly lurks in the night."

I frowned. "Oh. Uhm, I'd hate for you to get in trouble for falsifying a report. I'm not a cougar shifter."

"But you said…"

"Yes, but I didn't shift into a cougar for my first shift."

The officer frowned. "Then, what breed are you? I'll need something for the report."

"I don't think you'll have a code for me. Can you just put 'Feline Primogenitor?'"

The poor sod went bone white. Beads of sweat covered his forehead like BB-sized, clear polka dots. His entire demeanor screamed, "Please don't eat me," without saying a word.

He withdrew a digital audio recorder from one pouch on his duty belt, and I thought I noticed his hands shaking a little as he lifted it into view. "We can record your statement, and I'll transcribe it later."

"Uhm… don't I need to sign it? You had Amy and Mrs. Rodriguez sign theirs."

"It'll be fine, sir," the officer stammered.

I wasn't so sure about that, but it was the officer's head on the block, not mine. And he looked a little terrified of the idea that I'm a feline primogenitor. It took maybe fifteen minutes to record my statement and answer the clarifying questions he had.

By that time, the paramedics were ready to take the

perpetrator to the hospital, and the officer walked over and placed him under arrest for assault, battery, violation of a restraining order, and unlawful detainment. The officer read him his Miranda rights and handcuffed him to the gurney.

All three of us—Amy, Mrs. Rodriguez, and I—watched them leave.

Once the ambulance and police cruiser were out of sight, I turned to my landlady. "Mrs. Rodriguez, I'm sorry to pile more onto you after how the day has gone, but I need to discuss moving out of my apartment. I'm afraid I need to move closer to my new job."

"Well, normally, it would be an awful thing to break a lease," she replied. "But it so happens that I have a niece in need of a place, so if you're agreeable, she can sub-let your apartment until your current lease is up."

I grinned. "I am totally agreeable. I can be out by the end of the week. Thank you very much, ma'am."

She smiled and reached up to pat my cheek. "No, thank you. If you hadn't shown up when you did, I fear Amy and I wouldn't be standing here right now."

"No thanks necessary, ma'am. I was glad to help. I hope you have a nice day."

Mrs. Rodriguez smiled her reply and nodded, and I went upstairs to pack some clothes. I'd probably need to arrange for a storage unit until the local Alpha in Precious came back. I hoped he and I could work out some kind of agreement, because I didn't like the idea of a huge confrontation, not to mention being a new alpha on top of being a new shifter.

6

Gabrielle ran at a full sprint. Her lungs burned with the exertion as her paws kissed the ground in a distance-devouring gait. Sunlight sneaked through the leafy canopy overhead, mottling the ground in dots of illumination reminiscent of a jaguar's regular pattern.

She loved to run. Especially when she needed to think. A pleasant run would clear her mind and give her the peaceful foundation to see right to the heart of whatever issue was at hand, more often than not allowing her to see the solution at once. Alas... that was not the case this time. The issue at hand did not have any easy or straightforward solutions. The issue at hand was Wyatt Magnusson.

A scent wafting on the slight breeze told her she neared one of her favorite perches, and she slowed her sprint, padding through the forest until she stood at the shore of a small lake. It wasn't much larger than a pond, but it was too deep and too clear to be deemed such. A thirty-foot waterfall fed it, and a depression in the shore opposite the waterfall allowed the lake to feed the quintessential babbling brook.

She slinked up to a small rocky outcropping about twenty

feet below the waterfall's crest. The rocky perch was just close enough to the small lake to receive a faint, cooling mist from the waterfall's plunge. Even better, the overhead canopy never let direct sunlight bake the stone. Gabrielle wanted to purr as she stretched all her limbs and joints before curling up to enjoy the scene. That was a big downside to being a Genus *Panthera* breed for her; unlike the 'smaller' cats, she couldn't purr in her feline form.

It was difficult to keep from liking Wyatt Magnusson. He was a bundle of almost-child-like naivete wrapped up in a scary-powerful alpha primogenitor. She growled. A part of her wanted to rub her furry self against him right now. Stake a claim before anyone else could. But he was too new to this world. He wouldn't understand what the jaguar was doing... not yet. And when he finally understood, would he reciprocate or be angry?

Wyatt could have his pick of any woman in the shifter world, whether or not he realized that yet. *Gladys* would say 'yes' in a hot minute, and she was old enough to be his mother.

She growled again, though rather half-hearted this time. She'd never wanted a man to want to join her on a hunt before. Why did Wyatt have to make things so difficult?

Her stomach rumbled at the thought of a hunt, pulling her focus away from her thoughts. Yes. This area was rather well populated with deer. Perhaps a hunt would help... beyond just filling her belly.

BEING conscious made all the difference on the trip into Precious. The small town nestled in a river basin with rolling hills and grasslands all around it. It reminded me of what I'd read about frontier towns during the westward expansion, even if all the buildings were modern. I saw several park areas where wolf pups, kittens of various breeds, and young prey shifters all played together under the watchful eyes of adults.

THE SUN PEEKED over the horizon as I slowed to a stop in the parking lot of Precious's only hotel. It wasn't part of a chain, and everything about the place gave off an impression of maintenance and care. Opening the door rang an old-time bell mounted to the doorframe above it, and a smiling twenty-something with copper hair, vibrant green eyes, and an engaging smile appeared behind the front desk before I moved past the welcome mat.

"Hi, and welcome to the Precious Hotel," she said. "I'm Melody. How may I help you today?"

Melody was so upbeat and energetic that I couldn't keep from smiling. "Hello, Melody. I'm Wyatt. I was hoping to rent a room."

Wolf shifter, the growly voice remarked. *Not sure what breed...*

"Of course, Wyatt. How long will you need it?"

"I'm not sure. Probably at least until the local Alpha returns. I'd like to live here at least until I get a handle on... recent changes in my life."

Melody grinned. "It's okay, Wyatt. The few mundanes who live in the valley are all well aware that they're part of a shifter community. I'm a timber wolf."

"Ah, okay. That makes things much easier. Is it proper etiquette to offer one's... uhm..."

"We call them breeds; it can come across as rude to ask, but no one minds if you volunteer it during an introduction. I figured I'd be nice and share, since the entire town probably knows about you."

I fought the urge to wince. "Seriously? The *entire* town?"

Melody gave me a slow, smiling nod. The nod that almost screamed, 'You can run, but there's no point.' "Buddy Carrington and his crew have *never* pissed themselves in submission before, not even with Alpha Jace. Sorry, Wyatt, but you're news."

"You knew who I was when I walked in the door, didn't you?"

"Maybe," Melody replied, offering a smile and shrug.

I chuckled. It seemed impossible to be nervous or ill at ease around Melody. "Well, what do we need to do to finalize that room?"

"I'll need a payment of some sort. We can do a cash deposit now and settle up by the week, or if you have a card, we can use that."

I fished my wallet out of my back pocket and retrieved my bank card. Melody accepted it with a smile and turned to work with the front desk computer for a few moments. She ran my license through what looked like a document scanner and turned to a card swipe machine while the scanner did its thing.

"You know, you should probably visit a DMV office to update your license. Shifters all have a nice little 'S' in the star that shows it's a Federal ID, and it can make things a lot less complicated if you ever have to interact with law enforcement."

I couldn't keep from frowning. "I thought we were all some big secret, hiding in plain sight from humans."

Melody pursed her lips, something between a grimace and a pout. "We are, but we aren't. The government knows about us, but our existence is classified. Every branch of the military except the Air Force has its own shifter-only units. Mostly, the Feds and state authorities leave us alone, and we try to encourage that by policing ourselves and keeping problems out of the public eye. No one's sure how the big reveal would go, you know?" She turned away from me long enough to code two key cards before coming back to me and handing them over. "You'll be in Room 312. There's a big stairwell at the back with push-button controls on the outside door. That way, you can go for runs without having to stash your clothes and room key somewhere. Here are two keycards, but all the rooms have fingerprint readers, too. If you want to use it, just press a thumb or finger to the reader while you have the key card inserted to create the record of your print."

A run sounds nice, the growly voice remarked.

"Thank you, Melody."

She beamed at me. Then her eyes shot wide. "Oh! Very important. If you want to hunt, head into the eastern ranges. All the local prey shifters know to keep to the fields or west of town."

"Good to know," I replied. "Thank you."

Melody winked at me as I turned to leave. "You're very welcome, Wyatt. I'll be here till eleven tonight, so call the front desk if you need anything."

I nodded and went in search of the elevators. I found two side by side with one call button. I pressed it. The elevator on my right dinged and opened.

It took me little time at all to locate my room, and I swiped my thumb on the scanner while I had the keycard inserted. There was a double beep, and the door unlocked.

Entering the room, I saw nothing out of place or odd. I also *smelled* nothing odd either, which was good. Most hotels would probably be a nightmare now, with my shifter senses. I tested the King-size bed, which seemed to have the perfect mix of firm versus soft. I wouldn't be jumping on it in my cat form to test it; I'd probably break the poor frame. I retrieved the folding luggage stand from the closet and placed it next to a convenient wall, then returned to my car.

I SPENT PERHAPS twenty minutes getting 'moved in' before I stretched and felt the need to run echoing from the furry part of my mind. I walked over to the door and tested it a couple times, making sure it would latch on its own. I stowed my clothes on the bed and opened the door enough that I could push it open wider by shifting. Seconds later, a Smilodon trotted down the hallway in search of the back stairs.

GABRIELLE LOUNGED on her favorite perch over the small lake. The deer was delicious, and of course, she'd made sure it was only a deer and not a shifter. The eastern ranges were off-limits to the prey shifters in and around Precious, but life happened. So she always checked. She was sure a melanistic jaguar looked rather stupid sitting on its haunches and waving a paw at a herd of deer, but it was the best they'd devised. There wasn't any kind of animal telepathy or even something like it, and most shifters didn't smell human in their animal form. Maybe the new contact with the Magnusson clan could work with the Magi to develop something that would survive shifting.

It was so nice being out in the forest at her favorite perch. Things were so much simpler out here. No politics. No rogues trying to make the world burn or whatever it was they were doing. No human sensibilities or foibles. Just her and Nature. If she weren't so concerned about losing her human side, she would've given serious consideration to living out her days as Precious's one and only black panther.

Gabrielle shifted her position on the rock and yawned. She had nothing pressing that needed done. Another nap in the pleasant afternoon wouldn't be so bad, right?

SEVERAL DEER in the field tensed as I exited the hotel. I didn't know how one went about saying hello when in animal form, so I stopped and waved a paw as best I could before resuming my trot toward the eastern forest. I think a few deer and a rabbit or two waved back.

The trees I could see seemed to be conifers for the most part. The scents of pine and spruce filled my lungs with each inhalation, and trampling the grass of the field with my paws felt good. There was a time for careful stalking, but this wasn't it. No, it was time to run and frolic and get better acquainted with my feline self.

I crossed into the shade of the forest as a breeze came down off the hills and ruffled my fur. It reminded me of Vicki, and I chuffed in a feline version of an amused sigh. As much as I didn't want her to think of me as a pet, I'd probably let her rub my back and brush my fur from time to time because she seemed to enjoy it so much. For all her impishness, my sister had a heart of gold.

My mind continued to wander as I trotted through the forest. I probably should've paid more attention to my surroundings, but each time I stopped and considered it, I knew *exactly* how to get back to the hotel. So I put the human concern of getting lost out of my mind and just enjoyed myself.

A faint rustle caught my attention, and I slowed to a stop, examining my surroundings once more. It took a few minutes, but I soon spied a squirrel moving through the underbrush. The way it moved made me think it was looking for nuts or other forms of sustenance.

Okay. *Now*, it was time to stalk.

I angled myself toward the squirrel and padded in its direction. I let the animal portion of my mind take over, and I soon slinked my way closer to the squirrel without making a sound. That thought tickled me. A huge sabertooth cat making almost no sound as it snuck up on a squirrel. Something as big as I was shouldn't be capable of such silent movement. It was just unfair to the rest of the forest's denizens.

Taking my time and wisely using trees, clumps of underbrush, and other features of the terrain, I made my way to the squirrel. When I leaned out from behind a massive tree that looked like an oak, the squirrel was *right there*. I reached out my left fore-paw and flexed the proper muscle to extend one claw. The squirrel focused on the acorns in front of it and never realized a predator was so close... until I tapped its butt with my claw.

The squirrel jumped and turned, then froze at the sight of an apex predator that hadn't walked the Earth in thousands of years. I'll never know whether it *knew* what type of death I was or if it just knew I was a predator. All at once, it chirped out a fearful bark and leaped at the oak tree. In seconds, it had disappeared into the branches overhead, but we both knew I could've killed it if I chose. Fortunately for the squirrel, I never cared much for tree rats as a human, and I doubted they would taste any better when experienced with heightened senses. I chuffed my satisfaction at my first successful stalk and resumed my trot through the woods.

. . .

A SHORT TIME LATER, I picked up the sound of water running, and I stopped. I turned my head side to side for a better sense of the source and headed off in what I thought was its direction. A few minutes' trot led me to a decent-sized stream coming down out of the mountains in the distance, and I stepped close to sniff at the water. I don't know what I thought a sniff would accomplish, but it didn't smell bad. I tested it with my tongue and found it to be on the cold side of cool, even on a late summer day. It didn't taste bad, either, so I helped myself. The water felt good going down my throat, but lapping to get a drink felt odd. Maybe I would get more used to it with time.

I didn't feel like getting my fur wet, so once I drank my fill, I turned and trotted along the stream as it burbled and babbled its way down the hill. Before too long, I picked up the sound of a waterfall in the distance. In my mind, I smiled. I have no idea what it would've looked like to an outside observer. Probably frightening.

The stream led me straight to the waterfall. Stepping up to the ledge, I found a small lake about thirty feet below me. A rock outcropping jutted out from the hill some twenty feet below my ledge, and a black shape lay curled upon it. I realized what I saw when I watched a cat's tail twitch.

Sleeping, the growly voice remarked. *I should have some fun.*

No, I replied. *I'll just turn back the way I came. There's no reason to disturb anyone's sleep. Especially when whoever it is has teeth and claws.*

Not like mine.

I wanted to sigh, but I wasn't sure how I'd do it. *Oh, come on. I will not be that guy.*

Fine, the growly voice agreed, though sounding a touch petulant about it.

One last look. I'd never been this close to a melanistic

jaguar or leopard. I wasn't close enough to tell which specific breed it was, but it was a beautiful cat, regardless. Ah, well... maybe I'd meet whoever it is, eventually.

I exercised caution backing away from the ledge, and once I was ten feet away from it, I turned and began my trip back to the hotel. I should've probably checked in with Alistair after unpacking.

~

GABRIELLE YAWNED and stretched her legs and claws. That was a good nap, but it was time to go back to the 'real' world. She should probably check in with Alistair, see if he had any idea when Wyatt would be arriving. If she couldn't get out of being his orientation buddy, she might as well do a proper job of it.

She pushed herself to her feet and froze. The breeze coming off the waterfall carried a hint of feline shifter. But how could that be? As far as she knew, she was the only one who knew about this place.

The scent wasn't strong enough at the outcropping to know anything other than it came from a feline shifter that wasn't here. But if it wafted down with the waterfall, she knew where she might learn more.

A matter of maybe five minutes delivered Gabrielle to the ledge where the waterfall plunged into the lake below. There were tracks in the damp dirt. Big tracks. She leaned down to sniff one. Her eyes shot wide. Enough scent remained for her to recognize the shifter who left it.

Wyatt? He was here?

She looked at the tracks again. They looked large enough to match his massive paws. But what was he doing out here? And how did he find her lake? She looked over the tracks that approached the ledge then seemed to back away from it.

She followed them and saw where he turned and headed back to town.

She almost shot after him. The tracks didn't look too old, and he couldn't manage the speed she could. It would be simple to catch him. She came up with all kinds of human reasons to go back to town a different way, but he'd recognize her the first time she shifted around him. There was only one melanistic cat anywhere near Precious.

A resigned chuff. Fine. Time to play.

7

Refreshed and dressed once more, I opened my door intent on locating Alistair. I found Gabrielle leaning against the wall. Her posture communicated a relaxed nonchalance, and for a moment, it seemed she didn't care that I was standing in front of her. After three heartbeats, she met my gaze.

"How did you find my waterfall?"

I blinked. That was not what I was expecting. Her waterfall? Understanding clicked.

"I followed the stream that fed it. You were the melanistic cat?"

Gabrielle pushed off from the wall to stand upright. "I was going to stalk you back to town, but I guess you had just enough of a head start that I never caught you. I followed those ginormous tracks of yours right up to the back of the hotel, though."

I half-smiled and shrugged. "Yeah, my paws are a little big."

I turned toward the stairs, and Gabrielle matched me. We walked along in companionable silence, and I couldn't help but wonder why she was here. Don't get me wrong; every guy enjoys walking with a beautiful woman, and Gabrielle was... stunning. Even in faded jeans, a t-shirt, and sandals with straps, she was gorgeous. Up to now, I was the guy women called for computer help, and it always seemed like they were only interested in my utility. Weird error message on your computer? Call Wyatt. Cheap toner the company told you not to buy explode in your copier? Call Wyatt. Want to hang out with someone after work? Call someone *other than* Wyatt. Sure... I'd been on a few dates, here and there, but they weren't all that impressive. And I never felt like a second date would be anything other than punishment.

"How are you liking our sleepy little town?"

The question jerked me out of my spiraling thoughts, and I went with an ultra-cool, super-intelligent response, "Huh?" Then, my mind processed what I'd heard. "Oh! I like it well enough. I just came back to town today. Unpacked my luggage and went out for the run. Melody warned me about the eastern ranges versus the western ranges."

"She did?" Gabrielle remarked. "That was nice of her."

By that time, we reached the lobby and stepped into view of the front desk. Melody stood there, almost in the exact spot where she'd been upon my arrival. Only this time, she wasn't her previous upbeat self. Tears rolled freely down her cheeks. Every part of her I could see trembled, and my new senses caught a whiff of something on the air.

Hmmm... smells like... terror, the growly voice remarked.

"Melody, what's wrong?" I asked as I approached her.

Melody's eyes darted back and forth between me and Gabrielle for a couple seconds. It felt like a part of my soul wanted to die; she acted like a prey animal.

"Alpha Jace is back," she said, her voice small and vulnerable.

When no further information seemed to be on its way,

Gabrielle stepped forward. "What's wrong with Alpha Jace coming back? The town's his home."

"The Council came with him." Her voice made me think of a pup's whine. "They came here. I don't know how they knew you were in town, but they came here. They wanted to know your room number and where you were, but I told them hotel policy is that we only give out that kind of information for court orders." Melody's voice caught, and she gnawed at her lower lip with her teeth for a moment. "A councilor dominated me. He was even stronger than Alpha Jace. He made me tell them what they wanted to know."

The growly voice in my mind roared with rage. "Who? Who did that, Melody?"

"I know exactly who," Gabrielle answered. "It's okay, Melody. Don't worry about it."

Melody shook her head. "No, it's not okay. I... I... should've stood firm. I should've been better."

Without even thinking about it, I walked around the front desk and pulled Melody into a hug. "Don't worry about it, Melody; seriously, it will be okay. I'm going to go have a word with them. Do you want to watch?"

Melody shook her head.

I broke the hug and stepped back. "You'll be okay?"

She offered a small, tentative smile. "The hug almost made the entire experience worth it."

"Glad you liked it." I couldn't hold back the blush or the grin.

Before Melody could say anything else, I turned and walked with Gabrielle out of the hotel. The first thing I noticed was a collection of luxury SUVs parked in front of the town hall. I glanced toward Gabrielle, and she nodded.

"You said you know who did that," I remarked as we walked. "What can you tell me about him?"

Gabrielle sighed. "Thomas Carlyle. He's a wolf councilor,

and he's an entitled ass. A lot like Buddy Carrington, now that I think about it."

"So… he's a bully?"

Gabrielle nodded. "It seems like the really dominant wolves split about fifty-fifty between pleasant people and straight-up unrepentant assholes. The problem is, he's one of the strongest wolves in North America; that's how he ended up as the wolf councilor. The 'local' dire wolf doesn't want to deal with politics, so she keeps her head down, mostly. But it wouldn't matter, anyway. Thomas knows she would turn him into kibble if he ever moved on her."

"When you say local…?"

"No one really knows," Gabrielle replied, adding a shrug for flavor. "She avoids attention. There are only a few sightings every year. I think the current record is ten confirmed sightings in one year, but that was almost ten years ago now. She's basically a law unto herself. Oh, sure… she follows both the shifter and mundane laws, but only because she chooses to do so. We've been very lucky so far that none of the primogenitors have gone rogue. That would be a very tough hunt. As far as I know, she stays in North America. The other known dire wolf bounces around Europe."

"What should I expect when we walk in there?"

Gabrielle stopped and turned to me. "It will probably be a mess, honestly. There aren't enough vehicles out front for the *entire* Council to have come, so we're most likely looking at the predator councilors. Even then, that still means we'll have three wolves, three cats, three avians… oh. Pro tip: don't call them 'birds;' they really, really don't like that." Gabrielle's voice trailed off as she looked toward the line of SUVs. "You know… the more I think about it, I'm not sure what we'll be walking into. There are only eight of those luxury SUVs, but every shifter group sends three people to the Council. Even with just the predator councilors, there should be twenty-four to thirty cars. The three cat councilors makes sense; they will want to meet you. We already know the asshole wolf came to town. Beyond that? I'm sorry, Wyatt; I just don't know."

"It's okay. It's not like you have a lot of previous experience with feline primogenitors to draw on."

Gabrielle snorted a laugh. "Yeah, you are my first primogenitor, feline or otherwise. I wonder if we'll get more, now that you're here. And if we do, will they be Smilodons, too?"

"I hope you're not expecting me to know the answer to that," I replied as we reached the doors of the town hall. I held open the door for Gabrielle and followed her into the building.

The entry area held several cork boards with many announcements posted. I saw tasteful accents here and there, like pictures of town gatherings or events and some potted plants and flowers, and a reception desk sat beside the end of a hallway that led deeper into the building. A young man who looked thoroughly cowed sat behind the desk.

"They're in the council room," he said and dropped his eyes back to the desk.

I stopped and regarded the young man. "Are you okay?"

He jerked a choppy nod and remained silent. I wanted to draw him out a little, but right now, it was probably just as well that he kept his head down. I had a feeling the upcoming conversation would not go in any direction one could predict.

Gabrielle led me down the hallway to the town's council room. I didn't know how large the town council actually was, but the hall was short and wide. Gabrielle and I walked through the double doors together, and my first thought of the room beyond was how much it looked like a courtroom.

A large table sat in an area separated from rows of seats by a decorative wooden partition. The seating in the gallery was wood construction, with upholstery and padding on the seats and backs. I tried not to smirk at seeing the chairs around the big table without any padding at all. Good idea. Probably helps to keep the meetings from running too long.

Alistair lounged in the aisle seat of the gallery's front row, and a large group of people I didn't know stood or sat around the large table. At the sound of the door, everyone turned to look our way. Alistair smiled and stood.

"Hello, Wyatt," Alistair said as he held out his hand.

I gave him a respectable handshake as I answered, "Good day to you, Alistair. I apologize for not checking in with you when I arrived. The call of a run through the eastern ranges was just too strong."

Alistair smiled and nodded. "I know that feeling, and besides, never apologize."

"My grandfather says the same thing."

Alistair leaned close, almost whispering, "Where do you think I learned it?" Then, Alistair turned and gestured from the group to Wyatt. "Esteemed Councilors and Alpha Jason McCourtney, may I present Wyatt Magnusson?"

A young man standing to the side of the assembled councilors nodded when Alistair said 'Jason McCourtney,' and I saw several of the group fight the urge to gape at the mention of my family name. All except one. He stood out because his glare never wavered. He was maybe four inches shorter than me, with a full head of spiked, dirty blond hair that angled forward. His hazel eyes had a hard look to them, and I could tell he clenched his jaw tight.

"So, this is our supposed feline primogenitor?" he asked, and his expression quirked like he wanted to sneer. "I'm not impressed."

For as long as I live, I doubt if I'll ever know what possessed me to reply with, "I can't say that I really care whether I impress you. Shouldn't you be barking at some critter up a tree or peeing on someone's tire? Maybe licking yourself somewhere unmentionable? That's all wild dogs do, right?"

The sudden silence was so complete that a cough in the hall outside would have been deafening. Everyone stared at me in shock, some with their mouths agape. Again, all except the twerp with the blond spiky hair. His lips pulled back from his teeth in a silent snarl as a deep red flush came up in his neck. His hazel eyes shifted to a gold. His hands clenched into fists.

"I will kill you for such disrespect," he ground out between his clenched teeth.

I gave him my best uncaring shrug. "You're the guy who dominated Melody over at the hotel into violating policy, right?"

"She needed to learn her place, the same as you do."

"Whatever you say, Fido. Are we throwing down here, or is there someplace less breakable?"

Alistair lifted a hand, interjecting, "The town has a small arena for dominance fights. It's at the far end of the city park."

I nodded. "That works for me. What about you, Spot?"

He looked about ready to leap over the decorative divider at me, but he jerked a nod.

"Very well," Alistair remarked. "Let us proceed."

As EVERYONE FILED out of the town council chamber, Gabrielle pulled me into a vacant office. The moment the door latched, she spun, her face a mask of frustration and disbelief.

"Are you out of your mind? You just challenged a councilor! They don't get those jobs for being shy and retiring. He's won more dominance fights than he can probably count. Oh… and that's another thing. Dominance fights—at least when challenging a councilor—are to the death. Did you think about that before you popped off with your childish humor? Did you even *know* that?"

That put a whole new dimension on the situation.

"No, I honestly didn't, which I'm guessing you already knew. Almost everything I know about being a shifter I've learned from you. But instead of raking me over the coals for it, why don't you tell me about him?"

Gabrielle stopped and wiped her brow. "Okay. He's a Canadian timber wolf. He's about as large as a wolf shifter can be and not be a primogenitor. He likes to use his weight to his advantage, but that won't help him with you. Not against that ginormous cat I saw in the diner. He may try to get in behind you for a hamstring strike, and I've also heard he likes to jump on his opponent's back and break their necks with a bite."

I blinked and felt my eyebrows rise. "That's allowed?"

"It's a fight to the death, Wyatt. Anything's allowed. Oh, and there's one other thing. Your shifter healing won't help you much. It barely works against other shifters' natural weapons like teeth and claws. With time and a ton of food, you'll be okay, but don't go into this fight relying on it to save you."

Okay. *That* made all this a little scarier. Still, I wasn't about to back down. I took a deep breath and nodded.

"That's good to know. Thank you. Now, where is this arena Alistair mentioned?"

GABRIELLE LED WYATT to the arena. When they arrived, it seemed like most of the town was there, too. As they approached, all Gabrielle heard was the low-level, unintelligible noise a large crowd makes, but the moment Wyatt stepped into view, everyone started cheering and waving.

Pointing Wyatt toward the participants' entrance to the arena, Gabrielle turned toward the stands. She didn't expect she'd find a seat, not with such a large crowd, but she saw Melody sitting beside the sole empty seat in sight. It was right on the front row. Melody met her eyes and waved her over.

"I thought you didn't want to come," Gabrielle said as she accepted Melody's invitation to sit.

Melody shrugged. "I didn't, but it didn't seem right not to attend a dominance fight that's because of me. What do you think Wyatt's chances are?"

Gabrielle turned and met the woman's eyes. "I don't want to give you false hope, Melody. I don't think his chances are good. Thomas Carlyle has been fighting these types of fights for *years*, and he's still around. Wyatt has been a shifter now, for what? Five—maybe six—days? And awake and aware for only one of them? Even with his size advantage, I don't see how it can end any other way than in Thomas's favor."

"That's not right," Melody replied, her expression crestfallen. "Wyatt's a good guy."

"Yes, he is."

❧

I STEPPED INTO THE ARENA, and the crowd somehow cheered even louder. As loud as they already were, I wouldn't have thought it possible. The sheer volume hurt my ears a bit, but I refused to wince. I wouldn't give the jerk across the way the satisfaction of seeing that.

The arena was a large circle, easily sixty feet across and surrounded by an 8-foot palisade wall. At the top of the wall, a chain circled the arena from metal posts placed at

76

regular intervals. The first level of bleachers started there and went up. I saw Melody and Gabrielle sitting together; they both watched me. The other councilors sat behind Thomas.

Alistair stood and approached the chain. When he stopped moving, the crowd quieted.

"A dominance challenge has been issued and accepted between Wyatt Magnusson, our feline primogenitor, and Thomas Carlyle, a wolf councilor. As is our custom, once the challenge is accepted, there is no turning back. Participants, are you ready?"

I nodded just heartbeats before the jerk did.

"Very well," Alistair said. "Begin."

Alistair returned to his seat as Thomas started unbuttoning his shirt. I grinned and snapped my fingers twice, then whistled like I was calling a dog. "Here, Fido! Come on, boy! Heel!"

I watched rage color Thomas's cheeks purple, and he stopped bothering with being nice. There was an explosion of fabric, and a Canadian timber wolf made a sprinting leap at me, its lips pulled back from its teeth in a snarl.

Waiting until he committed to his leap, I rolled out of the way and let him collide with the palisade behind me. It was a gruesome hit that would've taken a regular wolf or dog out of the fight, but Thomas pushed himself to his feet and weaved as he stood there, rolling his head.

"Bad doggie, Fido! You're not supposed to hit the wall," I taunted, dancing away while carefully removing my own clothes. "You're supposed to hit me."

Thomas must have hit the wall harder than I thought, because he gave me more than sufficient time to get undressed for my shift. Right before I shifted, I took the time to wrap my clothes into a bundle and toss them to Gabrielle. Standing in the center of the arena naked as the day I was born, several women whistled or cheered. I could tell I blushed from the heat in my ears and cheeks.

I must choose wisely before adding any of them to the pride, the growly voice said.

That was new. *Who said I* wanted *a pride?*

Of course, I do, the growly voice replied. *It is my right.*

I pushed that line of thought aside and touched the part of my mind that wasn't human. I felt my feline form take over, and the whistling and cheering became awed—or fearful—whispers. Thomas turned to face me, snarling once again. I took a breath and put everything I had into a roar fit to rattle windows across town. I felt that odd burst as I roared, and for a split-second, I saw Thomas's snarl falter.

I don't know how long we stood there, staring at each other, but I grew tired of it. Well, bored to be honest. My cat form wasn't really built for it, but I lifted my left forepaw and waved it in a 'bring it on' gesture. I was rather proud I managed it.

Thomas refreshed his snarl and charged me. As he neared, I realized how much smaller than me he was. Next to my feline form, he looked like a half-grown pup. I bet *that* didn't help his mood at all, since Canadian timber wolves were one of the larger wolf breeds... if not *the* largest.

Once again, Thomas leaped at me mid-charge, but I was ready for him. I brought my right forepaw up and put all my weight and muscle into a 'slap.' The slap caught Thomas on the side of his head, my paw almost perfectly centered in the triangle created by his left eye, the base of his left ear, and the left mandible joint. The ghastly crack of multiple bones shattering almost overshadowed a lupine sound of pain as I dropped to my side and let Thomas 'frisbee' over top of me. I looked back in time to see him hit in an explosion of sawdust and dirt.

None of the damage I'd inflicted so far came from my

claws or teeth, so I knew Thomas would heal it in no time. I hoped the broken or shattered bones would take a little longer, but if I was going to win this, I needed to get in there and draw some blood. No… *a lot* of blood.

I jumped back to my feet and made my charge. Thomas was on his feet by the time I neared, and the swipe of my claws only caught his hind leg. He still yipped in pain, though, as he fled at a limping run. I tried to keep up with him, but my feline form wasn't built for speed.

Before I knew it, he was behind me. Then he was on my back, going for his 'signature' move. The odd thing was, I could feel a little pressure as he tried to bite my neck, but either his jaw hadn't fully healed yet or my hide was too tough for his teeth. The bite felt like those little pin-pricks people do to check their blood sugar.

It took no time at all for his gnawing on my neck to get *very* old, but I didn't want to 'just' roll over. I was sure other shifters tried that all the time. I wanted to be different. So I reared up on my hind legs. Thomas yipped as he pawed and nipped at my back and hips for some kind of traction, but he must not have found it. He hit the arena floor in another *poof* of dirt and sawdust, and I hoped he was watching for what came next.

Ever worked a nine-to-five in an office that put a lot of stock in those asinine team-building exercises like trust falls? That backward collapse where you trust your co-workers to keep you from hitting the floor? Yeah… I would've paid money to know what went through Thomas's mind as I forced myself to overbalance backward and come down on him like a thousand-pound furry tree.

Timber!

An immense cloud of dust and sawdust billowed into the air to the accompaniment of a solid, heavy *THUD* and many, many bones shattering all at once. The whole arena fell silent, and I saw several people cover a gaping mouth with a hand. I could've rolled over and finished it right there, but I wanted this fracas to be as memorable as possible. So, I wiggled like the wolf was my back scratcher. I heard a few more pops and snaps, with a whine or three thrown in for flavor.

Yeah... no one would mistake *that* for anything other than adding insult to injury; the only thing more humiliating would be to stand up and mark my territory on whatever furry mess remained.

Since I figured I'd made my point by now, I rolled to my feet and looked to see what remained of the inestimable Thomas Carlyle. It wasn't pretty. The wolf laid there, with blood oozing out of his ears and eyes, a red froth drooling out of his mouth. His deep barrel chest now looked more like a smooshed sandwich, and I think only the various tissues involved kept his legs connected.

I moved until I could look the wolf in his eyes, and I saw resigned acceptance there. He knew what happened next. I knew it, too. Every part of my feline form *ached* to end him, and I doubted anyone here would say he didn't deserve it.

But I—Wyatt Magnusson, the human—didn't want him dead. I just wanted him to be a decent person. I lifted my head and search the crowd until I found Alistair. He stood and approached the chain ring, then nodded once.

"Finish it, Wyatt. He wouldn't hesitate if your positions were reversed."

I touched the part of my mind that was still human and shifted. "I know that, so why should I sink to his level?"

Alistair heaved a sigh. "Because it is our way."

"It may be your way, but it's not mine."

I turned and knelt in front of Thomas the wolf. I met his eyes and held the gaze for several moments. Then, "Do you yield?"

A faint nod with an even fainter whine.

"Have you learned your lesson about being an ass to people? I don't want to have this discussion again."

Another faint nod.

I stood and addressed the crowd. "Thomas Carlyle yields. Honor and justice have been satisfied."

The silence blanketing the arena was so extreme that I figured my enhanced ears could hear a pin hitting the pavement on Main Street, a solid three hundred yards away. I approached the side of the arena where Gabrielle sat with Melody, holding the bundle of my clothes.

"Mind tossing me my clothes?"

Somewhere off to my left, I heard a woman mutter, "Does she have to?"

8

Gabrielle exited the arena in time to see the doctor from the infirmary and two assistants carrying a stretcher pass through the participants' entrance. This led her to notice Alistair and the remaining councilors standing off to one side and talking in hushed tones. More than one councilor's expression suggested the conversation was getting heated, despite being so muted. She watched Alpha Jace exit the spectator's access, and she thought he looked a little unsettled. Part of her said she should speak with him, but she knew her heart wasn't really in it. Gabrielle turned toward the participants' entrance to meet up with Wyatt, but Alistair saw her and motioned for her to join him.

"Yes, I understand your point, Norman," a female councilor said as Gabrielle approached, "but the fact of the matter is that our laws are sacrosanct. Wyatt defeated a councilor in a recognized dominance fight, which means Wyatt takes his seat on the Council."

The councilor addressed as Norman looked like he was

about thirty seconds from losing control. His nostrils flared as a deep red flush creeped up his neck, his eyes partially shifting toward golden wolf eyes, and he glared at the woman as he replied, "Dammit, Joanna! Thomas was a *wolf* councilor, and Wyatt is a *feline*. I will not accept a feline taking over a wolf seat and throwing the Council out of balance. Every shifter race has always had *three* councilors. I'm going in there and settling this once and for all."

Joanna and several of her associates regarded Norman with the expression of a patient parent dealing with a recalcitrant child. Joanna voiced what Gabrielle was sure everyone there was thinking, "And just what makes you think the outcome of your fight with Wyatt will be any different than Thomas's fight? Hmmm? You have always said that Thomas was a better fighter than you, a more vicious fighter than you. If he didn't succeed, how will you?"

Norman drew himself up to launch into a reply, but Alistair forestalled that by asking, "Gabrielle, what are your thoughts on the situation? You know Wyatt best out of all of us."

"I wouldn't say I really know him," Gabrielle countered, "but have any of you considered Wyatt might not *want* a seat on the Council?"

Every councilor present gaped at Gabrielle. Each person's expression communicated his or her confusion differently, but it was apparent that they had not even considered that possibility.

Alistair seemed to watch the councilors with barely restrained amusement, then asked, "Would you please explain your thinking on this?"

Gabrielle sighed. "Wyatt has been a shifter for all of... what... five days? He doesn't even understand what it means to be a shifter yet, let alone all the politicking and backstabbing and maneuvering that happens at the Council level.

Besides, we've already discussed how the dire wolf tends to keep to herself, and I would not be surprised at all if Wyatt decides to follow her lead.

"Keep in mind that Wyatt didn't choose the dominance fight. Yes, he was angry and offended at how Thomas had dominated Melody to violate the hotel's policies, but he didn't go into the arena to claim Thomas's seat. He went into the arena to defend Melody and everyone else who has been bullied by a more dominant shifter. We didn't—"

Alistair looked over Gabrielle's shoulder and smiled, interrupting her, "Ah, here he is now. Wyatt, would you come over here please?"

~

I COULDN'T TAKE the pained whines and yips as the medical people moved Thomas onto the stretcher, so I left the arena. As I stepped outside, I heard Alistair call me over to a group. I could see Gabrielle standing with him along with the rest of the councilors, and I couldn't help but wonder why they wanted to speak with me. I tried to keep my feelings from showing in my expression as I approached, and I arrived just in time to hear Alistair apologize to Gabrielle for interrupting her.

"The conquering hero arrives," Alistair remarked as I stopped at Gabrielle's side. I couldn't tell if he was mocking me or just joking in general.

"Hello, Alistair," I said. "You wanted something?"

Alistair glanced at the councilors before answering, "Yes... well, you see there's a bit of an issue arising from your victory. I suppose we should have foreseen it, but by defeating Thomas, you have the right to his seat on the Council, as per our laws and customs. That creates a problem because Thomas is a wolf. As a feline shifter, you would give the felines four votes, throwing the Council out of balance. There's no law that specifically *says* the Council must be balanced across all species, but we've kept the peace between the different shifter breeds for hundreds of years by ensuring we all have equal representation on the Council."

I made a dismissive wave. "Oh, that's easy. Thomas can keep his seat, or it can go to some other wolf. I certainly have no interest in being on the Council. The other primogenitor in North America isn't on the Council, so I see no reason to change things. Besides, I'm still learning about being a shifter and coming to grips with that fundamental change in my life; there's no reason to complicate that by adding something else."

By the time I wound down, I noticed the councilors all stared at me, wearing various expressions of shock and disbelief.

"What?" I asked. "What's the big deal?"

"Gabrielle just explained that she expected you were largely uninterested in a seat on the Council, my boy," Alistair explained. "I think they're having a difficult time processing a shifter of your strength not wanting power."

I grimaced and shook my head. "There are more important things in life than power. I need to understand and adjust to what my life is now. I don't need a seat on the Council for that. Matter of fact, I imagine a seat on the Council would only complicate that for me. So... was there anything else?"

Alistair smiled and shook his head. "No, my boy. I think you've answered the matter. Thank you much."

I turned to leave and noticed Gabrielle took the opportunity to leave with me, not that I minded. We walked far enough to be out of earshot for Alistair and the Councilors before Gabrielle threw me another curveball.

"I feel it's only sporting to warn you that many of the eligible ladies will make themselves known soon."

That hit me like a bucket of ice-cold water while I was fast asleep. I tried to keep from freezing mid-step and staring at her. My incomprehension was *that* strong.

"Uh... what?"

Gabrielle chuckled. "Don't act so surprised. You were already turning heads. With that display of both cunning *and* raw strength, anyone who thinks they might have a chance will be getting into line to make their case."

I looked at her, once again noticing just how attractive she was. "And just where do *you* fit into all this?"

Gabrielle worked her lower lip between her teeth, and damn if she didn't make that look sexy as all hell. "I'd be lying if I said I didn't feel it, too. My cat has wanted to climb you like a tree since you dominated Buddy in the diner; she was very put out that we let you slip away to go tie off the threads of your human life all by yourself. But that side of every shifter is much more primal than we are and doesn't always understand the human side of things. I get the impression that you're maybe two or three unexpected revelations away from going completely off the rails, and I don't believe following my cat's advice would help you with that."

My stomach chose that moment to interject a fierce growl into the discourse, making me aware of a gnawing sensation that almost felt like my spine or surrounding tissues might be in grave danger if I didn't get food soon.

"Say... not to change the subject, but it seems like I'm in need of food. You hungry at all?"

Gabrielle laughed. "I'm a shifter, too, Wyatt. It's rare when we're not hungry to some extent."

. . .

The steady, low-intensity background noise of people eating and chatting filled the diner, and even with my newly enhanced senses, I could only pick out a snippet of conversation or two as Gabrielle led me to an open table. One of Gladys's servers arrived before we finished sitting down to take our drink orders and leave menus and silverware wrapped in napkins.

Silence reigned for a moment until I said, "So, what's the next lesson on the journey to becoming a well-adjusted shifter?"

Gabrielle sat unspeaking for several moments more. At last, she shrugged. "I've never been a guide for new shifters before, and since I was born a shifter, it's a little difficult to know where to start."

"Well, what about an overview of shifters then? You said all the shifter races are represented on the Council?"

Gabrielle snorted. "Goodness, no. Every shifter type is represented, but for each race or species to be represented would make the Council so large it would be unwieldy. If I said 'race' earlier, it was a mis-speak on my part. By type, I mean wolf, feline, avian, and so on."

The server returned with our drinks, and Gabrielle took the time to browse the menu while I ordered three cheeseburgers with everything and a couple orders of fries. The server took the time to verify what I meant by 'everything,' which gave Gabrielle sufficient time to settle on what she wanted.

The server left to put our orders in, and Gabrielle snapped her fingers. "Oh, that's right. I ran into Doc. He asked me to tell you he'd appreciate it if you stopped by the infirmary. He'd like to get a medical baseline started for you if you plan to be around here for a while."

"Are you sure it's not just a cover for him to examine a feline primogenitor?"

Gabrielle shrugged. "I won't say 'yes,' but I can't say 'no' with any conviction, either. I know I'd be interested to find out if you deviate from the prehistoric natural Smilodons at all and, if so, how."

"Okay. You make a good point, there. I hadn't considered that aspect of it. Do you differ at all from natural melanistic jaguars?"

Gabrielle lifted her hand and tipped it back and forth. "I have a higher concentration of endurance muscle than has been recorded in my natural counterparts, but the difference is only a few percentage points. I don't really know if that counts."

Vicki would probably be able to give me chapter and verse on prehistoric Smilodons, but I knew next to nothing about them. I could do some research beforehand, so I'd be in a better position to understand the differences, too.

"Okay." I added a nod. "I'll do it. Want to stop by the infirmary after we eat to schedule it?"

"Sure, but I imagine Doc's going to have his hands full for a day or two with Thomas. You really did a number on him, you know. I heard those bones snap across the arena."

I shrugged. "I despise bullies with a passion. I was never bullied, myself; I think the family name kind of shielded me from that, but still…"

The bell over the diner's door jingled, and Gabrielle and I both turned our heads to look. Buddy Carrington stood halfway through the door, his eyes locked on me and his whole complexion pale. His posse piled up behind him. I could hear some grumbling about the sudden stop, and one of them leaned to the side to look around Buddy. He went a little pale, too.

It didn't take long for the background hum of the diner to fade, and I imagined everyone watched Buddy and his posse. I watched Buddy swallow hard a couple times, his

Adams apple bobbing like a harbor buoy in choppy seas, before he fully entered the diner and made his way to our table.

He stopped about seven feet from us, his posse arrayed out around him, and he asked, "Please, sir, may we come in?"

I scanned the faces looking at me without making eye contact and replied with my own question. "Are you going to behave?"

One by one, each member of the posse nodded. Buddy said, "Yes, sir."

"Then, why would I care? It's not even my diner."

Buddy jerked a quick nod and moved with haste toward an open table far from Gabrielle and me.

Once the background hum was back, I looked to Gabrielle, saying, "That was a little odd."

"No, it wasn't." She looked like she fought a grin or smile. Maybe a laugh. "Buddy has *always* looked to Thomas Carlyle as something of a role model or hero, even going so far as to model his behavior after the man. And you just schooled Thomas in the arena. I may be wrong, but I think we might be seeing a new Buddy in the making."

The server arrived with our food, and a comfortable silence descended on the table while we ate. My order was excellent, and Gabrielle didn't seem to have any complaints about hers, either.

I couldn't believe how hungry I was, going through my three cheeseburgers and two orders of fries like they were snacks. I finished everything only a minute or two behind Gabrielle and leaned back against my seat, a satisfied smile curling my lips. I had the 'pleasantly full' feeling you get when you eat just the right amount for your hunger, which was a little surprising considering how much food I had devoured.

"So, is this how it's always going to be now?" I asked.

"Will I go through what would be a month of food for a family of three each day?"

"Honestly, it'll vary, just like it did when you were human. On the days when you're very active and doing calorie-intensive work, you'll eat like an army battalion. On the lazy days, you might only eat like a squad."

"Doesn't a squad have something like ten or twelve people in it?"

Gabrielle smirked. "Usually, but look on the bright side. You can supplement your food budget by hunting."

The bell over the door dinged again, and Gabrielle and I both turned to look as the diner's background noise faded. Alistair stood just inside the door with a state trooper and a man and woman in suits just behind him. He scanned the diner, and his gaze settled on our table. He headed our way, the trooper and suits falling in behind him.

When Alistair reached our table, he rested his hands on the back of a chair across the table from us, his expression grim. After a heartbeat or three, he said, "Gabrielle, I regret to pull you away from mentoring Wyatt, but you're our best tracker. We need your expertise."

ALISTAIR'S WORDS circled through Gabrielle's mind as she examined his hangers-on. The trooper was easy (and human) enough. The man and woman in suits were human, too, but they carried faint hints of shifter. Too faint to tell what type. The man's suit jacket splayed open far enough so she could see a badge that looked suspiciously like one of the federal law enforcement agencies.

"Someone was taken?" Gabrielle asked.

Alistair started to reply, but the suited man pushed his way forward, saying, "Not here. Are you in or not?"

Gabrielle heaved an indifferent shrug. "I suppose so, but if you take me, you take Wyatt, too. He'll be useful, and I don't want to leave him to get into mischief."

"Wyatt getting into mischief isn't our problem," the suited man shot back. "Besides, he's not cleared. No deal."

"Fine, then. No tracker."

The suited man's eyes narrowed, and his nostrils flared. He smelled like budding anger. "This whole county is full of shifters. You won't be hard to replace."

Gabrielle offered the man an easy smile. "Good luck with that."

The suited man scanned the diner's patrons, his gaze settling on the table occupied by Buddy and his posse. "There, that man. We've used him before, so he's cleared. Let's go."

Gabrielle didn't turn to look. She didn't want to give the appearance of intimidation or interference, and Buddy surprised her.

"Nope," Buddy announced to the entire room. "The person you want is Gabrielle. I'll come along to help if she wants, but I'm not moving without her say-so."

The suited man's nostrils flared and compressed like a blacksmith's bellows. He definitely smelled like anger now. "How about I cite all of you for interfering in a federal investigation and get your charter revoked?"

"Ah," Alistair interjected, "you might want to be careful about that particular threat, my boy. Our charter—as you put it—is a legally recognized treaty between the Shifter Nation and the United States of America, duly ratified by the Senate with all the 'i's dotted and 't's crossed. What was your pay-grade inside the federal government again?"

"If the newbie's participation is her price," the suited woman said, joining the discussion for the first time, "we'll pay it. Every second we spend arguing over inconsequential matters is one more second we could've been making progress on this."

The suited man spun, saying, "But—"

"My authority, Jack. Now, let's go, please."

"The conference room in City Hall might be the best venue for the discussion," Alistair offered.

"Agreed," the suited woman said.

Gabrielle stood, prompting Wyatt to do the same. As she moved around the table, she pointed at Buddy and said, "Buddy, you might as well come along until we find out whether the extra hands will help. They probably don't want to give their briefing twice."

WOOD PANELING LINED the walls of the office. Tasteful knick-knacks decorated the windowsill and the mantle of the unused fireplace. A massive oak desk dominated the center of the space with understated elegance, and a cup of steeping Darjeeling tea sat atop a coaster within easy reach of the office's occupant, one Hector Olmstadt. Hector stood a few inches over six feet and possessed a massive frame and deep, barrel chest. He kept his hair and beard neatly trimmed and cared not at all that strands of gray creeped into its otherwise dark brown coloration.

Knocks on the door drew Hector's attention, and he called "Enter" without looking away from his computer's monitor. The door opened to admit Oscar Dunleevy, the head of their operations in Washington state. Oscar was a tall, broad-shouldered man, with dark hair and eyes, and he wore black fatigues with a tactical harness strapped to his chest. He insisted on hanging his holster from the harness on his chest, right over his left lung; Hector didn't see why he had to be different than the rest of the direct-action group, but hey… whatever. They had bigger problems.

Hector finished his immediate process on the computer and turned to face his guest. "Yes? How goes it?"

"It's going well. We had a line on the governor's children, but that turned into almost a bait-and-switch. We snagged three. I've rotated out the bait NAS with the version you sent last week."

Hector smiled. "Good. We just completed a tunnel connecting this place to the truck stop along the interstate a mile to the east, and the new bait devices all point to a raid here. I think they pair nicely with the charms that I just distributed to the staff; they allow the bearer to see through all illusions, no matter their source."

"Damn. I wouldn't mind having a few of those myself."

"I'd love to outfit the teams with them," Hector agreed, "but they're frightfully expensive. We're not exactly operating on an unlimited budget. Do you have anything else?"

Oscar shook his head. "No, I just thought I'd update you while I came for a re-supply. They've probably finished loading the trucks already and are waiting for me. How did you manage to hide our regional base as an orphanage?"

Hector grinned. "Well, like the man said, I'm not without skills."

9

A listair led the group to the conference room in the city's administration building. Gabrielle caught an expression of surprise from Wyatt out of the corner of her eye, and she guessed he hadn't realized he'd walked right by the door when he'd been in the admin building earlier. The walls were painted a soft, pastel blue... very close to the shade of a cloudless sky. A massive piece made from cherry and stained to perfection, the glass-topped, circular conference table dominated the room. It was so large that twenty chairs could surround it without making the room feel cramped.

Gabrielle went to her customary seat, and Wyatt sat beside her. Buddy sat as far from Wyatt as he could manage and still be grouped with the locals. She wanted to snicker and needle him about it but cared more about presenting a united front to the outsiders.

Once everyone was seated, the two suits shared a glance, and the woman began. "I am Winnifred Hauser, Special Agent. My associate is Special Agent Jackson Schumacher,

94

and our state liaison is Sergeant Thompson Rochester of the State Police. Over the past few weeks, we have noticed a dramatic upswing in reports of Missing Persons and Kidnapping. The victims have all been between the ages of seven and seventeen, and they have been regular humans, Magi, and shifters. We believe that the cases being spread across the three major populations slowed our recognition of the pattern.

"The most recent case happened yesterday in a small community just outside the state capital. Persons unknown abducted three children from the care of the woman who serves as the nanny for the governor's children. We believe the governor's twins were the intended targets, but due to an unforeseen re-shuffling of the schedule, they were not with the nanny. The children are all supernatural; one of them is a shifter, and the other two Magi. We've tried tracking the abductors with regular police canines, and we think they hid their trail with magic… which is where you come in."

"Why us?" Wyatt asked.

Gabrielle turned to him. "Shifters can sense magic, Wyatt. The most common is a scent that shouldn't be there, but I've known shifters who sensed it as sounds. One fox shifter I knew saw magic as gradients of color in a kind of wispy cloud-shape."

"That actually sounds kind of cool," Wyatt replied, his lips curling into a smile. "I wonder how I'll see it."

Gabrielle looked to their guests. "Please, forgive Wyatt. The most recent rogue cougar turned him, and he's still learning about his new world."

"Most cougar shifters I've spoken with tell me it's a scent for them," Hauser offered.

"That's not as cool," Wyatt remarked, "but I'm not a cougar shifter."

Schumacher frowned again. "But she just said a rogue cougar turned you."

Wyatt nodded. "Yes, she did."

"Then, how are you not a cougar?"

Gabrielle watched Wyatt glance her way first and then to Alistair.

"Go ahead, lad," Alistair answered the unspoken question. "They'll have access to the information as soon as we complete your medical profile and update our records."

Wyatt turned back to the agents and trooper. "I'm a feline primogenitor, a—"

"You're an American lion?" Hauser asked, her eyes twinkling as a child-like grin grew across her expression. Her associate and the state trooper exhibited fear under differing levels of control.

"No. A Smilodon."

Hauser's excited expression waned for a moment as she stared at the tabletop. It suddenly returned full force, and she met Wyatt's gaze once more. "You… you're a sabertooth?"

Wyatt merely nodded in response.

"Which species?" The case seemed forgotten.

"I'm not sure. I've never really looked in a mirror, but from what I've been able to tell, my main coloring is sort of tan like an African lion with faint tawny stripes."

"He's about as tall as the bottom of my ribcage at the shoulder," Gabrielle offered.

Buddy added, "And his paws cover a third of my chest."

Schumacher cleared his throat, and Hauser reined in her excitement, saying, "Yes, of course. I apologize. I minored in Paleontology, you see, and I absolutely loved the Pleistocene period and especially the big cats. But we should return to the case. We would like for you to visit the most recent abduction scene and try to track the abductors."

"You said Magi children have been taken?" Wyatt asked. "Have you spoken with the Magi Assembly?"

Schumacher looked like he wanted to growl again, and Gabrielle almost wished he had. Her cat almost salivated at the thought of Wyatt putting the man in his place.

Hauser pursed her lips for a moment before shaking her head. "We have tried multiple methods, but either the Magi won't admit that they received our requests for contact, or our information is out of date."

Without asking permission or forgiveness, Wyatt pulled out his cell phone and dialed a number. After a few moments, he said, "Hi, Grandma. Can you get Grandpa and Vicki, then put me on speaker? I have something here all of you need to know." Wyatt waited in silence for a few moments as the agents shared confused expressions. "Hi, everyone. Did you know there's been an uptick in abductions of Magi children? Some Special Agents came to town and want Gabrielle to try tracking the abductors from the most recent scene. Oh… uhm… okay. Bye."

Before anyone could say a word, a section of space between the conference table and the wall began rippling like the surface of a calm pond into which a stone has been thrown. The rippling effect quickly accelerated as motes of light swirled around it. Suddenly, the whole area around the effect flashed bright light, and when the light faded, Connor Magnusson, his wife Maeve, and Vicki stood in the conference room.

"Your grandfather is Connor Magnusson?" Hauser asked, almost glaring at Wyatt with her voice more of a hiss.

Wyatt nodded, adding a shrug. "You said you wanted to talk to the Magi Assembly."

"He's equivalent in rank and stature to the president!" Hauser hissed across the conference table again. "You don't just summon the president!"

"Wyatt didn't summon me," Connor said, his expression betraying amusement. "Now, what's this about abductions of Magi children?"

Hauser cleared her throat and went through the briefing she'd given thus far. She—and her associate—never lost their rattled demeanor, and the poor state trooper at their side just looked confused.

When Hauser wound down, Connor turned his attention to Alistair. "Have you heard anything else about this?"

Alistair shook his head. "No, I'm afraid not. I haven't had the chance to converse with Alpha Jace about the Shifter Council meeting as yet, so I don't know if anything about it was discussed there. I do know that none of my usual sources have mentioned it."

Connor nodded, and his gaze fell to the floor. Silence reigned for several moments before Connor turned to his granddaughter. "Vicki, you will serve as our liaison on this. Your task is to watch and learn, all while serving as a conduit of information both from us and to us. If they need Magi support within your knowledge and training, provide it. If what they need is beyond your comfort level, as our liaison, you will contact me and relay their need."

"Yes, sir," Vicki replied, adding a firm nod.

"I think…" Connor's voice trailed off as he turned to his wife.

She nodded, saying, "Yes, of course. You call the Assembly, and I'll gather the Order."

In the blink of an eye, Wyatt's grandparents vanished.

WELL, *that* was an experience. I looked to my sister and couldn't help but feel a swell of pride that she stood straight and betrayed no hint of uncertainty or inadequacy.

"The Order, sis?"

I watched Vicki's eyes roam across the non-family members in the room, before she sighed. "I suppose I might as well answer that, since they'll probably be involved anyway. The 'Order' Grandma mentioned is the Order of Merlin. As she is Merlin's granddaughter, she leads the Order as the Grandmaster. It's a sexist title, I know, but Grandma told me they argued like a horde of petulant children when she tried to change it to 'Grandmistress.' It will probably fall to me to change it when I inherit the position."

The agents looked very out of their depth, and I couldn't really blame them.

"May we ask what this 'Order of Merlin' does?" Hauser ventured, her voice tentative.

Out of the corner of my eye, I saw Alistair gesture toward the seat closest to Vicki, and my sister took him up on the offer. Comfortably ensconced in a chair, she said, "I can't tell you what the Order's entire role is now, because I don't really know. Grandma only first brought the Order up to me a month or so ago, and we're still going over its history. When he formed it, Merlin intended the Order to act as the Magi counter to the Order of Assassins from Persia and Syria."

A memory of my childhood flashed to the forefront of my mind. I was walking past my grandparents' kitchen on the way to my room, and I saw Grandma had a cutting block hanging against one wall. Grandma stood at the kitchen's center island chopping vegetables or something, and suddenly, she dropped the chef's knife and whipped her arm toward the hanging cutting block. The next thing I knew, there was a heavy *thwock*, and an impressively sized throwing knife now stuck in the center. I gasped and ran, and when I finally worked up the courage to look in the kitchen again, the hanging cutting block was gone. I never saw it again.

"I always thought Grandma faked throwing those knives, somehow," I blurted out. Now, everyone in the room except Vicki stared at me.

Vicki grinned—almost giggled. "No, Wyatt, she didn't."

"Wow... the things you learn about your family."

"So, the Order of Merlin are Magi assassin-hunters?" Hauser asked.

"That's what they started as. I know the 'normal' world believes the Mongols destroyed the Order of Assassins during their invasion of Persia, but from what Grandma tells me, that was just convenient timing. The Order of Merlin had already whittled their numbers across the Middle East and prepared a massive strike against their core strongholds, to be hidden as a series of earthquakes."

I wasn't the only one shocked at the thought of Magi causing earthquakes.

"You can create earthquakes?" Schumacher gasped.

"Well, *I* can't," Vicki replied, adding a demure shrug. I knew my sister well enough to interpret the 'yet' implied as part of her shrug.

Alistair interjected, "Seismic manipulation aside, I believe we were about to depart for the most recent abduction scene?"

The agents still looked unsettled, but Hauser rallied... mostly. "Uhm, yes, we should."

"I'll ride with Wyatt," Vicki chirped in her cheerleader voice as she stood, and I couldn't keep from smiling.

Seeing her again made me realize how much I missed my sister. We'd been virtually inseparable for most of our childhood, and it wasn't until our early teens that we started drifting apart... probably about the time my grandparents began teaching her Magi secrets.

. . .

WE LEFT THE ADMIN BUILDING, and the federal agents returned to their Suburban and the state trooper his cruiser. Buddy headed for his truck, and Alistair surprised me by asking to ride with him. Gabrielle led Vicki and me over to a matte black 4-door Jeep Wrangler with the license plate 'BLACKCAT,' and I couldn't keep from smiling.

"At least you're honest," I remarked.

Gabrielle and Vicki both sent curious expressions my way, and I gestured toward the license plate. Gabrielle broke into a huge grin and nodded.

Vicki frowned. "I don't get it."

"I'm a melanistic jaguar," Gabrielle said.

I watched Vicki's eyebrows go searching for her hairline as her lips curled into an almost perfect 'O.' Her mischievous side soon took over, though, and she grinned as she said, "Wow… that brings a whole new dimension to the phrase 'cat fight.'"

Gabrielle snorted a laugh as she unlocked the passenger door. "You have no idea."

"I'll sit behind you, Gabrielle, if that's okay," I remarked as I followed her around the Jeep. "Vicki sometimes gets car sick."

Gabrielle directed a concerned look Vicki's way, and my sister shrugged. "It hasn't happened for a few months, but it *does* happen."

"Good to know," my mentor in all things shifter replied and unlocked my door before slipping behind the wheel.

Moments later, Gabrielle eased us onto the road, and we became 'tail-end Charlie' in the four-car procession.

SILENCE RULED the vehicle for a couple miles until Vicki asked, "So, how good of a student is Wyatt? Is he doing okay adjusting to the shifter world?"

"Don't you think you should ask him that?" Gabrielle returned.

Vicki shrugged. "He doesn't always tell me. I know it's just because he doesn't want to worry me or seem like a whiner, but he hasn't figured out yet that I'll *always* worry about him."

"You do know he can hear you, right?"

"Yep, and I don't care."

Gabrielle sighed. "Well, he won his first dominance fight today… against a wolf councilor no less."

"Dominance fight?" Vicki didn't *quite* shriek.

"They can be rather common in shifter communities, especially if you have an overbearing asshole like Thomas Carlyle. He dominated the wolf shifter at the front desk of the hotel where Wyatt's staying, all to get information about Wyatt, and it really rattled her. She's usually one of the more dominant wolves in town, and it always rattles any shifter to be dominated like she was. Wyatt took exception to it and goaded him into a challenge."

Vicki glanced at me over her shoulder, and I could see her chewing on the inside of her cheek like she'd always done when she was worried. "Wyatt doesn't seem injured. I guess it went well?"

"For Wyatt, yeah," Gabrielle answered. "Carlyle? Not so much."

My sister turned toward me and smiled. "I'm proud of you, little brother."

"'Little brother?'" Gabrielle asked. "I thought you two were twins."

"Oh, we are," Vicki replied, "but I was born first by eight minutes."

"Which she has never let me forget, either," I added.

"Well, we can't have you developing any complexes, now

can we?" My sister gave me her mischievous smile. Then, she threw in a wink for good measure.

We soon settled into a comfortable silence as Gabrielle followed the other vehicles in our convoy. I knew the agents said the scene was just outside the capital city, which was about ninety minutes from Precious, but an address would've helped.

THE AGENTS LED us to a suburban community about thirty minutes outside the capital. The community wasn't gated, but it sported the tasteful stone walls and an arch over the entrance bearing its name. We traveled about five minutes past the entrance before we turned onto a dead-end street leading to cul de sac. I guessed the house at the very end was our destination from all the law enforcement and crime scene people roaming the place like an untamed herd. Our convoy stopped at the yellow police tape that crossed the street, and everyone stepped out of their vehicles to stretch after the long ride.

Hauser approached the uniform standing at the tape, and the two spoke for a moment. While we waited, I looked around the neighborhood, taking in the cookie-cutter houses that surrounded us. I didn't mind modern suburbia as such, but the uniformity of it all felt stifling to me.

The sole irregularity to the scene took the form of a woman maybe a couple inches taller than Gabrielle. She strode down the walk from the house neighboring the abduction site, and the only thing I could think was, *She has to be a model.* On further reflection, though, probably not. I couldn't imagine any model ever allowing such an expression of constrained disgust to show in public. Still, though, she was stunning, statuesque even.

Then, Hauser turned and whistled, waving everyone to follow. I couldn't help but wonder if she did it on purpose, given that Buddy was a wolf shifter.

I SMELLED it long before I saw it. Death. Did the kidnappers kill one of the parents?

"Aw, man," Buddy groaned behind me. "Not cool... not cool at all."

"What?" Vicki asked.

"They killed the family dog."

Vicki frowned. "How do you know that? We haven't even reached the scene yet."

"Wolf shifter, sweetheart," Buddy replied. "We have the best noses."

Hauser stopped to speak with the lead crime scene specialist and directed Schumacher to lead us around the house to the back yard. Sure enough, a collie lay dead by the gate, but the next thing I noticed was its bloody muzzle.

"Hey, it looks like the dog took exception to the kidnapping," I remarked.

Schumacher snorted. "Way ahead of you, Sylvester. The crime scene team already sampled the blood and tissue for DNA."

"Sylvester? Really?" Gabrielle asked. "You're going with the Looney Tunes cat?"

"Well, the kid's not fat or orange, so I can't call him Garfield or Heathcliff. What do you think I should call him?"

Gabrielle's expression hardened into a glare as she clenched one hand into a fist. I was at the right angle to see her eyes slowly shifting toward feline. "How about his name? Or is 'Wyatt' beyond your IQ?"

Schumacher pivoted to face Gabrielle full on, and I

watched red creep up his neck. Before he could say anything, though, Alistair stepped to his side.

"Young man," the old wolf spoke in his sagely grandfather tone, "you look like someone on the verge of making a colossal mistake. You might want to look up the statutes of the Shifter Treaty and give a very thorough perusal to the section that covers what is required for a normal human—especially a government agent aware of the shifters—to be challenged under shifter law. I'm not sure you realize it, dear boy, but you're one—maybe two—wrong sentences away from becoming a chew toy. And it would be one-hundred-percent legal... and beyond justified, given the degree to which you've been an ass. Just food for thought, you know."

"I'm not a boy," Schumacher growled, shifting his attention to Alistair.

Alistair responded with a patient chuckle. "I'm old enough to be your great-grandfather, so yes, you are most certainly a boy. Goodness knows, you've been acting like a child for most of the day."

I saw the muscles clench in Schumacher's jaw, and I couldn't keep from setting myself for a charge. Special Agent or no, if he drew back to strike Alistair, I would sack him like a linebacker hitting an inept quarterback.

"I've heard enough," Hauser said, our small crowd parting to allow her passage. "You've been a poor representative of our agency since we arrived in Precious, and I've reached my limit. You're relieved, and I'll contact our office to send Burke out to replace you."

Schumacher rounded on Hauser, and his eyes looked wild enough that I feared he was one frayed nerve from snapping. "You can't do that! You don't have the authority."

"Yes, as the ranking agent, I do. Officer Mays, please escort Agent Schumacher from the premises; he is no longer attached to this case. Jack, take the Suburban; I'm sure one of our associates will be kind enough to give me a ride back to the office."

Jack Schumacher's glare at Hauser seemed fit to reduce her to a pile of smoldering ash where she stood, and I felt a smidgin of wonder that he hadn't ground his teeth to powder, seeing how tightly he clenched his jaw. In the end, though, some angel gifted the man with a glimmer of wisdom, and he stormed off in the direction of our vehicles.

1 0

Sorrow and rage swirled deep within Karleen Vesper's soul, each warring for dominance. She sat with her sister and her sister's best friend. The friend relayed a story through halting gasps of words amid torso-wracking sobs. The friend's six-year-old child—her sister's goddaughter—was one of three children taken as part of the recent swell of abductions throughout the region, and the friend's husband spoke with law enforcement across the street at the actual site of the abduction.

"I... I don't know what the police are doing," the friend said at last. "No one is telling the distraught little woman anything."

That—more than anything else—tipped Karleen's internal battle to favor rage. She spoke for the first time in over thirty minutes. "Do you want me to see what the problem is?"

The friend declined with a timid shake of her head. Karleen's hackles rose further. As one of the two known lupine primogenitors, such timidity and spineless defeat were foreign to her psyche. The husband and law enforcement outside should be thanking their gods none of the children were *hers*. She would not be so meek or mild about the situation. *She* would be out for blood... and lots of it.

Using one of the hand gestures they'd developed over their childhood and adolescence, Karleen acquired her sister's attention, and she then nodded her head toward the house's foyer. Her sister excused herself and Karleen, then extracted her hands from the clutching grasp of the distraught mother. The foyer wasn't far enough that the mother's shifter hearing couldn't pick out their conversation, but it offered the illusion of privacy.

"What?" her sister asked, almost hissing the word in an urgent whisper.

"Yes, exactly," Karleen replied. "What am I even doing here, Nadine? I'm not law enforcement, neither that of the mundane or the shifter, and between the woman's broken blubbering and this artificial community, I'm starting to come out of my fur. I don't belong here."

Nadine sighed and pinched the bridge of her nose. She had always been too much of a city wolf for Karleen's liking, even before she met her mate. She'd tried explaining what the man did just the once, but after five minutes of arcane terms revolving around modern finance, Karleen came very close to offending her sister by summarizing it all as 'he plays with money.'

"I thought you might be able to help," Nadine said at last, almost sighing out the words.

"How, sis? I don't have the connections to get added to the investigation. I don't have *any* connections; you know that I have *purposefully* chosen to leave the shifter world to itself. And if you thought I'd be some kind of comforting caretaker, I'm taking you to the ER to get examined."

Another sigh. "I know. I didn't go into this expecting miracles of emotional growth. I... Look, you have a knack for getting what you want, regardless of whether others want to give it to you. I just thought you could use that to find the children; they weren't taken all that long ago. If they don't have a shifter on the team for tracking, you'd be a godsend in that aspect alone."

"Fine," Karleen sighed and growled out the word. "Fine. I'll see what I can do. Besides, the world at large needs to know that we will not tolerate attacks on our young, and if no one else will provide that lesson, I shall."

Without another word or even so much as a goodbye or well wishes to the sobbing woman in the sitting room, Karleen pivoted on her heel and left the house.

BEING OUTSIDE SHOULD HAVE SERVED as a balm to her unsettled emotions, but everywhere Karleen looked she saw only further proof that she was not among the trees and wilds she called home. Her eyes landed on the friend's husband—the father of one of the abducted children; he stood with a couple of the other men of the neighborhood and a couple police officers. It was an act of extreme will not to pull her lips back from her teeth in a wordless snarl. One of the few details beyond her baby being taken that the friend communicated was that the father wasn't a shifter. How *that* pairing happened boggled the mind; shifters normally avoided normal humans like a plague.

And how had the woman managed to keep from biting or scratching him during the throes of passion? Just one drop of saliva or blood would turn the man. No way the amount of caution and care required to keep that from happening would enhance the quality of their sex life.

She closed her eyes and took a deep breath, exhaling it across long seconds. None of this was her responsibility or concern. The shifter child. She had to stay focused on the shifter child. It wasn't her place to judge what kind of shifter the child would become growing up in such a place.

Another deep breath and slow exhale.

She wasn't sure it helped, but it did take enough time for the group at the sidewalk to separate. She heard the friend's husband stomp up the walk to his stoop where she stood. She identified him by scent with her eyes closed, and her ears tracked his movement as well—if not better—than her eyes would have.

"What's your problem?" he demanded.

Karleen opened her eyes and regarded the man in silence for several moments. Then, said, "You have failed in your duty to protect your young, and you smell like prey. It's a wonder the mother of your child hasn't eaten you yet."

The man couldn't decide whether to be afraid or angry; Karleen saw it in the emotions flitting through his expression. She felt certain her sister and the friend heard every word, but she didn't care. If by some miracle she recovered the children, she would never see this human again, and just as well. She despised what humans had done to the world.

Before the man could sort himself enough to reply, she pushed a sliver of dominance at him, saying, "Now, step aside."

The man didn't quite quail in submission, but Karleen hoped it was a near thing. Regardless, he almost leaped to move out of her way. She walked down the concrete path to the sidewalk that ran along the street, leaving the man and her thoughts of him behind her.

SHE WAS NO MORE than two-thirds of the way to the street when a convoy of vehicles pulled up to the police tape and stopped. The first was the classic government SUV, and the suited pair that exited it carried themselves like federal law enforcement of some flavor. The second vehicle was a state police cruiser with only one occupant. It was the last two vehicles that held her attention, though. The third vehicle carried two shifters, one young and one old… both wolves if she didn't miss her guess. The fourth vehicle carried two more shifters and, from the way her wolf's hackles rose, a Magi. The Magi's presence surprised her.

Who were these kids that their abduction provoked such a crew? From what little she knew of such things, the normal response to a request for shifter trackers was *one*. Two, if the local shifters felt generous or had an abundance of unoccupied labor. But four? And a *Magi*? There must be more to this than she knew.

She reached the sidewalk and stopped, unsure of how best to proceed. She savored her anonymity within the shifter world and didn't care to abandon it. But someone hunted and *claimed* shifter children. Every facet of her being cried out that she should act, anonymity be damned. She was one of the two strongest shifters in current existence as far as she knew. That had to count for something.

Her thoughts and musing occupied enough time that she saw one of the two agents come back around the house with a state trooper at his side. The man radiated anger and hatred of such strength it was almost palpable. Once again, Karleen cursed her ability to get lost in her own thoughts; she stood close enough to the scene that she might have heard what transpired. But no matter.

Karleen headed for the yellow police tape to the accompaniment of the agent slamming the door of the SUV and damn near peeling out as he whipped it around to leave the area at speed. She felt a moment of sorrow for whatever traffic cop pulled him over for speeding or reckless driving. *That* conversation wouldn't be pretty.

The uniformed city police officer at the cordon looked

young, like fresh academy graduate young. He held up his hand to stop her. "Only authorized personnel may pass, ma'am."

She pushed the tiniest thread of dominance toward him, a faint whisper carried by the breeze. "I'm one of the trackers."

The kid glanced over his shoulder, his entire demeanor suffused with indecision, and turned back to her. "Nobody told me about there being more of you, but okay. Go on through."

Karleen slipped under the tape as he lifted it and made her way toward the other shifters. Halfway there, she heard a woman discussing the magical aura that lingered over the area.

"This was a concealment spell," the unknown woman said, her voice almost sounding like she was teaching school. "Without knowing the precise spell used, I would guess it hides the scents associated with the abduction while masking trampled grass and tire tracks and such."

Listening to the woman discuss the magic, Karleen paid zero attention to her surroundings. A sharp *SNAP!* of a branch when she stepped on it drew everyone's attention.

The sole remaining government agent regarded Karleen with one raised eyebrow as she asked, "And just who are you?"

"My name is Karleen Vesper, and I'm here to help."

The suited agent nodded, as if accepting the statement at face value. "What makes you think you can be of use?" She gestured to the people surrounding her like someone on a game show displaying a collection of prizes. "I seem to be well-stocked in the help department."

There didn't seem to be any other way to get on the team than to come clean. "One of the children taken is my sister's goddaughter... and I'm the lupine primogenitor in North America."

~

THE LUPINE PRIMOGENITOR? Oh, shit... if this goes south, I'm probably the only person here who stands a chance of stopping her. Sure, there was nothing saying it would go south, but I couldn't help but think the outrage I'd been feeling ever since I learned someone was taking not just children but shifter and Magi children had to be amplified for her.

"Alistair?" Hauser asked.

Alistair stood silent for several moments before he shrugged. "It goes without saying that she has the potential to be a powerful ally in this. Beyond that, the fact that she has maintained her anonymity for years speaks to her skills at knowing when to share information. My only concern is that she isn't a proven team player."

"The drawbacks associated with not being a part of shifter society have never really affected me until now," Karleen remarked.

"We also do not know what or who we will face when we run these miscreants to ground," Alistair added, "and we would be fools to think there will not be a fight. For that alone, she is worth including."

Hauser gave a firm nod, saying, "Fair enough. Welcome to the team. I'm Winnifred Hauser, Special Agent and in charge of this case."

We ran through introductions, and I kept sliding my way out of it until I was last. Her gaze as she turned to me sent a tingle down my spine.

"And what of you?" Karleen asked. "I can tell you're a shifter, feline I think, but no more than that. I've never encountered your breed before, and that is strange to me."

"My name is Wyatt. About a week ago, I was turned by a rogue cougar about thirty minutes north of Precious."

"No. You're not a cougar; I've encountered cougar shifters before."

I nodded my agreement. "You're right; I'm not a cougar. I'm a feline primogenitor."

Karleen's eyes shot wide. "A *turned* primogenitor? I didn't know that was possible. My counterpart in Europe and I are born shifters."

"The best thought we have at this point," Alistair said, stepping into the topic, "is that he carried just enough Magi power to interact with the turning of the cougar. Not strong enough to prevent being turned but somehow strong enough to catalyze the turning to produce the first feline primogenitor I've ever heard of."

"Impressive." Karleen's eyes flicked back to me. "May I ask your breed?"

"Smilodon."

She frowned. "I'm not following."

"Sabertooth," I explained.

"Oh," Karleen said, drawing the word out as she grinned. "I'd like to see that sometime. You must be a majestic cat."

"He certainly makes an impression," Gabrielle interjected as she stepped to my side. Unless I was wrong, there a bit of an edge to her voice.

I watched Karleen's eyes flick from me to Gabrielle and back a few times before she pursed her lips and nodded. I wasn't sure what passed between the two women, but I couldn't escape the feeling that *something* had.

"Sorry to be such a killjoy," Hauser said, re-entering the conversation, "but we do have the minor matter of three abducted children."

Vicki cleared her throat, drawing everyone's attention. "I can break the concealment spell, no problem, but whatever it's hiding will merge with what we've done to the area. I mean, it might not be possible to tell if mashed grass is ours or the kidnappers."

Hauser nodded. "For this immediate area, sure, but anything outside of where we've stood obviously couldn't be our fault. The crime scene geeks will have some choice words for us, but they're a lot more bark than bite."

Hauser winced immediately after she finished speaking, and I guessed she realized she'd used the bark-vs.-bite analogy with a group of wolf shifters.

"Very well," Vicki responded. "Here we go."

I watched my sister lift her right hand and flex muscles as if reaching for something. In the blink of an eye, a dainty staff that looked hand-carved appeared in her hand, and I caught a faint scent of a crisp spring morning after a night of rain. Vicki closed her eyes and whispered a series of words that sounded ancient, not Latin but of that era. As her voice trailed off, I felt *something* difficult to describe. Pressure against my soul, maybe? Perhaps that feeling when your ears really need to pop but won't? Either way, the feeling began to fade, and with it, the pristine appearance of the backyard.

Lawn furniture that sat in an orderly fashion now lay haphazardly strewn about the place. The table with a large umbrella now lay on its side, the support shaft of the umbrella bent at an odd angle. Clumps of sod about the right size for a dog's paws lay off to the side of where they'd been torn from the yard, and blood congealed in an impressive not-quite-circle where the family friend and protector made the ultimate sacrifice for its human children.

"Look there," Gabrielle said, pointing toward the gate in the fence.

A now-obvious trail left the property and led toward the hills behind the housing development.

"I think that's our cue," Karleen remarked and began removing her clothes.

It took me a few moments to realize I stared, but in that short time, I couldn't keep from appreciating the wolf primogenitor's toned physique; she carried the hourglass figure of a 40's pin-up model very well. Buddy and Gabrielle also stripped out of their clothes, and soon, a wolf and melanistic jaguar stood in their places.

A massive wolf—almost as tall as my waist at the shoulder —trotted up to my side and looked up at me, wagging its tail. It looked very similar to Buddy's wolf in many respects. The general body shape. Body features such as ears, tail, and muzzle. But Karleen's wolf looked more than just scaled up, compared to Buddy. She looked fundamentally sturdier, more massive and resilient. She opened her mouth to loll out her tongue in a canine grin, and the first thought in my mind was, 'My, Karleen, what big teeth you have.'

I staggered for a moment as the wolf leaned against me, and Gabrielle promptly snarled and hissed. Karleen leaned around me to look at Gabrielle and replied with her own snarl and growl.

"Ladies," Hauser said, "I completely understand that Wyatt here is a fine hunk of a man, even to the sensibilities of a lowly human such as me, but we have a job to do."

Both snarls vanished as if they never happened, and I noticed both ladies' ears and tails drooped. Buddy chuffed his amusement as his tongue lolled out one side of muzzle in a canine grin, and the sound carried hints of amusement before he loped through the open gate and began following the trail. Gabrielle moved to follow him and made the point of rubbing her entire length along my right side as she looked at Karleen as if to say, 'And just what are you going to do about it?'

Karleen replied with an amused chuff of her own and trotted along in Gabrielle's wake.

I hurried to collect everyone's clothes and store them in a

duffle bag Alistair handed me, then moved to fall into step beside Vicki.

Vicki gave me a look, and I couldn't process what was behind it. I'd never seen that expression before. After some moments and a few dozen yards away from the house, she lifted an eyebrow and asked, "So, you're a fine hunk of man now?"

About fifteen yards in front of us, Karleen stopped and turned to look back at us, making three very obvious human-style nods before resuming her trot alongside Buddy and Gabrielle.

Vicki chuckled, though I could tell she tried to hold it in. "Well, I guess that's settled."

The trail led us up into the hills, and before long, the two-legged members of our group scrabbled over and up rocky terrain that seemed ready and perhaps waiting for a careless moment to send us sliding backward toward a cliff. Alistair and Vicki made their way fairly well, but Hauser was not prepared for a hike at all in her skirt suit and dress shoes with a medium heel. Not even a tenth of the way to the top, I moved closer to offer her my arm. She accepted, taking a firm hold on my wrist and bringing her other hand up for a steadying grip on my bicep.

We spent the better part of thirty minutes climbing the hill in pursuit of the trail, until we pushed our way through some underbrush and found ourselves standing at the edge of a trailhead for one of the more popular hiking destinations in the area. The wolves and Gabrielle stood around a set of tire tracks. The wolves wagged their tails and looked from us to the tracks and back as if to say, 'Look what we found.'

"Finally," Hauser sighed as she approached the tracks and knelt. "We have a break in this case."

She thrust her hand into the pocket of her suit jacket and retrieved a cell phone. She stood and walked well away from the area, then began pacing as she made a call. "This is Special Agent Hauser. I need a full crime scene team at the trailhead for Mercy's Peak hiking trail." She paused for a moment, and my enhanced hearing could pick up someone speaking, but she was too far away for me to tell what was said. "Yes, the site is very well preserved. We should be able to get impressions from tire tracks and possibly shoe prints. Oh, and please grab my duffle from the site before you leave. I was not prepared at all for the hike we just took." She listened for a few moments again. "Excellent. Thank you."

Hauser returned her phone to a pocket and walked back to us. "Okay, you three. Let's get you back on two legs before some hikers come off the trail. Oh, and let's do that back away from the tire tracks, so we don't risk fouling the impressions with paw prints."

The two wolves and jaguar bounded over to one of the parked cars, and I followed, laying out their clothes on the hood. Then, I turned my back and rejoined Hauser and Vicki.

"Agent Hauser," Vicki said as she knelt, "I think this is hair… and blood."

"Okay. Don't touch it. The crime scene people will collect it and run an analysis."

"But I could use it to track the owner," Vicki replied.

Hauser stared at Vicki, a frown creeping into her expression. "What? You can use that to find them?"

Vicki stood. "I can use it to find the owner. There's no guarantee it's who we're looking for, but a divination might tell us that."

Hauser pursed her lips and paced away from the scene. Once she reached a good distance from the tracks, she turned and paced back and forth as she thought her way through the matter aloud.

"I've never heard of Magi talents being used in court," Hauser muttered. "I don't even know if a divination is admissible." Pace. Pace. Pace. "But ultimately, our first duty is to see the children home safe. Yes, the people responsible need to be in prison, but the children's safety is paramount." Hauser stopped and turned to look at Vicki. "Do it. Try not to disturb the tire tracks if you can at all, but get enough of a sample to tell if it's from either a kidnapper or a child and track them to their location."

Vicki pulled her satchel from her shoulder and held it toward me, saying, "Wyatt?"

I stepped close enough to accept it, and Vicki lifted the flap and rummaged inside.

"Where did you get this?" I asked as she searched. "I don't remember you having it back in Precious."

My sister stopped her search long enough to meet my eyes and grin. "I didn't have my staff in Precious, either."

Returning her attention to the satchel, Vicki soon produced a specimen jar small enough to fit in the palm of her hand and a plastic tongue depressor that tapered to a dull point. She looked at the red dot and strands of hair on the ground for a moment, chewing on the inside of her cheek, then nodded firmly before delving back into the satchel for a second specimen jar. She knelt and made quick work of collecting bloody dirt in one jar and the strands of hair in the other.

Vicki pushed herself to stand and, gesturing for me to follow, walked away from the tire tracks. She stopped near the center of the trailhead's parking lot and handed me the jars and plastic tongue depressor before delving back into the satchel once more. You could've knocked me over with a feather when she pulled out a two-foot-square folding table and a folding chair with a cushioned seat and back.

"Seriously, sis?"

Vicki merely grinned as she leaned the chair against my leg and unfolded the table and its legs.

"That's nothing, my boy," Alistair remarked, arriving at my side. "Some of the things I saw your grandfather do during the war makes that satchel seem like a child's parlor trick."

I directed my astonishment toward him. "Really?"

Alister simply nodded. "Oh, yes. One time, our platoon got trapped in a nasty blizzard and separated from our unit. Your grandfather pointed out the direction we needed to go to rejoin everyone and told us the distance, but the weather was such that many of us would've died of hypothermia— even with our shifter metabolisms—before we reached the base. I watched him spin a thirty-man bivouac out of thin air, complete with heating stoves and firewood."

"Wow."

Vicki arrived in front of me then, retrieving the specimen jars and fishing a ceramic bowl the size of a large mixer out of the satchel. "Wyatt, would you be a dear and fill this bowl with some water from that stream over there?"

"You mean your amazing satchel can't carry a water jug?"

My sister gave me a flat look before returning to the chair. "Oh, it can, but something about it makes the water unusable for magic or rituals. Gives the water an odd flavor, too, even through a Nalgene."

I handed her the satchel and accepted the bowl. It was a simple matter to fill the bowl from the burbling stream that flowed down the hill on the far side of the parking lot, and when I returned, a number of other specimen jars sat on one side of the table, arranged in neat little rows.

The filled bowl went in the center of her half of the table, and I stepped back to watch her work. The thought that magic existed and that my family was part of it still felt a little odd, but I couldn't resist watching my sister show off her skills. She left her seat to retrieve a twig just large enough to be a stirring rod for the bowl and began taking the caps off the specimen jars. She added pinches, dashes, and one small jar's entire contents as she swirled the twig through the water and whispered what sounded like a chant in that language I didn't recognize.

After several moments, she removed the twig from the water as it became a cloudy purple, and the water continued swirling on its own. Vicki set the twig aside and retrieved the specimen jar with the bloody dirt. Still reciting the whispered chat, she twisted off the lid and dumped all of the dirt into the water. The water began to bubble and froth, and mere moments later, a purple cloud poofed into the air in front of her.

As the cloud dissipated, it left an image in its wake, fringed with a gray fog. The image showed two men facing each other, and their expressions and gestures made it clear they disagreed about something. Vicki traced a series of odd signs with her right hand, adding more of that strange language, and the image began speaking.

"Dammit, Oscar, I'm serious. We're not safe here anymore." This came from the man who wasn't the focus of the image. He looked young-ish, so thin he was almost emaciated, and his sweat-soaked brown hair lay plastered to his scalp and forehead.

"Lyle, what part of 'I cannot help that' don't you understand?" the focus of the image shot back. This man was tall, broad-shouldered, with dark hair and eyes, and he wore black fatigues with a tactical harness strapped to his chest. A holster hung from the harness on his chest, right over his left lung. "The buyer is already on the way, and we don't have any way to contact them. Even if we could, they're not the most trusting sorts, so changing the meeting place isn't a way to engender good feelings. I get that you think your illusion or whatever broke, but so what? We'll be long gone by the time any law enforcement or anyone else gets here... if they ever do. Get it together."

The image started to fade but not before Oscar gestured at Lyle with his right hand. A blood-soaked bandage encircled his forearm.

"I'll bet he's the one the dog bit," Hauser said, announcing her presence at my side. I'd been so focused on the exchange between Oscar and Lyle that I hadn't noticed her approach. "Thank you, Vicki. I just wish he'd said when they expect the buyers. I hate having a deadline I don't know."

Vicki didn't respond as she rummaged once more in her satchel. This time, she produced another sample jar, only it was a cylinder about two inches across and three tall. She unscrewed the lid and held it up to me. "More water, please, Wyatt?"

I smiled and accepted the jar. As I walked to the stream, I heard at least one engine approaching and tires crunching gravel. I brought the full jar back to my sister and saw a length of twine and a metal arrow in her hands. She tied the twine to a loop on the arrow and set it aside. She gave the water level an appraising look before pouring out a smidgeon of it.

"Wyatt, be a dear and empty the bowl, please," my sister said, making an exaggeration of batting her eyelashes at me.

I chuckled and shook my head as I retrieved the ceramic bowl and carried it to the far side of the parking lot, where I emptied it. As I walked back, I heard Karleen almost growl, "Just who is she that she thinks she can order around a shifter primogenitor like a pet?"

Gabrielle stood at Karleen's side, and since I barely heard

Karleen's question, I doubted Vicki or Hauser even suspected she'd spoken.

My shifter mentor gave Karleen a smirk as she whispered, "She's his twin sister."

Karleen's glare faded. "Ah. That makes sense. My sister and I still romp like pups every now and then, and she's a city wolf through and through."

Just as I arrived back at Vicki's table, a tan truck with the state's Park Service logo pulled into the lot. Hauser hurried to point them away from the crime scene as she lifted her badge. A man and a woman in park ranger uniforms exited the truck, and I heard them exchange introductions with Hauser.

"Your people contacted us just as we were leaving the ranger station at the park entrance. They're about thirty minutes out." one of the rangers said. "We decided to head up here and do what we could to help until they arrive."

Hauser nodded. "I appreciate that. We need to keep everyone out of a thirty-foot radius centered on the Number 37 parking spot over there. I believe those tire tracks are evidence in an ongoing investigation."

The rangers returned to their truck and produced a couple stacks of the orange hazard cones I've most often seen along the highway. They then walked over to about fifty feet from the parking spot and ringed the space with those cones.

When the woman reached the path we'd followed up the hill, she froze. "Hey, Frank? We have some damn big paw prints over here."

Hauser shot the rest of us a glance before walking over to the rangers. "You don't need to worry about those."

"Agent, I don't know what you're on about, but if wolves or big cats..." Her voice trailed off as she turned to take in the rest of us, and I could see the color drain from her face.

"Oh... oh, my." Then, she leaned close to Hauser and whispered, though we could still hear. "You mean the stories are true?"

Hauser gave the woman the best poker face I'd ever seen. "What stories, Ranger?"

"You mean you don't know? The werewolf stories... supposedly, hikers have seen huge wolves and cats up in these hills for years, but aside from scattered paw prints that really aren't all that exceptional compared to the average wolf, there's never been any proof. I have a couple friends in the national forestry service who found massive wolf prints about half the size of a dinner plate over in Cascade National Forest." She stopped and frowned, looking down at the three sets of paw prints and pointed at Karleen's tracks. "You know, the pictures they sent me looked a lot like these prints right here."

The ranger whipped her phone out of her pocket like a professional Old West gunslinger.

Now, Hauser's poker face shifted to a glare. "If you take that picture, I will confiscate your phone and request a warrant to seize any cloud storage you may have. I appreciate your help thus far, but I think it's best for all concerned if you and your fellow ranger maintain position at the entrance to the parking lot."

The rangers almost stared at Hauser for several moments before they meandered over to stand a few steps beyond the entrance to the parking lot. They whispered among themselves, and every so often, they'd cast wary looks toward us over their shoulders. From what my shifter hearing could glean, they were whispering about what those big paw prints meant and what they should do about them. For their sake, I sincerely hoped they decided to do nothing; I know I didn't want to run afoul of anyone with the title 'Special Agent' in front of their name.

The sudden absence of Vicki's whispered chanting drew my attention, and I turned just in time to see her dunk the arrow to which she'd tied the twine earlier into the larger specimen jar I'd filled with water. She whispered more words I didn't understand, and there was a brief flash of light and a small poof of smoke. She lifted the arrow out of the liquid mixture and eyed the metal with an appraising expression.

The arrow began spinning and soon settled on pointing toward something a few ticks east from due north. Vicki stood and walked in a circle, but regardless of the direction she faced, the arrow still pointed in the same direction.

"Agent Hauser?" Vicki called.

Hauser spun, and Vicki pointed to the arrow dangling from the twine. Hauser's eyes widened just a moment, then gleamed as she broke into a smile. "Does that mean what I think it does?"

Vicki shrugged. "I don't know what you think it means, but it's pointing to the owner of those hair strands."

"How long will it last?" Hauser asked.

"Uhm, maybe an hour? I'm not really sure, honestly, but it's renewable. If the effect fades, I'll just dunk it in the solution again and repeat the spell."

Hauser nodded and sighed. "Now, we just have to wait for the rest of the team to arrive. Damn. I didn't ask them to bring our vehicles, and they couldn't have brought yours anyway."

"It's fine," Gabrielle remarked. "Buddy and I can run back and bring vehicles."

"Unless you know a shortcut to get here," I said, "you'll probably have to follow the same path as the crime scene people, which means an hour. Maybe more."

"Fine, then," Gabrielle replied. "You'll come too. We'll strap the duffle to your cat. Now that I'm thinking about it, I doubt my cat or Buddy's wolf are large enough for it."

She, Buddy, and Karleen led me over to the underbrush that would hide us from the park rangers. Buddy and Gabrielle stripped again and shifted. Karleen and I gathered their clothes into my duffle, and then, Karleen did the same for me after I stripped and shifted.

For what seemed to be the longest time, Karleen just stood there staring at me. Her expression flitted through awe, admiration, and a few other emotions I couldn't identify. In fact, it took a growl from Gabrielle to break her focus enough that she gathered my clothes into the duffle and helped me step through the shoulder strap, then clicked the waist strap into place and snugged it tight to keep the duffle from flopping around as I ran.

Gabrielle chuffed her approval—at least I think it was approval—and darted off down the hill. Buddy was quick to follow.

Both the black cat and *the dire wolf would be fine additions to the pride*, the growly voice in my head remarked. It was the first time I'd heard it in a while.

Where is this 'pride' stuff coming from? I don't need a pride, and besides, I can't even get a girlfriend.

It felt like the growly voice scoffed at that thought but made no reply otherwise.

When we arrived at our vehicles, a woman in black tactical clothes—cargo pants, shirt, boots, the works—strode up to us. She was tall and willowy, and I felt like I should double-check that she even cast a shadow. She wore her straight dark hair in a tight bun and projected an air of barely contained pugnaciousness.

"You Magnusson?" she asked.

I glanced to Gabrielle and Buddy, both of whom shrugged, before turning back to her. "Who's asking?"

She pulled a folio out of a pocket and opened it one-handed to reveal a badge and photo ID. "Special Agent Edwina Burke. Hauser said you'd lead me to her."

I so wanted to ask how she came to be named Edwina in the twenty-first century, but she probably had enough childhood trauma from her name that I didn't need to add to it. In the end, I shrugged. "Okay. Follow us."

"Nah. I'm not exactly the trusting sort. You ride shotgun with me, and they can follow."

I wondered if she realized just how much danger she'd be

in if I was indeed hostile, but I didn't want to make a scene. Besides, I couldn't help but feel that would just be dirty pool.

"Okay," I replied, adding an indifferent shrug for flavor. As she led me over to a government-issue SUV, I asked, "Are you a cat person?"

She froze mid-step and gave me a confused glare. "What does *that* have to do with anything?"

"Hopefully, you won't have to find out." I said no more about it, opening the passenger door instead and climbing inside.

Burke walked around the SUV and climbed behind the wheel. She maneuvered the massive vehicle like an expert, and soon, we led Gabrielle and Buddy out of the cul de sac.

AS WE WENT, I directed her to take the backroads that connected most of the trailheads in the state, if you knew the proper turns to make. No stop signs. No traffic lights. No idiot drivers. I figured this route would cut off at least a third of the travel time back to Mercy's Peak, but secretly, I hoped for half or better. Agent Burke passed the trip in silence, and I never once saw any expression other than a vague scowl. Hauser was very expressive, especially when she found out I was a Smilodon. So, what was Burke's problem?

"So what is it?" I asked after enduring the silent scowl as long as I could. "Are you constipated? Is it a bad day for you? Did a pet shit in your shoes? Oh... and take the next right."

Burke slowed to take the turn and glanced at me, adding a frown to the scowl. "What are you talking about?"

"Well, you've been scowling since the first time I laid eyes on you, and I'm just trying to figure out what the deal is."

"You don't think missing children are scowl-worthy?"

"I think missing kids are more than scowl-worthy, but I

can't afford to let it affect my overall outlook. If I let myself get mad, I'm sure no one would enjoy the aftermath."

Burke heaved a sigh. "Fine. I don't like that we've resorted to outside contractors. You people have no place in law enforcement and, more often than not, create more problems than you solve."

Ah, so that's it. "Was that Schumacher's problem, too? He was an ass the whole time he was around us."

Burke snorted. "No. Schumacher believes in werewolves and all that paranormal or supernatural nonsense. He swears they're real and should be caged like the wild animals they are."

"Oh, a bigot then. That's nice."

This stretch of road was straight enough that Burke could afford to give me A Look without endangering us too much. "You don't seriously believe that crap, too, do you? Magic and wizards? Werewolves and werecats?"

I wasn't sure whether I should educate her or not, and it certainly begged the question of why Hauser requested her to replace Schumacher if she hadn't been clued in about shifters and Magi. Agent Burke was in for an awakening; only time would tell whether it was rude or pleasant.

WHEN WE ROLLED into the trailhead's parking lot, it looked like we weren't too far behind the crime scene guys and extra officers who secured the scene while the CSAs worked. I noticed all the extraneous vehicles were gone, and I guessed the rangers went up the trail collecting hikers and asking them to leave.

I saw Hauser chatting with one of the crime scene types as we rolled into the parking lot, and she now wore attire almost exactly like Burke. Black cargo pants. Black pull-over shirt. Black tactical boots. She saw us arrive and ended her conversation to head our way.

"Thanks for collecting my wayward agent," Hauser said as she approached. "Now that the crime scene people are here, we're free to head out."

Gabrielle and Buddy arrived at my side just then, and I didn't see how proceeding with Burke still in the dark could be good at all. No part of me believed whoever took the children would simply hand them over at our polite request, and Burke would become a major liability if she learned shifters and Magi were real in the middle of a firefight. Nothing for it, then...

"Agent Hauser," I said, "before we do that, I think someone needs to bring Burke up to speed on a couple things."

At first, confusion dominated her expression. Then, Hauser glanced at the three of us—shifters all—and my sister —the Magi liaison, and understanding dawned. "Oh. Right. We're too exposed here, and she'll want proof." She looked around until she found the rangers. "Where's your ranger station?"

"At the bottom of the hill," one of them replied.

"That'll do." Hauser remarked, nodding once.

TEN MINUTES LATER, we pulled into the parking lot of the local ranger station. It was tiny. Maybe fifteen hundred square feet total. The rangers pulled in behind us, and Hauser was quick to intercept them.

"I need to commandeer your ranger station for a few minutes. One of you, come with me to help speed things along. The other can wait out here to be joined shortly by your associates."

"What associates?" one of the rangers asked. "We're it for this station."

"Perfect, then. Stay at the far end of the parking lot until we come back." With that, Hauser turned and almost marched into the building. "Burke, Wyatt, Vicki... with me."

I was surprised that the rangers left their station unlocked when they'd come up the hill, but maybe there wasn't enough traffic around here that they felt the need to lock it. A main room that seemed to be both a reception area and office dominated the building, but a separate office and full bathroom with a shower occupied a third of the space. Hauser walked straight to the desk, spun, and leaned against it. She waited for me to close the door behind us, then ripped off the bandage.

"Burke, they're not called werewolves or werecats or were-whatever. Under the terms of the treaty they have with our government, the proper term is 'shifter.' And magic is real, too. Vicki, here, is heiress to one of the most prestigious and powerful Magi families the world has ever known."

Burke looked at Hauser like the senior agent was off her meds. Before she could verbally respond, though, my sister took a step closer and asked, "Agent Burke, do you smoke?"

Burke glowered at Vicki for interrupting but still answered. "Yes, but I'm trying to quit. Why?"

Vicki lifted her right hand and snapped her fingers to distract Burke from the word she whispered, and a tiny flame—about the size of a lighter's flame—winked into existence and danced on the tip of her index finger. My sister was just irreverent enough that she didn't bother to rein in her smirk. "Need a light?"

Sweat beaded on Burke's forehead. Her breathing became short and ragged, almost gasps, and she stared at the tiny flame on my sister's fingertip as if she couldn't look away.

"Wyatt," Hauser said, "your turn, I think."

I fought the urge to sigh. I wasn't sure Burke could handle any further shock to her system, but Hauser's expression didn't give me much choice. Besides, she hadn't been all that secretive about wanting to see me in my feline form. I crossed to the separate office and stepped inside, pushing the door most of the way closed but not latching it. Stripping to shift was almost old hat at this point, and I made short work of it. I turned to face the door, because the office wasn't exactly spacious, and touched the part of my mind that hadn't been human since I woke up in the Precious infirmary.

The shift felt smoother this time. Maybe it was easier the more times I did it? Either way, we had a job to do, and we'd spent too much time already on Agent Burke. I hooked a claw on the door to pull it open and padded back into the main office. Hauser looked like a child faced with a mound of presents when she saw me, but Burke still stared at the flame dancing on my sister's fingertip.

I couldn't ignore my enhanced senses in my feline form like I could when I was human, and Burke's rapid heartbeat sounded like a steady, fast-paced stream of waterdrops on tin to my ears. She approached full-blown tachycardia. My reluctance to be a part of this erupted, but before I could slink back into the office, Hauser touched Burke's shoulder and nodded toward me.

Burke seemed to exert willpower to look away from the flame, and Vicki dismissed it as soon as she did. She turned and dropped her eyes, though not too far as my jaw was the same level as her belt; my curved incisors reached almost halfway to her knees. Her heartbeat became a machine gun to my ears... and she promptly collapsed. Eyes rolled back in her head, the whole bit. Elvis definitely left the building.

Vicki caught her with a cushion of air before Burke could bounce her head off the concrete floor and directed a glare at

Hauser. "Wasn't that a bit irresponsible, Agent Hauser? What if I hadn't been here to catch her? You could've caused her some serious harm with this little stunt of yours."

"She would have argued with us until our ears bled from listening to her otherwise. Besides, it's how they read me in on the situation, and I turned out okay. Mostly."

I let the ladies argue while I padded back into the separate office to shift back and get dressed. I returned and added my two cents. "You couldn't hear her heartbeat, Hauser; I could. You risked her life with this."

"What's her heartrate like now?" Hauser asked.

I closed my eyes and focused. Then leaned closer. "It's still rapid, but it's slowing. Not as bad as it was."

"All right. Do you mind carrying her to the SUV? It's time we gave the station back to the rangers."

Part of me couldn't believe how callous she was about all this, but I guess it wasn't my problem in the long run. I knelt long enough to scoop Burke into my arms, and Vicki helped me with the doors. Hauser stood beside the open back door by the time I arrived, and I took extra care as I laid Burke in the back seat. I made a pillow out of a handy jacket and backed away. Hauser closed the door, and Burke didn't stir at all.

"Let's go, people!" Hauser shouted as she opened the SUV's driver door and stepped up on the running board. "The vehicle with Vicki leads."

Vicki and I hopped into Gabrielle's Jeep, and off we went.

As she drove, Gabrielle kept glancing at the arrow, which Vicki held high for maximum visibility and freedom of movement. I wondered how long she could hold it like that. Turned out, it wasn't long. Maybe five miles down the road, Vicki tied the other end of the twine that held the metal arrow to the rear-view mirror and let her arm fall to her side.

Our trip was the most zigzag, inefficient travel I'm sure three vehicles ever took. Whenever possible, Gabrielle followed a path that kept the arrow pointing straight ahead. When that wasn't possible, she made the best compromise she could. More than once, we had to stop and turn around to find a better route.

We spent over three hours following that arrow's direction. It led us to a run-down, decommissioned industrial site situated on the south bank of a major river that flowed west to the Pacific. A rusted, patchy fence-line surrounded the facility about five hundred yards from the actual site, and the remains of a security gate before them held a (mostly) legible but very weather-beaten sign that read, 'Industrial Steel & Fabrication, Inc. Est. 1953.'

We backed our vehicles far enough away that anyone roaming around the facility wouldn't see us standing at the fence-line. Most of us had been sitting so long we took the opportunity to stand up and stretch our legs. As soon as I left the confines of the Jeep for the bright, sunny afternoon, I became aware of a shouting match that seemed to be happening in the agents' SUV. My shifter hearing picked up enough of the exchange to tell that Burke didn't appreciate Hauser's 'rip off the bandage' approach to educating her about supernaturals and Magi. Like I didn't see *that* coming...

Vicki took a few steps toward the agents, but I held up my hand and shook my head.

"What?" my sister asked.

Karleen and Gabrielle arrived at my side, their eyes locked on the government SUV. Karleen said, "Burke and Hauser are having a 'Come to Jesus' talk about Hauser's methods. You don't want any part of that."

The rear passenger door of the SUV abruptly shot open. It happened so fast that I would've believed the mechanism was spring-assisted. Burke jumped out and clamped her hand against the doorframe. Aw, crap... if she slammed that door, five hundred yards and change might be close enough for even humans to notice the sound. She looked for all the world like she wanted nothing more than to slam the door so hard it went *through* the SUV, but her better angels held sway. Burke closed the door with so little force that I barely heard the latch engage. She then turned and stomped toward us, her cheeks and neck flushed, her hands clenching into fists and then unclenching, her expression granite.

Burke stopped about ten feet away from us, and her eyes landed on me. In a heartbeat, her expression softened. She closed the distance until she was close enough that she had to look up to meet my eyes and said, "For the record, I happen to like cats quite a bit. I prefer them over dogs, in fact."

That said, she pivoted on her heel and strode back to the SUV.

Vicki turned to me and lifted one eyebrow. "You go, little brother. If you don't end this case with her digits, you're doing something wrong."

Karleen and Gabrielle glanced at each other, then shook their heads almost in unison. Gabrielle explained, "It'll never happen. As far as we can tell, she's just a human. A relationship between her and Wyatt would carry too much risk of turning her, and I'm not sure anyone wants to see the result of Wyatt turning someone."

Karleen added a shudder and shook her head. "I know I've never considered turning someone. I mean... in theory, they'd just be a regular wolf shifter, but what if they weren't? What if anyone I turn becomes a primogenitor like me? And let's take that one step further. Suppose primogenitors beget primogenitors when we turn humans; what happens when one of us turn someone like a violent career criminal? What happens then?"

"You didn't see the dominance fight between Wyatt and the wolf councilor," Gabrielle remarked. "This guy had more dominance fights under his belt than any three other councilors, and Wyatt made him look like a pup still learning how to fight. And don't even get me started on how Wyatt chose to end it. That was plain humiliation, pure and simple. We do *not* need the mess we'd have on our collective hands if a primogenitor turned a career criminal into a primogenitor."

Hauser stepped into view at the back of the SUV and gestured for all of us to gather around. Our conversation faded as I followed the ladies over to the agents. I saw the back hatch of the SUV was up, and Burke stood off to one side with her hands on her hips.

"Okay," Hauser said, opening the impromptu briefing. "First, major point... Vicki, how certain are you of your tracking spell? On a scale of one to ten, what is that spell's reliability?"

Vicki took a deep breath and blew out her cheeks before exhaling. "In a lot of ways, it's like a computer, in that it follows the 'garbage in, garbage out' principle. The person who lost those strands of hair is in there. You could take that bet to Vegas and break the house. Is that person one of the missing children? I can't say. The blood we found with the hairs did seem to connect to someone associated with the children's abductions, but if you recall, we never actually *saw* any children when we looked in on Oscar and Lyle."

Hauser gnawed at her lower lip for a moment or three. "Do you have any of the hair left, or did you need all of it for the tracking spell?"

When my sister replied, a smile tugged at the corners of her mouth. "Why, Agent... only a green apprentice would need all *three* strands for a tracking spell, and if those three strands weren't from the same person, the tracking spell would... well... matters would not go well for the Magi in that case."

"So, can you do another divination but use one of the hairs?" Hauser asked, her eyes alight.

Vicki's response was to produce the specimen jar containing the other two strands of hair and remove the lid.

"Hauser," Burke interjected, "what's your plan here?"

"If we can lay eyes on the abducted children and use Vicki's testimony as an expert in the field regarding the efficacy of the tracking spell, I consider that sufficient grounds for an 'exigent circumstances' warrant, and I'll call the US Attorney's office right now."

Burke blinked, and I heard her heartrate tick up a bit. "Wait... you mean there are judges who know about... about... all this?"

Hauser's eagerness vanished. "Shit. I would assume there are, but I have no idea if any of the judges in this district do."

"Grandpa would know," Vicki replied. She held the open specimen jar in her left hand, looking for all the world like she only waited for Hauser to say 'go.'

Hauser turned to me, but before she could utter a word, I had my phone in my hand. Three of five bars? Should be good enough. I unlocked it, opened the dialer, and keyed in our grandfather's private number.

"What do you need, Wyatt?" Grandpa asked by way of greeting after the second ring.

I tapped the control to put the call on speaker. "Hi, Grandpa. You're on speaker with me, Gabrielle, Agent Hauser, and the rest of the team. We need to know if there's a federal judge in this district who's aware of shifters and Magi."

Silence extended for about three seconds before I heard him sigh. "It would appear not. The Magi Assembly's contact in the federal courts for this district apparently retired two months ago. Agent Hauser, I assume you're in need of a warrant?"

"Dire need, sir," Hauser replied. "Your granddaughter used a strand of hair—"

"I taught her the spell," Grandpa interrupted, "and you're on-site now? Do you need reinforcements?"

"Reinforcements, sir?" Hauser asked, shooting me and Vicki a wide-eyed expression.

My sister and I shrugged as Grandpa answered, "Besides human children, both Magi *and* shifter children have been abducted. Under the terms of the Shifter Treaty and ours, both groups have sufficient grounds to put boots—or paws—in the field. Is Alistair still with you?"

Alistair stepped closer so the phone would pick up his voice. "I'm here, Old Wizard."

"How soon could the Shifter Council deliver a war party?"

Hauser's gaze locked on Gabrielle, and eyes wide, she mouthed, 'A war party?'

"Unknown at present," Alistair replied. "My immediate support structure is back in Precious, and we're about three or four hours northwest of there. The facility Vicki's spell led us to is rather large, as well. I certainly wouldn't mind having an additional shifter or four for reconnaissance."

A few more seconds of silence, punctuated by muffled discussion.

"Vicki," Grandpa said at last, "your grandmother has dispatched a unit of the Order to your location. They are experienced Magi, all possessing Master certification in long-distance teleportation. She made it clear they report to *you*. Agent Hauser, I need a name."

Hauser blanched. "Sir?"

"What federal judge in this district do you prefer to work with?"

"Oh… uhm… Judge Gerald Buckman, sir."

Grandpa replied, "You'll have your search warrant in thirty minutes or less."

The phone clicked as the call ended.

13

W ithin a minute of the call ending, perhaps less, a section of reality about ten feet away from them began swirling like a two-dimensional whirlpool. The swirling intensified until motes of light began winking within the swirls. Fifteen people—seven men and eight women—stepped out of the effect, before it vanished as if it had never been. They marched straight to Vicki, clapped their fists to their chests, and bowed their heads.

"Lady Victoria," the man closest to her said, "we stand ready to serve you."

There were times in the past Vicki had longed to hear those words. Times she looked upon their treatment of her grandmother with envy. But she knew now what that treatment cost. Blood at least, if not lives. She wasn't sure the price was worth the accolades.

"Thank you. Please take Alistair Cooper to Precious and return with whatever shifters he assigns. They will be our eyes, ears, and noses within that facility as we prepare for the assault."

"Wait," Hauser interrupted. "What about us while they're

gone? There's supposedly a buyer on the way, and we have no idea of the timetable. I don't know that we can afford to be stuck out here with no place to hide."

One of the other Magi—this one a woman—stepped forward. "Move your vehicles a good ten feet from this road."

The rest of the original party looked to Vicki, who replied with a nod. Soon, the vehicles rested in their new location.

"I need one hair from each of you," the same woman said, as the other Magi arranged themselves in an odd, off-center circle. All of them—from Vicki to Karleen—plucked a hair and held it out for her.

When she reached Wyatt and took his hair in her palm, she paused and regarded the hair with a surprised frown before returning her focus to him. She bowed her head to him, saying, "Lord Wyatt."

Everyone—Wyatt included—shot questioning glances to Vicki, but she didn't understand, either.

All hairs collected, the woman moved to the middle of the circle, and the entire group began chanting. Vicki recognized it as Sumerian and wondered how many people her grandmother had trained over the years. Maeve Magnusson was the only person Vicki knew who taught students the ancient Sumerian language to use for their spellcasting. Her grandfather used ancient Gaelic.

The area swelled with power, though Vicki doubted the agents could sense it, and as the Magi reached the climax of the spell, the woman leaned forward and scooped a handful of dirt from the road. She stepped outside the group and waved her hand in front of the vehicles from end to front, letting the dirt fall from her hands as she did so. The vehicles vanished from back to front, until all of them—even their tracks in the grass—disappeared from view.

"Now, step past the horizon of the illusion to be hidden behind it," the woman said. "Master Alistair?"

Alistair Cooper left the group to approach the Magi. "You've been to Precious before?"

The woman smiled. "You wouldn't believe the sheer list of places we've been when compiled from all our travels. As it stands, I am the one who has visited Precious before, and as such, I'll guide the teleportation."

"Then, I shall place myself in your capable hands," Alistair replied. "I'm ready when you are."

Without further discourse, the woman lifted her hands and began reciting ancient Sumerian. Moments later, the Magi and Alistair vanished.

Vicki turned to those who remained. "Come. We might as well sit in the comfort of the vehicles."

At most, fifteen minutes passed since Alistair left with the Magi, and those fifteen minutes crawled by. *Crawled.* Just when I was going to ask Gabrielle about going for a run, two people appeared in the road. I recognized one as my grandfather; I had no idea who the other one was. He was young, wearing dress slacks, dress shoes, and a sleeveless vest over his dress shirt. The thickness of the lenses in his glasses would put the finest telescopes to shame. His entire demeanor betrayed his fright.

We all piled out of the vehicles, and I watched Grandpa look around before his gaze locked on our general area. We started walking to meet them but were still within the illusion's radius when the young man spoke.

"I... I thought you said they'd be here."

"Patience, young man," Grandpa replied.

"It's just that... that Judge Buckman ordered me to deliver this warrant to Agent Hauser in person. I've never s-seen the judge so unsettled. Do you know what's going on?"

Grandpa gave the young man a reassuring smile. "Oh, yes, but you shouldn't trouble yourself with it. Now, gird yourself. You're about to see something that might unsettle you further."

"I don't see how..." the young man began, then gaped as we stepped through the illusion's event horizon and seemed to appear out nowhere. "Where... where did they come from?"

"They waited behind an illusion. Now, go find Agent Hauser and complete your charge."

I watched the young man scamper to the two agents, the only ones of our group in tactical garb.

"A-Agent H-Hauser?" he asked, clutching his packet to his chest like a life preserver.

Hauser raised her hand in reply and greeting, and the young man shifted course to approach her. When he stopped, he held out the packet. "Judge Buckman charged me with delivering this packet to you and you alone, ma'am."

"Thank you," Hauser replied as she accepted the packet.

The young man pivoted and scurried back to Grandpa. "May we go now, please?"

"In a moment," Grandpa replied and crossed the short distance to Vicki and me. "Are you two well? Do you need anything?"

Vicki took a step and threw her arms around Grandpa, then beamed when she broke the hug and stepped back. "We're fine, Grandpa. Please, thank Grandma for the Order Magi. They took Alistair to Precious to gather shifters."

Grandpa nodded, then turned to me. "How are you holding up?"

I shrugged and nodded. "It's a lot to get used to, and then, there's all this. But I'll be okay."

He smiled and clapped me on the shoulder. "I know you

will, my boy. I'm just as proud of you as I am your sister. Always have been."

I smiled. "I know, and I never felt like I was the odd one out."

"I'd better return Buckman's clerk to him," Grandpa said and held out his hand.

I gave him a firm, respectable handshake, and he turned back to the law clerk, whose eyes darted all over the place as if he were under imminent threat of attack.

"All right, young buck," Grandpa said as he stopped in the center of the road, "stand close."

The clerk stepped closer, and Grandpa recited a short phrase in Gaelic as he flicked his hand through an equally quick series of gestures. In the blink of an eye, they were gone.

By some unspoken agreement, we all turned and began walking back to the vehicles. The event horizon of the illusion felt like ice crystals dancing across my skin, and Hauser fell in step beside me. I noticed she held the folio with far less reverence than the clerk had.

"I cannot imagine what it was like to grow up in Connor Magnusson's house," she said, her tone laced with wonder.

"For me, at least, it was the simple difference of being in a home where I was loved versus one where I was scorned. If you want to know what it was like growing up around two leaders of the Magi community, you'll have to ask Vicki."

Hauser flinched as if physically slapped. "Ah. Right. Sorry about that."

I chuckled. People always seemed to think it was something to tip-toe around. I never did. "Don't get wound up about it. It took most of my teenage years, but I made my peace with my parents."

"You did? They spoke with you?"

That thought caused me to snort my laughter. "If they

didn't want anything to do with me as a child, I'll wager they definitely don't now. No... I meant that I came to terms with their decision toward me. I don't understand it, and frankly, I would never treat a child the way they treated me, especially if the child was my own. But it is what it is."

Hauser nodded.

"So, is that your search warrant?"

"I imagine so, but the way that clerk held it, I wouldn't be surprised if it turns out to be an engraved invitation to dine with the Archangel Gabriel." She lifted the folio and opened it, reading over the sole document inside. "Yep, it's our search warrant. As soon as we have more of you furry types for perimeter control and scouting, we'll go in."

"'Furry types,' is it?"

Hauser gave me a quizzical expression in reply, which faded into a playful smile. "Am I wrong?"

"No," I answered, chuckling. "I can't say that you are."

As we approached the waiting vehicles, Hauser gestured for everyone to gather. Once we had, she said, "Is there any point to begin planning the raid on this site before we have all the elements?"

Gabrielle looked up to the sky. As it was mid-afternoon, the sun was about two-thirds of the way across the sky. "While it would be a disadvantage for you and Burke, I think we should move in about two to three hours after nightfall. Magi can augment night vision with spells, yes?"

"I think we can," Vicki answered. "But I don't know how yet."

I smiled. "I'll bet one or more of the Magi Grandma sent can. I may be wrong, but it seemed they were almost too ready for something like this."

Vicki chewed on the inside of her cheek for a moment before venturing a nod. "You noticed that, too? I don't know anything about the Order as it exists in the modern day, so maybe they have a quick reaction force ready to go. Still, it seemed like they went from 'what's going on' to 'here's what we're doing' rather quickly."

"Rules of engagement," Gabrielle said, drawing several pairs of eyes to her. "We need to discuss the rules of engagement for when we go in there."

"How so?" Burke asked, frowning. "We're law enforcement. If we find the missing children, we arrest and detain everyone."

Gabrielle gave the woman a blank look for a moment. "*You* might be law enforcement, but *we're* not. If we're right and these people have abducted shifter children, that is an act of war to us. We have no interest in arrests or evidence or prosecution. The threat to our children must be ended."

"Yes, that's true," Vicki agreed, "but we must also exist within the wider world, Gabrielle. The human authorities will not respond well to this use of resources with nothing to show for it. At least nothing they can show the people at large. This is as much a public relations piece as it is anything else. Sad to say, I know, but most things are that garner national media attention."

The growl that was Gabrielle's response sounded decidedly feline and not friendly at all.

Before anyone else could say anything, the first group of fifteen shifters arrived with a Magi. All of them were in their human form, and as the Magi led them to our side, I noticed scents for shifters I hadn't met yet. Then, the next group arrived, fifteen shifters and one Magi. They cleared the area, and before the second group passed into our illusion, the third group arrived. And on. And on. And on. The arrivals continued until each of the fifteen Magi brought fifteen shifters.

Hauser gaped at them as they milled about behind our

vehicles but still within our illusion. "Fifteen times fifteen… two-hundred-twenty-five?"

"Two-hundred-twenty-five," Gabrielle affirmed. "A smaller war party than we might normally field, but this facility isn't too large."

The hair on the back of my neck rose, and I turned just in time to see Magi almost literally fill the road. No fanfare. No poof or swirly reality. They were just *there*. A final three appeared at the head of the massive group, and I smiled as I watched my grandparents and Alistair lead the Magi toward us. Grandpa and Alistair carried folios of some kind.

Grandpa, Grandma, and Alistair walked straight to us when they passed through the event horizon of the illusion. When they stopped, Grandpa scanned the area as if looking for something, then turned to Grandma.

Grandma nodded. "Yes, I agree. The illusion needs to be expanded to account for all the recent additions."

Grandpa handed the folio he carried to Grandma, then took a deep breath and exhaled slowly. He brought his hands up to his chest and wove them as if rolling up a ball as he rattled off ancient Gaelic. At the climax of his recitation, he pulled his arms out to his sides, fingers spread wide. I felt *something*, but my senses weren't fine-tuned enough to tell what it was.

"Oh, yes, dear," Grandma remarked, smiling. "That will do nicely." She turned to regard the Magi still clearing the road. "The illusion extends two hundred yards back now and seventy-five to either side. Let's hurry and get inside it."

The Magi stepped up their pace as Grandma turned back to us and returned the folio to Grandpa. I couldn't help but notice the mischievous twinkle in her eyes.

Grandpa lifted the folio and thumbed it open. He cleared his throat and read, "Be it known to all concerned that the Magi Assembly has decreed that the rampant abduction of

Magi children is an existential threat to Magi as a whole. In response, the Assembly voted unanimously to form this, the 7th Magi Expeditionary Unit since the Assembly's establishment, and to commission Victoria Catherine Magnusson as its commanding officer. Do you accept?"

Vicki gaped at our grandparents, her eyes flicking back and forth between them as her jaw gradually slackened. Silence extended until she caught up to the fact that Grandpa waited for her response, and she stammered, "Y-yes."

"Victoria Catherine Magnusson, you are hereby charged and directed to take command of the 7th Magi Expeditionary Unit for the purpose of tracing the perpetrators of the abductions to the full extent of their organization and visiting upon them such fate as you deem appropriate."

Grandpa closed the folio and extended it to Vicki. I scanned the faces around me, and everyone looked on as if this was a major deal. I didn't understand why, but I also felt like I shouldn't speak up. Once Vicki accepted the folio, though she did so with trembling hands, Grandpa turned to me, and his expression softened into the understanding, patient, friendly grandfather I'd known my whole life.

"Wyatt, this is the seventh expeditionary force commissioned by the Assembly, as its name implies. The Assembly has existed for over two thousand years. Normally, we prefer to work behind the scenes or make the human governments aware of a problem and let them handle it."

Oh. And my sister was going to be leading this? Wow.

And then Alistair stood at Grandpa's side. "Wyatt, know that I argued stringently that you should be given command of our war party. After all, it seemed only fitting when the old wizard told me what the Assembly decided."

"Uhm, no. I'm too new to all this, and... and... I've never managed or led anyone. You shouldn't give me command of the shifter side of things, simply because my sister commands the Magi contingent. She's been training her whole life for this, and I'm... what... maybe a week old? As far as the shifter community is concerned?"

Grandpa and Alistair shared a look. Grandma smirked and winked at me as Grandpa said, "Told you, Old Wolf. My boy has a good head on his shoulders."

"Yes, you did indeed tell me," Alistair agreed as he extended his folio to Gabrielle. "Gabrielle, the Shifter Council has decided that you shall lead our war party and coordinate with Vicki to ensure all persons behind this face a suitable fate."

Just then, Hauser's phone rang. She blanched at such a trite interruption to such a momentous moment. Witnessing the commissioning of a Magi Expeditionary Unit *and* a shifter war party? She wasn't sure any other human alive could claim seeing such.

Before she could silence the call, Grandpa turned to her and stated, "You should take that call."

Hauser keyed the command to accept the call and said, "Agent Hauser." She listened for a few moments, then pulled the phone away from her head and thumbed a control on the screen. "Okay, sir; you're on speaker."

A man said, "Agent Burke, are you there as well?"

"Yes, sir," Burke replied.

"Very well. For any who may also be present and not know me, I am the Deputy Director for Paranormal Affairs, and no, you will not find my name, title, or department anywhere on my agency's table of organization. Agents Hauser and Burke, I have spoken with your supervisors to let them know I would be calling you, as this is technically a breach of the chain of command, but the exigent nature of the situation warrants it. Effective immediately, the United States cedes all jurisdiction over the rash of children abductions to the task force assembled by the Magi Assembly and

Shifter Council. The two of you will act as liaison between federal law enforcement and the task force and claim federal jurisdiction in any encounters with state or local agencies. Do you understand this directive as I have communicated it?"

"What of the perpetrators, sir?" Burke asked.

"The Magi and shifters will decide whether the perpetrators will face their justice or ours."

Burke looked ready to say more, but Hauser shook her head in silence. Burke scowled but left her arguments unspoken. "Thank you, sir."

"Very well. Agents, I expect glowing reports about how well you represented both our agency and government. Be safe out there."

The audio clicked when the call ended, and Hauser looked to Grandpa.

Grandpa replied with a half-shrug. "Events escalated faster than I anticipated. Apologies that your search warrant is basically wasted effort at this point."

"How is it wasted?" Burke asked. "We still need it to search the premises for the children."

Hauser shook her head. "No, we don't. This isn't our case anymore. *They* don't need a search warrant, just a formal hand-off of jurisdiction."

Burke's expression suggested she was less than pleased about that turn of events, but no one else seemed to care.

"Well, we'll leave you to get this organized," Grandpa said, stepping into the silence that edged toward awkwardness. "Care for a ride home, Old Wolf?"

Alistair nodded. "Why, thank you, Old Wizard. Don't mind if I do."

My grandparents and Alistair turned and left the illusion, then vanished. Remaining were around four hundred and fifty people, all staring at us as they waited for orders.

1 4

Three hours after sunset, we set off. To say a Smilodon and dire wolf drew odd looks when running with wolves, foxes, and a few different big cat breeds while several breeds of predator birds flew overhead was—perhaps—an understatement. It seemed the Magi spent almost as much time staring at me and Karleen as they spent focused on their objectives. When we neared the fence, Vicki had to remind the Magi with the lead elements to check for wards not even ninety minutes after we'd finalized the plan. I was tempted to suggest to Karleen that the two of us should go back to the vehicles, change back to humans, and retrieve our clothes before re-joining the assault.

And that's what it was. An assault. There was no way it could be anything else when over two hundred Magi combat veterans and a like number of equally skilled and experienced shifters descended on the defunct Industrial Steel & Fabrication complex in the dead of night.

After conferring with both my grandparents and Alistair, Vicki and Gabrielle settled on using the unit model developed during World War II: one to three Magi rounding out a squad of shifters in their animal forms and one to three shifters rounding out a squad of Magi. And despite Karleen's preference, she and I were *not* in the same unit; Gabrielle and Vicki both agreed that would be an inefficient use of such powerful shifters. Karleen's puppy dog eyes in her dire wolf form were brutal in their sad pleading, but my sister and Gabrielle stood firm. Just to twist the knife, she added a sad puppy whine as she trudged off to her assigned unit.

Vicki and Gabrielle also laid down simple rules of engagement: prisoners preferred, except in cases of direct threat to life. My unit tested those rules not even fifty yards inside the perimeter fence. We set off to the left once we passed through the main gate, circling west or downstream to be the point unit in securing that section of the complex. Given my sheer size, I served as a kind of stealth reinforcement, doing my best to stalk through the tall grass that ringed the facility. As we neared the first building we had to clear and secure, the wolf on point ran into a roving guard... quite literally. The guard—a short, stocky guy who looked like he spent too much time in the gym using steroids—stood at the corner and turned to walk toward us just as the point wolf trotted around the corner and ran his snout into the guard's crotch. The wolf let out a startled yip as the guard doubled over and groaned. The closest Magi lifted her hands to put the guard to sleep, but she was too late. I was already on the move, charging out of the tall grass at a tangent to the building; I shoulder-checked the guard into the block wall.

I don't care how fit you are or how protective your equipment is. Force *always* equals mass times acceleration, and I weigh upwards of a thousand pounds in my feline form. The guard's head hit the wall hard enough to concuss a bowling ball, and he slid to his knees before falling forward... totally unconscious.

The Magi glared at me and leaned close to whisper, "I had that! You did not have to intervene!"

I gave her a flat look in response. If she did indeed 'have that,' why did I have time to run fifteen yards from the tall grass to reach the guard? I'm nowhere close to a cheetah. I'm a tank, not a race car. But unlike Smilodons, magic moves at the speed of thought. I held the Magi's eyes for a few moments longer and attempted a contemptuous snort before I returned to the high grass.

The Magi and other shifters in my unit moved into the building, dragging the unconscious guard with them. They soon stepped back outside, and the Magi at the end of the formation wove a ward to seal the building and mark it as cleared.

OVER THE NEXT hour or so, we moved through the eastern portion of the complex's outer-most perimeter. We encountered five more guards, and I'm proud to say we handled them much more professionally than the first. We did not locate the barracks or the children, but honestly, I didn't expect that we would. No one in their right mind would place high-value targets or buildings on the perimeter of their location.

We completed our assigned zone of patrol when we reached the river. While the company was in operation, they installed locks where their property touched the river, and as such, both riverbanks were in truth concrete structures much like loading docks, with the outer-most lock gates in line with the property fence at the eastern and western edges of the complex. And there, on the far side of the river, was our first anomaly of the night: three roving guards, even though there were supposedly no structures on that side of the river.

The Magi who failed her first test of the night stepped forward and lifted her hands. She rattled off a series of words that sounded like the language Vicki used to work magic and waved her hand from right to left as she completed the spell. The three guards across the river dropped, fast asleep, but the guard closest the river slipped over the edge and splashed into the water, some ten feet below. In his state of magically induced sleep, he'd soon drown, and for all we knew, he had crucial information we needed.

Every shifter in my unit looked to one another, and every feline promptly sat down. Tigers usually didn't mind the water, but we didn't have any with us. Besides, I didn't even know if I'd float in my feline form. One of the larger wolves chuffed at us before making a running jump into the river. He paddled over to the sleeping form drifting downstream with the river's current and worked at it until the guard was on his back. The wolf held him by biting the shoulder strap of his tactical harness, then pulled him ashore.

When the wolf emerged from the river on the muddy bank outside the fence, he released the guard once the man's boots were clear of the water and then looked at the rest of us as if to say, "See? That wasn't so hard."

Heh… with my incisors, I would've killed the poor guy just trying to roll him over so his face was out of the water.

GABRIELLE PADDED along at Vicki's side, taking in all the sounds and scents her enhanced senses allowed. Her nose wasn't as good as a wolf's, but it was more than good enough for their task that night. She didn't want to stray far from Wyatt's sister, either. Granted, Vicki could take care of herself, but this wasn't Gabrielle's first raid. For Wyatt's sister, she was fairly certain it was.

The faint sound of a boot scraping gravel reached her ears, and she patted Vicki's foot with her paw. Vicki gave the hand signal to communicate a hostile contact. Gabrielle stalked forward and peered around the darkened corner. A lone sentry paced in front of the building's door. She slinked around the corner and lunged at the sentry for a take-down. She was mid-lunge, lips pulled back from her teeth in a silent snarl, when the sentry turned. He froze, his expression a mask of fright. Gabrielle's front paws connected with his chest, and she rode him down to the ground. His rifle clattered against the concrete but didn't discharge. Before the guard could do more than piss himself, Vicki was there and put him to sleep.

The building behind the guard turned out to be an operations center of sorts. Gabrielle couldn't see too much from her position, but she saw maps tacked to a corkboard on one wall. Vicki seemed rather elated. The rest of their unit fanned out to clear the building while Vicki plundered the area for whatever looked even vaguely important.

At one point, Vicki leaned close to Gabrielle, and her whisper was as close to a cheer as Gabrielle had ever heard while still being a whisper, "This is *everything*, Gabrielle! *Everything!*"

Gabrielle tried to share her excitement. She thought she would once she was able to see everything. Instead, she chuffed her agreement and padded off to do a circuit of the building. She didn't want any roving guards to interrupt them.

~

KARLEEN PADDED along with a squad of Magi at her tail. The rest of the teams worked their way through the facility, while she had one goal and one goal only: find the children. She remembered enough of her sister's friend's scent to use that as a base for locating one of the children. A 'normal' canine couldn't do that, but wolf shifters weren't wholly canine even in their lupine form. Unlike the 'lesser cousins,' wolf shifters could invoke higher reasoning and cognition. A faint breeze blew through the facility from the mountains in the distance, and Karleen froze. There. It was faint. Just a hint. But the scent was close enough to that of the city wolf so Karleen had no doubt. She felt her muscles tense in preparation for the long, loping stride of a wolf on the hunt. Then froze. She wasn't alone this time. She couldn't just dash off into the night. The constraint made her want to growl and take off anyway, but the thought that she might *need* the Magi when she reached the children held her back. She lifted her right paw and made a very unnatural motion of swiping at the air, doing her best to mimic the human 'come on — this way' wave, before she set off at a trot.

By this point in the night, the facility felt largely deserted. It wasn't. But Karleen didn't know how far the other elements of the assault force had progressed in securing the facility. No one would make a sound until she howled that the children were safe. The scent she followed grew increasingly stronger until she stood at a small storage building. One wall was a shop or garage door, and each wall also had at least one human-sized door. In her circuit of the building, she passed a section of the wall that fairly reeked of the city wolf that was her sister's friend, and she *knew*. The children were just on the other side of the wall. She trotted back to her Magi and led them to the door closest to where she'd picked up the strong scent and pawed the air in front of it. She didn't want to paw the door itself or try to open it herself. If anyone was in there with the children, that might give them away.

The Magi in charge understood, though, for she approached the door and tried the knob. It was locked. But that didn't stop her. She placed her hand flat against the door with her thumb curled around the shaft of the doorknob. A quick recitation in a language Karleen didn't know, and her lupine ears picked up the faint *click* of the lock releasing. The Magi then grasped the knob and turned. The door opened.

As soon as there was enough room, Karleen surged forward and shouldered the door wide. She stood in a tiled entryway of the small warehouse, dust and dirt thick on the floor with shoe prints betraying the abductors. It was a simple matter to follow both the shoe prints and the scent to what looked like an office door on the side of the warehouse. She stopped a foot away from the door again and pawed the air.

The Magi who'd stayed right on her tail came forward and tested the knob. It opened. The light in the room came on as the Magi swung the door wide, and three children huddled together on a ratty mattress, their hands and feet tied. Other Magi stepped into the room and untied the children while the team lead assured them they were safe now. The children free, a Magi lifted one each into his or her arms while the team lead opened a portal. The Magi carrying the children stepped through and were gone. Karleen pivoted and charged back to the door leading outside. It was still ajar, so she turned her muzzle away and hit the door at full speed with her shoulder. The door flew open and slammed against the wall as Karleen ran some ten feet outside, then skidded to a stop.

She lifted her muzzle to the night sky and howled her triumph for all to hear.

∽

I TURNED my head when the howl split the night. The wolves in my unit turned their muzzles skyward and added their own. Then, more howls joined. And still more. Soon, the whole facility bathed in the exultant song of our wolf shifters.

It was over... for now. All that remained was to collect our prisoners and whatever intelligence the other teams found. Then, clear out. We weren't even going to mask our presence. I maintained my vigilance as we backtracked our path through the facility, just on the off-chance we missed someone, but there was no need. We returned to our vehicles without encountering any active 'hostiles.'

As the groups filtered in with prisoners, we laid them out in the tall grass. Those of us wearing fur collected our packs and padded away long enough to shift back to human and pull on our clothes. Then, we rejoined the Magi.

After a discussion between Vicki, Gabrielle, my grandparents, and Alistair, the decision was to deliver all of our prisoners to the Magi for interrogation. Vicki and Gabrielle would take the documents, maps, and everything else from their ops center to Precious where Alistair would lead the analysis with shifters from the Council specifically trained for intelligence work.

I lost track of the number of trips I made with a sleeping prisoner over each shoulder in a fireman's carry. The portal Grandpa opened didn't look like anywhere on the manor grounds that I'd ever seen, but I figured I should keep my questions to a minimum, since I was now a shifter and all. I didn't want to put him in any awkward positions because he was 'Grandpa.'

It wasn't long until only shifters and two Magi stood around our vehicles. The Magi opened a portal to Precious large enough for our vehicles and several shifters standing shoulder-to-shoulder, and we vacated the area.

15

The infirmary in Precious occupied a space three lots down from the city's administration building. Given the nature of shifter healing and the relative lack of any wars at the moment, it wasn't very busy. In fact, the only patient when I walked in with Gabrielle was Thomas Carlyle, still in wolf form and dozing on a gurney.

The infirmary's sole doctor looked up as the door opened and broke into a huge grin. He almost jumped up from his seat and strode across the room. The moment he crossed within arms' reach, he erupted in a huge smile and thrust his hand out to Gabrielle.

"Excellent job you did, getting those children back," he said, pumping Gabrielle's arm like the handle of a hand-pump. "And to bring them back unharmed! Capital, my dear; simply capital!"

Gabrielle endured the enthusiastic hand-shake until he released her and indicated me with her left hand, "You wanted to examine Wyatt, Doc. Well, we're here."

"Excellent! We'll start with the basics, and then I'll ask you to shift." He added a self-deprecating shrug. "I'm afraid the nature of our existence is such that I have as much experience as a veterinarian as I do an MD. If I thought it wouldn't scandalize the state medical board into revoking my license to practice, I'd get a degree in Veterinary Medicine, too."

That kind of hit me. "You mean shifters don't have their own medical board? I would've thought we would."

"Oh, no, dear boy... not at all. Most shifters' concept of medicine is... well... not too current with the times, I'm afraid. In that respect, we're on par with the Magi. They don't have to bother with medical studies, though; a Magi who's strong in his or her healing talent can remove diseases and afflictions modern human medicine considers terminal. Oddly enough, though, almost every Magi whose strongest talent is healing has also pursued some level of medical degree. From what one told me, a more thorough understanding of the body can help them when they set out to heal someone. But! I digress. You're here for your medical work-up, and I'm just chattering away. Let's get you over here and start your complete physical."

When Doc said 'complete physical,' he wasn't joking. He poked, prodded, tickled, or measured me in more places than I realized I had places. He weighed me. Then, he took tissue, urine, and blood samples. After that, a full body x-ray. And after *that*, a full-body PET scan.

And after all that, he told me to shift, and we did it all again.

Gabrielle led Wyatt into the administration building's conference room. Doc already waited, sitting in a chair near the projector screen that hung down from the ceiling along one wall, and Alistair, Alpha Jace, and Vicki trailed in behind them. Karleen slunk in behind Vicki, looking for all the world like she hoped no one would notice her.

Doc's eyes narrowed at seeing Karleen trailing along in the group's wake. "And just who are you, Miss?"

Everyone turned to look, but the other shifters had to have known she was there. As the dire wolf primogenitor, her scent wasn't anything like any other wolf shifter.

"Karleen Vesper," she answered.

Doc lifted the file on the table in front of him and flicked it open. "Let's see... Gabrielle Hassan, Alistair Cooper, Jason McCourtney, and Victoria Magnusson. Nope. There is no 'Karleen Vesper' on this medical release authorization. So, which are you? Wyatt groupie or shifter journalist?"

An almost-predatory smile curled Karleen's lips as she answered, "Oh, I am most definitely a 'Wyatt groupie,' as you put it, but I'm also the North American dire wolf."

Doc gaped. "You are?"

"Yep," Karleen replied, adding a nod for flavor.

Gabrielle watched Doc scan the others present with his eyes as he gnawed on his lower lip, then flicked his eyes back to Karleen as he asked, "I don't suppose you'd agree to a medical baseline and comparison to the historical dire wolf?"

Karleen shrugged and leaned against the wall near the door. "I dunno. Why don't you let me sit in on this discussion to see how it works?"

"Oh! Well... I don't know. I mean, there's patient privacy to consider, and..."

Wyatt trooped around the table and took his folder out of Doc's hands. Before Doc could even ask what was happening, Wyatt added Karleen to the medical release order and initialed his addition. Then, he returned to the seat he'd claimed, saying, "Find a seat, Karleen."

The dire wolf shifter exploded into motion and claimed

the seat to Wyatt's left before the people in front of her had a chance to take more than a step. The part of Gabrielle that was always a predatory cat of the genus *Panthera* tried to growl, but Gabrielle didn't let it out. She wasn't sure what kind of game Karleen was playing, but she wasn't about to let the dire wolf claim Wyatt without making a fight of it... possibly literally.

"Uhm... yes..." Doc muttered as he looked over the edited release form. "Well, everything appears to be in order here. So, let's take our seats and begin."

Everyone who wasn't already seated found one, with Alpha Jace sitting at the head of the table with Alistair on his right.

Doc cleared his throat and began, "Three days ago, I collected all of the data I will now present. At that time, Mister Wyatt was on Day Eight of his life as a shifter."

A silence settled over the group that felt both awed and expectant.

"And he has already won a dominance fight with a councilor," Alpha Jace remarked.

"Yes," Doc replied, bobbing his head in a nod.

"How is Carlyle anyway?" Alistair asked.

Doc flicked his eyes to Alpha Jace, who nodded. "He's recovering well. Almost completely healed, in fact. None of the injuries were anything that our accelerated healing would normally have a problem with, but it was the sheer scope of injury that proved the most challenging. I insisted he remain in the infirmary while we get him back to a healthy weight, because his body almost devoured itself to feed the healing process. Right now, I doubt he could win a fight with an enthusiastic puppy."

Alistair nodded his understanding.

Alpha Jace said, "Very good, Doctor. Thank you. Please proceed."

"Uhm, yes. So the bulk of the delay in having this meeting has been the struggle to obtain Mister Wyatt's human medical records. Even after he gave me a signed release authorization, the doctor's office was still difficult about it all. But I digress."

Doc clicked to the first slide in his presentation.

"Mister Wyatt has benefitted from almost a doubling of his muscle mass as well as a major reduction in his body fat, which is the norm for a turned shifter. Furthermore, his body is still refining the improvements granted to Human Wyatt. This is in line with what we've seen with other turned shifters, but the sheer scope is unlike anything in the medical database. At the time of the examination, Mister Wyatt could already deadlift six hundred kilograms. The deadlift record for turned shifters is eight hundred kilograms and change, and it was set by a shifter eighty-six years into his shifter life. For those present who are uninitiated to turned shifters, it is not uncommon for their physical prowess to keep improving as far as ninety days post-turn. In just eight days, Mister Wyatt's deadlift capacity increased by an order of magnitude.

"As interesting as the improvements to Human Wyatt are, the disparity between his feline form and its historical coun-terparts is far more startling. First of all, Wyatt's feline skeleton is eighteen-point-seven percent more massive than the largest *Smilodon populator* fossil we have found to date, which was the largest of the three *Smilodon* sub-species iden-tified thus far. Just to put this in perspective, *Smilodon popu-lator* was itself about twenty percent larger than modern Bengal tigers, the second-largest example of Genus *Panthera* after their Siberian cousin. Paleontologists have singled out the *Smilodon* breed of saber-tooth cats for having weak jaws and fragile incisors when compared to the other species of sabertooth cats, and my examination of Wyatt's feline form led me to conclude that he *does not* have these weaknesses.

Many people who study shifters have said that we all start off as the best versions of ourselves we could possibly be, and I believe this applies to Wyatt as well, for both his human and feline forms."

"Does your data or examination give you any indication of where he'll plateau?" Alpha Jace asked.

Doc emphatically shook his head side to side. "Not at all. Right this moment, his front paws are large enough and his entire form powerful enough that he could remove a man's head with a lateral swipe if he put his whole body behind it. Despite having more of the fast twitch muscle present in modern cheetahs than cheetahs themselves do, Wyatt's feline form is built for endurance almost from the paws up; I ruined three treadmills trying to run him to exhaustion. The only reason he doesn't have a higher *percentage* than cheetahs is the simple fact of having so much more muscle overall than they do."

Everyone in the room—besides Wyatt—gaped at the doctor. Alpha Jace voiced the prevalent thought, "*Three* treadmills?"

Doc shrugged. "Well, to be fair, I didn't pay close enough attention the first time and told him to get on the light duty one we use for sprinters. The poor thing just collapsed when Wyatt put his full weight on it. But even after moving him to the heavy-duty treadmills we use for lion and tiger shifters, he *still* burned out the bearings and gear boxes. Not to mention that the frames of those two treadmills now look vaguely U-shaped."

Vicki leaned forward and shot a mischievous grin toward her brother. "I guess it's time for you to go on a diet, brother mine."

"Oh, no... not at all, Miss Magnusson. If anything, we need to increase his caloric intake, favoring protein and carbs. We discussed what—and how much—he has been eating since waking up in the infirmary, and my calculations suggest he's consuming less than three-fourths of what he should be. I'm surprised there's any fat left in his body at all. Shifters aren't quite as bad as humans when it comes to consuming muscle mass if he or she isn't getting enough food, but his eating habits are absolutely holding him back."

"Doc," Wyatt protested, "I already eat like a squad of trainees in basic."

"Then, eat like a platoon at least," Doc shot back. "You are not *quite* starving yourself just yet, Wyatt, but if you don't step up your caloric consumption, you will be and soon. Gabrielle, at the risk of creating a conservation crisis, take him out and teach him how to hunt."

THE REST of the presentation faded to the background for me as my mind swirled around Doc's unequivocal statement that I wasn't eating enough. I wasn't hungry... was I? Sure, I kinda felt like I could eat, but I wasn't anywhere close to what I'd call ravenous. And if I followed his advice, what would I look like in eight more days? I mean, my physique already pushed the limits of what a plain old human could achieve with nutritional min-maxing and obsessive exercise and weight training. What more did he want from me?

But I'm not human anymore, the growly voice opined. *Why should I compare myself to... them?*

That was the first time the growly voice tiptoed around the edges of frightening me. For a split second, I had the impression it was going to say 'food' instead of 'them.'

I've never been a very competitive soul. Well, not really. Most of my competition has been with myself. Could I correctly solve an IT problem faster than an estimated time? Could I hike a section of trail faster than my personal record? Stuff like that. As for external competition? Being better at something than Joe Schmo? Nah. That's just not healthy. I mean, sure. If a person approaches with the proper attitude and viewpoint, external competitiveness can be a good thing, but oftentimes, it serves only to catalyze a lack of self-esteem or self-worth. *That Guy is so successful at underwater basket-weaving; I'll never be able to compete with him.* And other senseless crap like that.

So, I was more than a little surprised to realize parts of me *wanted* to find out just how ripped I could get with enough quality food and a proper exercise regime.

"Hey, Wyatt... you in there?" Gabrielle's voice pulled me out of my thoughts.

"Oh, uhm, sorry, Gabrielle. What were you saying?"

"I said that Doc gave me two copies of his recommended dietary guidelines for you, since you're kind of my ward in the shifter world for now."

I blinked. "Oh, he did? What does he recommend?"

Gabrielle chuckled. "Well, he goes into a lot of detail, but you can basically boil it all down to one statement: Meat and a lot of it. If you're a numbers guy, he wants you to aim for six thousand to eight thousand calories per day, divided between protein at seventy-eight percent, carbohydrates at fifteen percent, and fat at seven percent."

"Oh," I replied, wincing. "That's a lot of food, Gabrielle."

"The best way to do it, probably, is to eat six to eight one-thousand-calorie meals spread throughout the day. I split my caloric intake into meals like that as best I can, and on the weeks where I actually manage it, I don't feel hungry."

"Oh." I still felt a little overwhelmed by the sheer mass of food Doc wanted me to eat each day. "Do you think he's right? About my metabolism and body still growing and changing?"

I caught Gabrielle's nod out of the corner of my eye. "I

absolutely think he's right, Wyatt. It's a proven fact among turned shifters that the turning process isn't a one-and-done kind of thing. Sure, *most* of it happens within the first seventy-two to hundred-and-twenty hours, but the process doesn't complete for something like sixty to ninety days. You're the first turned primogenitor we know of, but so far, you're following the trend. Your baseline just started out so much higher than most shifters."

A surprising thought came to me. "He didn't say anything about why I'm a primogenitor and not a cougar, either."

Gabrielle chuckled. "That's because we don't know *why* you're a primogenitor and not a cougar. We don't know why Karleen is a dire wolf, instead of either breed of wolf that her parents are. For all that we as shifters have looked into primogenitors, there haven't been enough of them to assemble any kind of body of knowledge about them beyond the basics. Stuff like 'do not piss them off.'"

"Seriously?"

"You heard Doc, Wyatt," Gabrielle insisted. "Right now, your cat is big enough and strong enough to send an adult human's head flying toward the fences. If you came at me intent on my death, the only way I come out of that—the *only* way—is to run like a terrified kitten. Sure, I know stuff that you don't. I have a lot of experience fighting in my feline form, but all it would take is one good hit from you to put me at your mercy. If you don't believe me, look what you did to Thomas Carlyle just by falling on him."

That was a terrifying thought. But at the same time, repugnant. The part of me where the growly voice lived outright recoiled and snarled at the thought of trying to kill Gabrielle. What struck me about the growly voice's reaction was the sheer, overwhelming disgust and contempt it radiated at the mere thought of attacking Gabrielle out of an intent to harm. It was over and above what I would have said was my normal rejection of harming others without due cause.

It's because she's mine. *I will not harm my own unless they betray me*, the growly voice explained.

Wait, what? Just when did I lay claim to Gabrielle? I don't remember that happening.

The growly voice almost snarled. *How can I be so stupid? Or am I perhaps blind? Do I not remember both Karleen and Gabrielle rubbing against me in their true forms?*

Images exploded in my mind. It was from my human perspective, and it took me a heartbeat or two to realize it was from the backyard where the children were abducted. Karleen leaning against me in her dire wolf form—pressing herself against me, if I'm going to be honest. And then, Gabrielle rubbing herself along my other side from jaw to tail.

Oh. Oh my.

Did that mean they claimed me?

Of course not, the growly voice replied. *I do the claiming. They just made me aware that they were agreeable to me claiming them.*

"Is there something wrong, Wyatt?" Gabrielle asked, pulling me from my thoughts once again. "You look a little unsettled."

Well, crap. How was I going to ask her? I mean, guys just don't walk up to women and say, 'Hey, cutie, interested in being claimed?'

The growly voice seemed to scoff. *Humans always complicate things too much.*

There. There was no way I could bring up the whole 'claiming' thing without being as red as a tomato, but I could ask her about the growly voice.

"Uhm, I don't really know how to say this, but ever since I woke up in the infirmary here, I've had another voice in my head. I don't really know how to describe it, but it's sort of growly and always talks as if it's me."

Gabrielle grinned. "That's because it *is* you, Wyatt. That voice is the manifestation of your feline's thoughts and instincts."

"It's a lot more articulate that I would've thought a big cat would be."

Gabrielle threw back her head and laughed. "Well, of course, it is, silly. Our human side influences and enhances our animal side as much as the animal influences and enhances the human."

"So, it's normal for it to identify an elk shifter for me?"

She gave me an expression that screamed 'Well, duh,' as she said, "Of course. Your feline is *you*, Wyatt. If you know what a timber wolf shifter smells like, your feline will, too."

"What if I'm pretty sure I've only met one elk shifter, though?"

Gabrielle froze mid-step and turned to me. "What? I'm not sure I understand."

"Okay," I said, heaving a sigh. "When I went to tie off all the remnants of my human life, I walked into a situation that ended up with a police response. My growly voice identified the officer who responded as an elk shifter, and I've not encountered anyone that smelled like him... before or since."

"That... how is that possible? You shouldn't be able to identify shifter breeds you've never encountered before. Did you identify me as a jaguar when we met in the infirmary?"

I shook my head slowly as I went back over the memory. "No... I don't remember hearing the growly voice until after my first shift. I think the first time I heard it was in Alistair's office when we met Grandpa and Vicki."

"Hrmm..." Gabrielle frowned. "What did it say?"

I couldn't keep from blushing. "Uhm... I'm not sure I want to say."

"Oh, come on, Wyatt. It could be important." Then, a faint smile curled her lips. "Will it help if I promise not to change my opinion of you?"

"That kind of begs the question what opinion you have of me. I mean, I wouldn't want you to have a bad opinion, you know."

An unreadable expression slowly took over Gabrielle's face. "You wouldn't?"

I shrugged one shoulder and looked away. "No. I think you're an amazing person, and..." another half-shrug "... well... I enjoy spending time with you."

I was not prepared for Gabrielle's reaction at all. Her entire expression lit up. But just as quickly as she flared, she schooled herself back to a teacher's non-expression. "Once we're past the point of you being my orientation ward, I want to re-visit that topic, Mister Wyatt. Now, what did the growly voice say the first time you heard it?"

I felt my face and ears heat again. "I was thinking about the life I'd had up to encountering the cougar, and it had a rather pointed opinion of how I'd been living my life up till then."

"Don't make me pull it out of you with a herd of horse shifters. What did it say?"

"I don't remember the exact phrasing, but it basically said I had been wasting my life and potential."

Now, Gabrielle's eagerness faded somewhat. "Oh. Yeah, our animal sides can be a bit... uhm... blunt. I think I told you once before they're much more primal than our human sides are, and they don't really understand white lies or letting someone down easy, especially ourselves."

"So, it's not common for a new shifter's animal side to know things like shifter breeds I've never met?"

Gabrielle shook her head in place of answering 'no.'

"What about explaining concepts of shifter culture that I

didn't already know?"

"Wyatt, what you're talking about sounds like racial memories. That hasn't happened for shifters in over a thousand years, and even then, it only happened with *born* shifters. You'd better tell me whatever it told you. I'd hate for it to give you the wrong idea about something."

If my ears and cheeks weren't already flaring red, they did now. "Uhm, it's okay. I wasn't planning to act on what it told me or anything."

"That's not fair," Gabrielle countered. "After you get some experience with shifters, your animal side is very good about instinctual or intuitive judgments. So, come on. Tell me already."

I closed my eyes and shook my head; I couldn't help it. I *really did not* want to have this particular conversation right now. Especially not in the middle of Main Street in Precious.

"Come on, Wyatt. If I'm going to help you learn the ways of shifter culture, I have to know whether your animal side is pushing you astray."

I motioned for her to lean close. She sighed and rolled her eyes, but she still leaned close.

All in a rush, I rattled it off in an urgent whisper as quietly as I could. "It told me that you and Karleen want me to claim you because of how the two of you rubbed against me in that backyard where the children were abducted."

When I leaned back, I saw Gabrielle's eyes were wide. Before I could process any more of her expression, she pivoted on her heel and started striding away from me.

"I just remembered something I need to do, Wyatt," Gabrielle said, waving over her shoulder. "I'll catch up with you later."

As I watched Gabrielle hurry off, I couldn't help but wonder if I'd said something wrong... or maybe—just maybe —I'd said something right.

16

Gabrielle's mind splintered across myriad thoughts as she hurried away from Wyatt. She thought she'd have more time. He wasn't supposed to know about shifters claiming their mates yet. That's not how this was supposed to work. It was supposed to be fairly simple. She'd guide Wyatt into an understanding of the shifter world, and then— when the time was right—tell him how she felt and what she wanted. She'd already given him a hint about it, after all, when she talked about how her cat wanted to climb him like a tree. It worked out better that way, if men had at least an inkling of what was coming.

But this? No. This was... well... it wasn't wrong *exactly*, but it certainly wasn't how events were supposed to unfold. She needed to be very careful about this, or she'd scare him away. And if she wasn't with him most of the time, one of the others in town might steal him out from under her.

Gabrielle pulled herself from her thoughts to survey her surroundings. She was almost down to the infirmary, but she really wanted to go back to the administration building and speak with... huh. Alpha Jace couldn't help her; he was a few years younger than she was. Alistair? Yes! Alistair was old enough that he might know what was going on. No need to tell him what Wyatt suspected about the way she and Karleen had rubbed against him, even though he was right there when they'd done it.

A quick glance over her shoulder showed that Wyatt was no longer in sight. Good. She didn't want him to see her backtrack to the admin building. That would cast the reason for her rapid departure into doubt, and she didn't want that. She turned and hustled back down the street.

Just as she approached the admin building's entrance, the door opened, and Alpha Jace led Alistair outside. Alpha Jace smiled when he saw her.

"Ah, Gabrielle," he said, "there you are. I'm afraid I need an unofficial word with Wyatt. Is there somewhere we might be able to chat, just the two—well, four—of us? Alistair says I can resolve the matter with a simple conversation, but that's not really how things work among shifters."

Gabrielle frowned. What Alpha Jace was saying was too far removed from what had been her sole focus just moments before. She was usually quicker on her feet, but she felt like her mind was mired in molasses. Then, all at once, it was like her mind broke free, and she knew without a doubt what Alpha Jace feared. Wyatt was an alpha, too, and so much more powerful than Jace. It would be so simple for Wyatt to take control of the community from Jace that he was probably afraid for his life.

"Oh! I really don't think you need to worry about that," Gabrielle said, "but sure, I can find Wyatt. Uhm... do you know the lake back in the hills at the base of the waterfall?"

Alistair nodded. "I can take him there."

"Okay. I'll find Wyatt and bring him."

Gabrielle turned and headed off. She had no idea where

Wyatt went, but she hoped enough of a scent still remained that she could follow in human form. When she reached the spot where she left Wyatt, she glanced behind her, hoping to find Alistair and Alpha Jace gone... and they were. With a soft sigh of relief, she closed her eyes and concentrated on the faint scent of Wyatt that still hung in the air.

"Whatcha doing, kitty cat?" a voice jerked Gabrielle out of her concentration. She opened her eyes and found Karleen standing in front of her. For the briefest moment, Gabrielle felt an urge for an irrational anger toward the dire wolf. Wyatt was *hers*. But that passed almost before she recognized it.

Gabrielle sighed again. "I'm trying to find Wyatt. I wasn't watching to see which way he went, and now, Alpha Jace wants to see him."

"Oh." All playfulness evaporated from Karleen's expression. "He's in the diner."

"Thank you," Gabrielle replied, adding a grateful nod. Without further ado, Gabrielle turned and headed that way. She was not surprised when Karleen fell into step beside her.

"So," Karleen began, "once you tell Wyatt that Jace wants to see him—"

"Alpha Jace," Gabrielle corrected her.

Karleen scoffed. "He's not *my* Alpha. I am my own Alpha. But anyway, once you send Wyatt off to see Jace, do you think we could talk?"

A deep dread settled around Gabrielle's shoulders as a growing suspicion of why Karleen wanted to talk grew in her mind. Karleen was going to ask her to back off Wyatt... and... well... she didn't want to.

"Alistair and Alpha Jace asked me to go with Wyatt," Gabrielle replied, hoping she kept herself nice and calm. She didn't want any sign of her nervousness or dread to express in ways another shifter could detect.

Karleen smiled and reached out to pat Gabrielle on the shoulder. "You don't need to be afraid of me or nervous. I was just hoping for some girl talk. Find me once you're finished with Jace and Alistair?"

Gabrielle nodded. "Sorry to chat and run, but I really need to find Wyatt."

"Here," Karleen said, pushing a piece of paper into Gabrielle's hand. "My number. It'll make finding me easier."

Gabrielle wasn't all that sure she *wanted* finding Karleen to be easier, but she accepted the paper and hurried on her way.

I LEANED back in my seat as I pushed the now-empty plate away from me. Well, it was really more like a platter. Three steaks—medium rare—with steamed vegetables on the side was my conquest of choice. The delicious smells wafting out of the diner's kitchen no longer made me want to drool, and the background noise of the lunch rush made for a pleasant ambiance. People nodded to me as they passed my table, some even giving me a thumbs up or other form of encouragement over my role in returning the abducted children. At first, I thought it was just community building with the new guy, but I noticed those people doing the same with Buddy. He saw me noticing and stood up from his table, heading my way.

"May I sit?" he asked when he reached my table.

I nodded and gestured to a seat.

"You looked a little confused there," Buddy said as he planted himself about ninety degrees around the table from me.

"Maybe I was. Everyone still seems to be congratulating

me for being on the team that found the abducted children, and we're—what—four days past that now?"

Buddy grinned. "I can see how that might seem odd. It'll die down around the week to two-week mark. Everyone wishes they could've been a part of it, and unlike the humans, we don't need an advertising campaign to support our fighters. Plus, everyone knows you're the new blood. Most newbies—no matter how dominant or what their background was—would've sat this one out until they had more experience being a shifter. You dove right in on all fours, and people remember that kind of thing. And people are talking about how you put that distracted Magi in her place when Fido bumped into the guard. Relations between shifters and Magi haven't always been sunshine and roses, and given your family, a lot of us thought we knew where you'd come down in a disagreement. You proved us all wrong."

I grinned and fought to keep from laughing. "Fido? Really?"

"Nah. His name's Harold Perry, but people usually call him Harry. For being so oblivious on point that he nosed a guard in the crotch, he's Fido for a while. I've heard a few people have even asked him to fetch the paper or whistled while they waved a stick like they're going to throw it."

Now, I did lose it and burst out in a huge belly laugh. "Oh, damn... that is too funny. How's he taking it?"

Buddy shrugged. "Ehh... he knows it's all in good fun, but at the same time, he also knows he screwed up. By the time he earns another place on point, he won't make the same mistake again."

The bell over the diner's door drew my attention, and Gabrielle walked in with purpose in her stride. I watched her scan the diner until her eyes landed on me, and she betrayed the briefest hint of surprise at seeing who sat at my table. But that didn't keep her from heading my way.

"Hey, Gabby," Buddy said, nodding his head in greeting when she arrived at our table.

"Hey, Buddy," she replied, her eyes never leaving me. "Wyatt, do you have a few minutes? Alistair asked me to find you."

"Well, that's my cue." Buddy slapped his knees and almost jumped to his feet. "I'll catch you kids later."

I pulled my wallet and dropped sufficient bills on the table to cover the meal and a generous tip, then nodded to Gabrielle. Without saying a word, she turned and led me out of the diner. I decided something was amiss when she led me around the corner of the diner and started walking toward the western hills.

"Uhm, Gabrielle?"

She responded with a questioning expression.

"I thought you said Alistair asked you to find me. Why are we—"

"Ssshhh," Gabrielle shot back. "You'll see."

WE HIKED into the forest where I stalked my first squirrel and marveled at how that seemed so long ago. I kept expecting Gabrielle to shift to her jaguar, but before I knew it, we approached the lake where I'd seen her sleeping... still human. When we stepped through the underbrush lining the lakeshore, I saw why. Alpha Jace and Alistair sat on a rocky outcropping almost opposite the waterfall.

"Thank you, Gabrielle," Alistair said as we approached, then looked to me. "Lad, you're here because Gabrielle said you might prefer a quiet conversation over other ways of settling a man's mind. But given the minds involved, it had to be something low-key that wouldn't step on anyone's dignity or give others the wrong idea."

I wracked my brain trying to figure out what Alistair

meant, but all I had were proverbial crickets. "Okay. Well, help a guy out. Whose mind is unsettled and why?"

"What are your intentions for Precious?" Alpha Jace asked, his tone sounding like he was wound a little tight.

"My intentions for Precious? Do you mind clarifying that? Because I don't know what you mean."

Jace's expression hardened toward a glare. "Don't be coy with me. Answer the damned question."

All of a sudden, this didn't feel like such a quiet conversation, and the part of me that was no longer human tried to growl. I was sufficiently aware of the situation that I stifled that urge, but that didn't mean I thought it was inappropriate.

"He's not being coy, Alpha Jace," Gabrielle said, stepping into the conversation. "He doesn't understand. He's not even two full weeks into being a shifter yet."

I watched Jace's eyes flick to Gabrielle and back to me before he took a deep breath and relaxed a little bit. "Look, you are the most powerful alpha I've ever encountered. Whether that's because you're a primogenitor or because of some weird confluence of your Magi family or just random chance, I don't know. What I do know is that smarting off to Thomas Carlyle the way you did and provoking that dominance fight would've been a death sentence for anyone else aside from maybe the dire wolf. So, I would really appreciate knowing if you're planning to challenge me."

"Isn't that a little too soon to tell?" I asked. "I mean… I'm just recently in town, so I'm not familiar with all the rules and laws and such. I don't really appreciate Buddy and his people being left off the leash like I found them the day I woke up, but I don't suppose that's any of my business."

Then, it clicked. Alpha Jace didn't mean 'challenge,' as in calling him out in public over stuff I disagreed with. He meant 'challenge,' as in challenging him to a dominance fight.

Which, if my altercation with Thomas Carlyle was any indication, he stood no chance of winning.

"Oh… you mean challenge you for Alpha of Precious or whatever your domain is? Nope. Not interested in that at all. I have too much going on with learning what it means to be a primogenitor shifter; I don't need the added hassle of trying to run a town or county or whatever. That's all yours. I will say that I like Karleen's idea of staying out of shifter politics and such, so I'd like to find some kind of agreement where I get to stay in Precious and learn about being a shifter without being drawn into a pack or pride or whatever you call it."

Alpha Jace blinked. "Are you serious? An alpha as powerful and dominant as you not wanting to claim territory?"

I shrugged. "That may change; I don't know. Right now, I'm about three major surprises away from running off into the hills screaming, and I don't need more shocks to my system. I will say this, though. If you were to do something heinous, say, like let a murderer walk away, I will kill the murderer and find you for a chat you probably won't enjoy. You should consider my reactions to Buddy Carrington and Thomas Carlyle as a kind of bellwether for how I'll respond to bad people. I don't *want* to kill anyone, but if someone pushes me far enough, I'll end them without a second thought."

Exactly as I should, the growly voice contributed.

Alpha Jace looked like he wanted to bristle. "If you think you're going to be some kind of free agent—"

Alistair laid a hand on Jace's shoulder. "Peace, my friend. There's no reason to turn this into a confrontation."

"Of course there is!" Jace shot back. "He's standing there dictating terms and threatening me. I'm not about to stand for that."

"Look," I said, "I've already told you I don't want your job, and I was honest. I'm also not about to bow down to you, either. Like Karleen, I am *outside* the traditional shifter hierarchy. If that's a problem for you for whatever reason, you're welcome to start a fight I'll finish."

Alpha Jace growled through gritted teeth, and his eyes took on the amber hue of a wolf. He launched himself off the rock where he sat and looked for all the world like he wanted to choke the life out of me.

Like this, the growly voice offered, and I felt conscious control over my body fade away. I side-stepped Jace's leap and put most of my torso into a powerful haymaker that struck his left temple as he sailed past me. He hit the ground a few feet away and rolled until a tree trunk stopped his motion. A faint groan indicated he was still alive but without his full faculties.

"Well, that tears it," I remarked and started removing my clothes. I stood on four legs and felt the mountain breeze through my fur before Alpha Jace even started to shake off the effects of my punch. When Jace stood up, the pupil of his left eye was about twice the size of his right, and he wobbled on his feet. I sat on my haunches and waited to see how he wanted to play this.

"Vin dok ebber gohn," Jace said, his voice slightly slurred. "Bog rad nosum."

Alpha Jace took a step toward me. Then a second. Midstep of the third, his support leg buckled, and he collapsed like a felled tree. Alistair and Gabrielle ran to him, and when they rolled him over, an almost petulant frustration dominated his expression as he said, "Gobber nom."

"I think we need to get him back to Doc," Alistair remarked.

I shifted back and donned my clothes, asking, "How do we do that without making whatever it is worse?"

"We have rescue litters back in town," Gabrielle remarked. "They're designed to strap to a rescue-trained shifter. It won't do his dignity any good, but I don't see how else to do it without jostling him."

Alistair looked at Gabrielle. "Neither of us are strong enough to pull him, though."

I started unbuttoning my shirt again. "I'll pull it. I did whatever this is, so the least I can do is get him to the infirmary."

I had my t-shirt over my head and didn't see Gabrielle strip and shift. By the time I pulled it off, I watched a melanistic jaguar dash off into the forest. She returned in a little under forty-five minutes, bearing a bundle strapped to her back.

Alistair went to her and released the straps, unfolding the rescue litter. The rescue litter looked to be heavy-duty canvas wrapped over what looked like the material used in heavy-duty ratchet straps that was woven between all four posts of the litter. The large, heavy wheels on one end made me think that was the bottom. To complete the litter's utility, the canvas sported thick straps resembling medical restraints.

Alpha Jace did not seem to appreciate the litter, setting off on a string of heated gibberish while he kept trying to stand. All he accomplished, though, was random waving of his arms and legs during his rant.

I stood and padded over to Alistair, who set about strapping the litter's harness on me. By the time he finished, the straps were uncomfortably tight, not tight enough to restrict my breathing or motion but still not comfortable at all.

"Damn," Alistair muttered, then spoke at his normal volume. "Wyatt, you'd better not take a deep breath till we get Jace back to town. The straps look close to rupturing as it is."

I nodded my agreement and turned around to see Gabrielle back in human form and dressed. She took one side of the litter and helped Alistair lay it out beside Jace. Jace still jabbered, and his tone grew increasingly frustrated and angry. He didn't seem to have any significant control over his limbs, as he waved them hither and yon while he expressed his displeasure with the situation.

"Jace," Alistair said, "if you can understand me, shut up and nod your head."

He stopped jabbering and nodded his head.

"Okay. That's good," Alistair replied. "Now, I'm willing to let you try standing one more time, but if you can't manage it, we're taking you back to town on the litter."

I watched from a safe distance as Jace managed to roll over and tried to stand. He almost managed it before his legs started trembling, and he collapsed again.

"Right then," Alistair remarked. "It's the litter. Will you be smart about this and not struggle or do we need to strap you in?"

"Dorf banu," Jace grumbled.

Alistair and Gabrielle shared a look, and both shrugged. Jace moved as best he could onto the litter. Once he laid on the litter, Jace moved to cross his arms and only smacked himself in the face for his effort. *That* didn't improve his mood at all.

"Wyatt, we need you over here by the head of the litter," Gabrielle said.

I trotted around and positioned myself as they directed. I soon felt weight settle onto the harness.

Gabrielle and Alistair both checked each other's work in securing the litter to the harness before we set out for town. I meowed my thanks when Gabrielle collected my clothes and folded everything into a bundle inside my button-down shirt while she carried my shoes in her other hand.

Alistair looked around the area for a few moments before nodding. "Okay. I think we have everything. Take it nice and easy, Wyatt, until we get to level ground. Oh… and try not to cut across an incline at an angle. All sorts of complications could develop from that."

I nodded my understanding, and we set off for town.

Gabrielle followed Alistair and Doc into the conference room of the administration building. She didn't want to be here, but Alistair insisted. She forced herself to remain impassive as she moved to a seat on Alistair's right.

"Two visits from the Shifter Council in as many days," one of the councilors waiting for them remarked. "It almost makes one wonder just what is going on out here. Have you lost your touch, Alistair?"

Gabrielle felt her cat rise toward the surface, and she fought the urge to strike out at the snide wolf councilor.

Alistair chuckled. "Councilor Markos, if you think administering a shifter community with an emerging primogenitor is any kind of easy, I invite you to take my job so I can return to the peace and quiet of Boston." Markos did not say a word, and Alistair snorted. "I thought not. Shall we proceed with the grim business that brought us here today?"

"Doctor, give your report if you would," Councilor Edelson—a feline shifter—said.

Doc cleared his throat and began. "Alistair, Gabrielle, and Wyatt Magnusson delivered Alpha Jason McCourtney to the infirmary three days ago on a rescue litter. He presented with aphasia and significantly reduced motor control. Under an x-ray, the left side of his skull displayed spider-web-like fractures consistent with significant blunt force trauma. Using other imaging techniques, I have determined that the blunt force trauma that shattered the side of his skull sent bone fragments ripping through his brain like shotgun pellets. Hmmm... perhaps flechettes might be a better description. Either way, those bone fragments shredded his speech center and primary motor cortex. I have seen significant healing of the skull and brain tissue since he first arrived, but he still presents with aphasia and has difficulty controlling his limbs. He also seems incapable of shifting to his wolf form. If Jason McCourtney had been human, I find it unlikely he would have been alive when he hit the ground."

Several of the councilors' eyes shot wide. The feline councilor turned her focus back to Alistair, saying, "How did this happen, Alistair?"

Alistair took a breath and released it as a heavy sigh. "Alpha Jace came to me the day we brought him to the infirmary to discuss his concerns about Wyatt. Wyatt is a very powerful alpha, and to Jace's view, it was only a matter of time before he challenged Jace to a dominance fight Wyatt would almost certainly win. I doubted Wyatt was interested in running Precious as Alpha, and I tried to explain this, but Jace didn't accept it. I persuaded him to have a quiet conversation with Wyatt, somewhere they could talk without Jace having to present himself as Alpha of Precious, and engaged Gabrielle to deliver Wyatt to the meeting place." Alistair broke off and shook his head. "The conversation started well enough, and I thought we were actually making progress... right up until Wyatt told Jace he considered himself outside our normal shifter structure like Primogenitor Karleen. He reinforced his point rather strongly, and to be quite honest,

I'm not sure what happened. Jace just snapped and launched himself at Wyatt, and Wyatt defended himself with a punch to the left side of Jace's head."

The feline councilor's eyes narrowed. "The *left* side, you say?"

Alistair nodded his confirmation.

The councilors turned to each other, and Markos remarked, "There *is* precedent for undeclared dominance fights."

"There is precedent for non-lethal dominance fights as well," the avian councilor present opined.

The feline councilor regarded her associates for a few moments—including the two that hadn't spoken—before she asked, "Are you suggesting we treat this as an undeclared dominance fight and award the position of Alpha of Precious to Wyatt Magnusson?"

Councilor Markos scoffed. "He's responsible for putting us in this position. I see no reason he can't be responsible for solving it."

"No," Gabrielle countered. "You make it sound like he committed a crime. Alpha Jace *attacked* him during the course of a conversation intended to prevent a confrontation. He had every right to defend himself."

One of the silent-thus-far councilors—a bear shifter according to her scent—nodded her agreement. "She has the right of it by my sight. The day we chastise our people for defending themselves is the day I resign from the council and take my people with me."

Silence descended on the conference room as several present expressed shock.

"And yet," the bear councilor continued, "Precious *must* have an Alpha, and nowhere in our laws and traditions is there a precedent for Interim Alphas. By blood and might, Wyatt Magnusson is the rightful Alpha of Precious."

Gabrielle closed her eyes and shook her head, forcing herself not to scoff or do anything else that the councilors might construe as disrespectful. "And what of Wyatt's desire *not* to be Alpha? During the conversation with Alpha Jace, Wyatt said he felt like he was little more than three surprises away from running screaming into the hills. Does the Pacific Northwest *need* its first Smilodon in ten thousand years?"

"Three surprises, you say?" the bear councilor asked.

"Yes, that's what he said," Gabrielle replied.

The bear councilor grunted. "He still has two left; we're good. I motion that we declare the altercation between Wyatt Magnusson and Jason McCourtney an undeclared dominance fight and award Wyatt Magnusson the position of Alpha of Precious."

"I second the motion," Councilor Markos chimed in without missing a beat.

The feline councilor who served as presiding officer for the meeting looked at each of her associates in turn as she said, "Motion submitted and seconded. Right hands for 'yay,' and left hands for 'nay.' Cast your votes now."

"THEY DID *WHAT*?" My heart thumped against my chest like it wanted to abandon me and take up residence somewhere else, and quite frankly, I didn't blame it. I felt... I felt... I didn't know what I felt. Panic? Absolutely, and it blotted out whatever else I may have felt about my sudden elevation in Precious's society. "Didn't they realize I don't know *anything* about being a shifter? How am I even remotely qualified to be an Alpha?"

I couldn't decide whether to put my head down on Alistair's desk and try to hide or high tail it out of Precious as fast my feet—or paws—will carry me. Grandma and Grandpa would let me hide out at home, right?

"Lad, for what it's worth," Alistair began, his tone resembling Grandpa's when I was too keyed up to sleep, "the laws and traditions aren't exactly brimming with qualifications to be Alpha of a pack, pride, or community."

I speared him with what I felt was a bewildered expression. "And just what does *that* mean?"

"According to the laws and traditions, a person earns the title of Alpha by winning a dominance fight against the current Alpha. Those are normally fights to the death, but there have been enough that were not to set a non-lethal precedent as well."

I gave him what I felt was an expectant look as I waited for him to finish. He didn't.

"That's it, lad. If you're a twenty-year-old full of piss and vinegar and manage to beat the fifty-year-old veteran, you're Alpha."

I groaned and again considered the idea of bugging out. "So, why wasn't I consulted on this?"

"Well, lad, it all came together kind of quick. To be fair, Gabrielle spoke up for you. She was very clear that you didn't want to be Alpha, but the crisis council chose otherwise."

"Wait… what was that? What's a crisis council?"

Alistair retrieved a toothpick soaked in mint and tea tree oil from a container on his desk and leaned back against his seat as he slipped it between his teeth and began chewing on it. "Whenever there is an exigent situation that requires outside adjudication, the Shifter Council dispatches a five-councilor team that they call a crisis council. As a group of five, they're equipped to accomplish things without being so large they're unwieldy."

"So, they speak with the full authority of the Shifter Council?"

Alistair nodded. "Afraid so, lad."

I need to quit being a whiny kitten, the growly voice said. *Of course, this crisis council awarded me the title of Alpha. It is my right as the strongest alpha shifter in the area. Give the community a week to get used to the change in leadership, and I can finally begin building my pride.*

Well, damn. I did not need *that* on top of everything else. But for all that my cat has his head up his butt about this pride business, he was right that I needed to quit being a whiny kitten.

"So, there's absolutely no way I can get out of this or postpone it until I get my feet under me?"

Alistair shrugged. "That depends. Do you want to be a respected member of the shifter community?"

"Yes," I answered in unison with the growly voice in my head.

"Then, not really, no."

A SHORT TIME LATER, Alistair led Jace's betas into the administration building's conference room. Against my better judgment, I sat at the head of the table. A couple of the betas bristled at seeing me in Jace's seat, but that didn't surprise me at all. Alistair invited everyone to sit around the far end of the table and withdrew a folded paper from his vest pocket.

"Per unanimous vote of this 374th Crisis Council, the North American Shifter Council hereby recognizes the undeclared dominance fight between Jason McCourtney, Alpha of Precious and Godwin County, and Wyatt Magnusson, Feline Primogenitor. As the dominance fight left Jason McCourtney medically unable to perform his duties as Alpha, the Crisis Council hereby bestows the title and position of Alpha of Precious and Godwin County upon Wyatt Magnusson, witnessed by Alistair Cooper and Gabrielle Hassan. This directive constitutes official notification and is effective forthwith."

No more than two seconds after Alistair stopped speaking and returned the paper to his vest pocket, the beta who sat at the opposite end of the table shot to his feet. "I challenge you for the position of Alpha."

I turned my attention to Alistair. "Is that valid? I mean… can he do that so soon after an investiture of a new Alpha?"

Alistair worked his jaw for a moment before he replied, "Technically, there is nothing in the laws or traditions about how soon after taking over an Alpha can be challenged. However, it has always been accepted practice—considered polite, really—to wait at least one day before anyone challenges the new Alpha."

"Hell with that," the beta growled. "I'm not going to wait a day before I beat this upstart's ass, and this will be a fight to the death."

Silence claimed the room as everyone turned to me, awaiting my response.

I took a slow, deep breath and exhaled it as a sigh. "I didn't want to be Alpha. Matter of fact, I don't particularly want to kill you. But if you feel so strongly about this, I suppose it's just as well that I do. I'm not sure I want you walking around creating who knows what kind of turmoil. So be it. Shall we go now?"

My matter-of-fact evaluation seemed to set my challenger back on his heels a bit. At least, he didn't look as gung-ho about fighting me as he had mere moments ago. Was he expecting me to vacate the position without a fight? Either way, it was his problem. He couldn't withdraw his challenge and still be a respected member of the shifter community. I knew *that* much.

"Fine!" my challenger growled, his whole demeanor almost screaming that he fought to maintain his bravado and ire. "Let's settle this now."

I stood and made eye contact with each of the remaining betas. "The rest of you might as well tag along. I would just as soon get all the executions out of the way at the same time."

Without waiting for a response, I left the conference room.

As we all trooped out to the arena, I heard snatches of conversation behind me. It seemed more than one beta questioned my challenger's sanity or good sense, especially after witnessing my performance in the fight with Thomas Carlyle. As far as I noticed, my challenger never responded.

When we reached the arena, Alistair led the other betas into the stands, while my opponent and I strode through the participants' gate. The moment we crossed into the fighting ring, I started removing my clothes, which meant I stood naked as the day I was born for a solid five to seven minutes as my opponent crossed the fighting ring and stripped as well.

"Last chance to call this off," I shouted.

The beta across the ring from me sneered. "What... are you afraid?"

I shrugged and muttered, "So be it. I tried."

Then, I nodded to Alistair. He stepped to the edge of the ring and repeated the spiel from my dominance fight with Thomas Carlyle. The moment 'begin' left his mouth, my opponent and I shifted. Then, we charged each other.

A gray wolf sprinted toward me, and I knew nothing of his preferred tactics or fighting style. But as we grew closer, I realized I didn't care. We didn't have to be here. He didn't have to be an ass about all this. The fight with Jace had not been my choice. But it's just like Grandpa said; if a person doesn't choose their path, a path will be chosen for them. But those were thoughts for another time.

I pulled my head back to the present circumstances just in time to see the wolf flex his muscles, and I remembered Carlyle flexing almost the same way right before he leaped at me. I dropped to the ground mid-stride and slid in the dirt and sawdust that made up the arena's floor. The wolf was too far into the motion, because he still leaped. The moment his paws left the ground, an idea came to my mind, and I tried to judge when to strike.

In my mind, I lunged up to rip out the wolf's abdomen with my massive incisors, a fight-ending move if ever there was one. Instead, I lunged too soon, and my jaws clamped around the wolf's neck. Following through with my premature lunge, I brought my right paw up to press against the wolf's side as I brought us both back to the ground. The wolf yipped at his impact with the ground, and that yip was his last sound. I flexed my claws to spear into the wolf's torso and put my shoulder into holding him down. I then put every ounce of strength I had into my jaws and pushed away with my right paw while I jerked my head away. There was a gruesome ripping sound, punctuated by ghastly crushing of vertebrae, as I ripped the wolf's head and half of his neck away from his body. Blood fountained out of the torso as I pushed it away, and I opened my jaws to fling the head in the opposite direction.

I turned to face the betas sitting in the row behind Alistair. Each and every one stared at me with sheer, unadulterated terror dominating their expressions. I shifted and met each beta's eyes in turn.

Then, I shouted, "Next!"

The betas fled.

Gabrielle entered the diner and approached the table where Karleen waited. She was not looking forward to this conversation, but she didn't feel like she had any way to decline without damaging whatever relationship she had with Karleen. After all, Karleen was a member of the team investigating the abductions, the first time Gabrielle ever heard of the lupine primogenitor getting involved with shifter society. She didn't want to mess up so bad that Karleen returned to her self-imposed isolation.

Karleen looked up from the sheaf of papers she held when Gabrielle stopped at the edge of the table and smiled. "Hi. Thanks for agreeing to speak with me. Have a seat."

"You're welcome. I have to admit a certain curiosity about why you wanted to talk," Gabrielle replied, returning the smile as she sat.

Karleen collected her papers and shoved them in the expanding file folder at her elbow. Then, pushed the folder away. "So... I'm sure you're aware that I do a *very* good job of keeping information about myself away from the public view. Being one of the only two—well, now three—known primogenitors makes for a certain amount of notoriety in our world. I have never liked the limelight, and I also have never found anyone interested in me for me, instead of what I am. If Wyatt hasn't noticed the groupies yet, he will. It's very apparent that you are interested in him. I'm interested in him, too. This presents an excellent opportunity."

Gabrielle fought to keep her nerves and heart settled. She didn't want Karleen to hear or otherwise sense any heightened emotion from her. She took a deep breath and released it slowly as she nodded. "I can think of at least two possible opportunities, but what opportunity do you see?"

"I argue that both of us are fine specimens of female shifters, and I think Wyatt might be interested in both of us." Karleen answered. "At least, the potential is there. It isn't uncommon among shifters for the Alpha of a pack or pride to have multiple mates. I thought you might want to discuss teaming up and expressing our mutual interest to Wyatt. Once we have him, we could approach him together with the idea that both of us would have to agree on future mates after us. What do you think?"

That was a good question. Gabrielle never considered that Karleen might want to conspire with her so that Wyatt claimed them *both*. On the surface, it was a great idea. She knew the chances of winning a challenge against Karleen, and she didn't want to risk that the dire wolf shifter would demand a fight to the death if she did challenge her. There was just one potential problem...

"Do you care that I'm not really into women?" Gabrielle asked.

Karleen made a dismissive wave. "Not in the slightest. I'm not really into women, either. Depending on how many mates Wyatt ends up with, it may become a thing... or it may never become a thing. I have two concerns: one, I want to see if Wyatt wants explore a relationship; and two, I don't want to fight the Huntress for him if he does."

Gabrielle blinked. "Excuse me? The Huntress?"

"Yes," Karleen replied, adding a smile as she nodded. "Within about a thousand miles in any direction you pick, most shifter communities have heard of the melanistic jaguar who has yet to fail a hunt. While they may or may not know your name, they have absolutely heard of the Huntress."

Gabrielle slumped against the back of her seat. Yet another thing she never considered. Oh, sure… the Shifter Council had contacted Alpha Jace or Alistair to request her on rogue hunts as far east as North Dakota and as far south as the Nevada desert. But she never once thought about having a reputation.

"I can see I've surprised you at the least," Karleen remarked. "Have I overwhelmed you?"

"No… well, I don't know really. It's always been a matter of pride that I am the Council's first call when they need a tracker. I never considered that I might have a reputation because of it."

Karleen nodded. "I can see that. So, aside from how I blindsided you with your reputation, what do you think?"

"I certainly like your idea better than the prospect of fighting you," Gabrielle replied, as she smiled. "You say you don't want to fight me, but I don't know of any regular shifter ever winning a one-on-one against a primogenitor. I —" The buzzing of Gabrielle's phone drew her attention away from the conversation. "Excuse me for checking this. Vicki promised to contact me as soon as the intel team finished with everything we captured at the steel mill."

Karleen nodded as Gabrielle picked up her phone and unlocked it. The notification was a new text message from Vicki: Meet in admin conference ASAP!

"Come on," Gabrielle said, standing and pushing her chair close to the table. "Vicki said ASAP."

Karleen stood without a word and dropped a fifty-dollar bill on the table as she collected her folder.

THEY CAUGHT up with Vicki leading the representative of the intel team into the administration building. The intel rep carried a thick satchel as he hustled to keep up with Wyatt's sister, and from what Gabrielle could hear of their heartbeats, they were wound up about something. They walked right past the young man at the reception desk without saying a word, and Gabrielle saw Alistair and Wyatt already sitting at the conference table. Gabrielle frowned at the sight of Wyatt in the seat Alpha Jace normally chose, with Alistair at his left. Wyatt caught her eye and nodded to the chair at his right. Karleen followed and sat to Gabrielle's right while the intel guy pulled a laptop out of his satchel and connected it to the room's projector, while Vicki retrieved a clutch of papers and laid them out for him.

"Where is Alpha Jace?" Vicki asked. "I would've thought he'd be here, too."

Alistair and Wyatt shared a look before Alistair sighed, then said, "Yes, about that… I've called a general community meeting in the town hall tomorrow, but the short of it is that Jason McCourtney is no longer Alpha of Precious and Godwin County. The crisis council decided that the altercation between Jason and Wyatt constituted an undeclared dominance fight, and as Jason is no longer medically capable to perform his duties as Alpha, that title and its responsibilities fall to Wyatt as 'victor.'"

"What?" Vicki asked, the papers she held forgotten. "What does that mean?"

"It means that Wyatt is now the ultimate authority in

both the town and the county as a whole in respect to the shifter community," Alistair explained, "but we can talk more about that later. Why did you call for us?"

Vicki took a deep breath and looked to the intel rep. He shrugged and gestured for her to proceed. "Okay, since Grant over here doesn't want to step up, I guess I'll present what the intel team found. The operations center at the steel mill was a figurative gold mine of information, and the intel team has spent the intervening days analyzing and compiling everything.

"From what we're seeing, one highly organized and well-funded group accounts for over ninety-eight percent of the recent up-swing in abductions, going as far back as eight months ago. The steel mill was their operations center for the state, and aside from a bunkhouse, mess hall, and the ops room, it was the first stop for abducted children. Looking at the data, it appears these people are using the children as the 'product' in some kind of child trafficking scheme. I can't for the life of me understand why anyone would think they could kidnap Magi and shifter children old enough to remember their families and think that would work out well long-term, but I suppose there's always the chance they don't realize some of these children are shifters or Magi. It's not like there's a visible difference between them."

Vicki nodded to the intel guy who brought up a picture of a massive complex with what looked like a mansion or manor house at the center of it.

"The reason I tagged the text with ASAP is that it looks like this group is planning to hit the largest orphanage in the tri-state area: The Millicent Guthrie Home for Children. The children here are all human, as Magi and shifters take care of their own orphans. The facility has just enough security to keep up appearances, and with the facility receiving freight deliveries of food and other consumables almost every day, the traffickers have a perfect cover. It would be very simple to roll up in a couple 53-foot semis with enough heavies to take the facility and then load all the children into the trailer and drive away. The facility is far enough away from major towns in the area that law enforcement response time would be upwards of an hour, and that assumes a notification to law enforcement in the first place. If they're smart enough to cut the phone and electrical lines right when they start, no one will know anything happened until the facility staff become missing persons."

Wyatt asked, "Do we have a timetable for this raid?"

Vicki grimaced. "Yes. The raid will happen the day after tomorrow."

"That does not leave a lot of time to develop a response plan," Alistair remarked. "Have you informed your grandparents yet?"

"They're my next call," Vicki replied.

"Call them now, please," Alistair said. "We need to have a high-level discussion about how much force we can bring to bear in forty-eight hours. One option is bringing Agent Hauser into the conversation, but the feds might require even more time to mobilize than we will."

Vicki withdrew her phone from a hip pocket and started the call. After a few seconds, she said, "Hi, Grandpa. Is Grandma close?" Pause. "Okay, good. Alistair suggested I call you right away to discuss what we learned from our raid on the steel mill." Pause. "Thanks, Grandpa. I love you both. Bye."

Before Vicki had enough time to return the phone to her hip pocket, reality began rippling in the corner of the conference room, and less than five heartbeats later, Connor and Maeve Magnusson stood there.

"Your tone suggested some urgency," Connor remarked.

Vicki nodded. "We have credible intelligence that the

people behind all the abductions are going to raid an orphanage. The Millicent Guthrie Home."

Connor's eyebrows shot up. "That's not a *small* orphanage. Bit audacious, isn't it?"

"I thought the same thing," Alistair agreed, "but the analysts say that all the data hang together for a very convincing picture."

Wyatt smiled as he gestured toward the available seats. "Please, make yourselves comfortable."

"Don't mind if we do," Connor replied and helped Maeve with her chair before claiming one for himself. "What does the local Alpha think of the data?"

Wyatt blushed, and Alistair cleared his throat before saying, "Yes... there's been a change in leadership since the last time you were here. Wyatt is the new Alpha. Jason McCourtney made the mistake of attacking Wyatt, and Wyatt's self-defense rendered him medically incapable of performing as Alpha. The Council sent a crisis council, and they decided to award the position to Wyatt since he won an undeclared dominance fight."

Connor beamed. "Well, congratulations, my boy! I'm proud of you."

"I don't want it," Wyatt replied. "It should have been a quiet conversation to work out how I could co-exist with the shifter community here in Precious, but I guess I said the wrong thing or something."

"You'll do fine," Connor commented. "Be sure to find a few stable, level-headed seconds to give you time to learn what it means to be a shifter, and you'll be set. You've always been down-to-earth and very sensible. But we digress...

"I think our first step should be confirming that the orphanage is in operation with children. Despite the credibility of the intelligence analysts, we need to be absolutely sure this isn't some kind of trap. Given the available time, we should start moving our people toward the orphanage, regardless. If it is a trap, no harm no foul; everyone just gets a nice sightseeing trip. But if it's *not* a trap, we could be critically out of position by the time we confirm the state of affairs." Connor fell silent as he lifted his face toward the ceiling and tapped his chin with two fingers. "Yes, we can supply the same people for this as we did for the raid on the steel mill. Alistair, how soon can you round up an equivalent number of shifters?"

Maeve touched Connor's forearm and looked to Vicki, asking, "Does your information say how large a force they'll use to raid the orphanage?"

Vicki shook her head. "I'm afraid not. It seems like they're planning to take ten teams, but your guess is as good as mine what constitutes a team for these people."

"What did the leadership at the steel mill consider a team to be?" Connor asked.

"The only teams mentioned in relation to the steel mill were four-person abduction teams."

Maeve scoffed. "No one in their right mind would try raiding the Millicent Guthrie House with just forty people. That facility is too large."

"Agreed," Connor replied. "So be it. Overwhelming force it is, then. Alistair, can you field combat-ready shifters later today?"

Alistair adopted a thoughtful expression for several moments before he nodded. "Yes. It'll be tight on the timing, but I think I can."

"Very well," Connor said. "I'll send a few to assist with investigating the orphanage and round up the Magi half of the assault team. Gather here in Precious?"

"That sounds fine," Alistair agreed.

With that, Connor stood, and Maeve followed him. Then, they vanished in the blink of an eye.

Alistair turned to Wyatt. "It seems we'll have to advance our plans for formal notification of the change in leadership, but we are fortunate that there are sufficient combat-experienced shifters in Precious to fill the roster. The rest of Godwin County will have to wait to learn there's a new alpha until after the orphanage operation."

"Should I sound off the old air-raid siren?" Gabrielle asked.

"As much as I hate that thing, it is the prudent thing to do," Alistair replied, then explained for Wyatt. "Precious has an air-raid siren that dates back to World War II. Since then, the town has repurposed it to be the call for an emergency town meeting. They test it every month on the first day of the month, but if it sounds off any other time, everyone gathers at the high school stadium for a town meeting."

As Alistair started explaining the siren to Wyatt, Gabrielle stood and left the conference room.

GABRIELLE HADN'T BEEN GONE for more than ten minutes when a piercing wail split the air. It was *beyond* painfully loud for me, and the other shifters in the room didn't seem to like it, either. At least shifter healing would repair whatever hearing damage we accrued.

After a couple repetitions, the siren wound down, and not a moment too soon. I sighed my relief into the silence that settled in the siren's wake and smiled. "Ah, blessed quiet."

"Come on, lad," Alistair said, tapping my arm and standing up from the table. "The whole town will be migrating to the stadium, and we should do the same."

"Can I come, too?" Vicki asked.

"Of course," Alistair replied.

. . .

ALISTAIR LED me and Vicki toward a section of town I hadn't seen yet. We hadn't any more than stepped off the curb outside the administration building when a group of shifters caught up with us on their own way to the stadium. I listened to them chat among themselves, debating the cause of the emergency town meeting, as I followed along in their wake and at Alistair's side. They seemed pleasant enough from what I could tell by listening to their tone and watching their body language. None of them were swaggering braggarts like Buddy had been the day we met.

By the time we walked across town to the stadium, I could hear the dull roar of everyone in the stands talking. We were among the last people to arrive and passed the stands to walk onto the field. As we cleared the entryway, Gabrielle waved to Vicki and motioned her to a seat she saved.

A small stage on a trailer frame with fold-down steps sat in the middle of the field, centered on the 50-yard line and hitched to a small garden tractor. Whoever had pulled the stage into position was not near the tractor, and I supposed the person found a seat in the stands. Personally, I wanted to find a seat in the stands, too.

What surprised me the most about the stadium was how *clean* it was. With my IT studies and career, I've spent some time in and around sporting locations, and no matter how efficient and dedicated the custodial staff is, the places always seemed to have a low-grade funk. Then, it clicked. *Of course*, these people would go overboard cleaning the stadium. With a shifter's enhanced senses, a barely discernible funk to a human would almost be the area-effect miasma that surrounded sewage treatment plants to shifters. Now that I thought about it, I wouldn't be surprised if the cleaning staff washed everything down with bleach and then rinsed with firehoses to wash away the bleach smell.

As Alistair and I approached the trailer, a young woman

brought a camera on a wheeled tripod out to the stage. She stopped about ten feet away and watched a monitor as she cranked a handle to raise the camera up to center on the microphone that stood on a stand in the center of the stage. She fiddled with the fine adjustment on the camera lift and then locked it in before she turned and waved. As Alistair approached and stood behind the microphone, the massive screen at the far end of the stadium came to life and displayed a close-up of Alistair and the microphone.

"People of Precious," Alistair began, "thank you for responding so quickly to the call for a town meeting. I called the meeting to inform you that Jason McCourtney is no longer Alpha of Precious and Godwin County. As most of you know, we have a new primogenitor—our first feline primogenitor in known history—in town, and he recently won a dominance fight with Thomas Carlyle, one of the wolf councilors. To make a long story short, Jason McCourtney felt it was only a matter of time until the new feline primogenitor challenged him for his position, and I suggested having a quiet talk behind the scenes to calm his concerns. During this conversation, Jason McCourtney attacked the primogenitor, and in the course of defending himself, the primogenitor delivered sufficient harm that Jason McCourtney was no longer medically capable of performing his duties as Alpha. The Shifter Council sent a crisis council, which ruled that the attack constituted an undeclared dominance fight and—as the victor—the primogenitor earned the position of Alpha. Citizens of Precious, I give you your new Alpha, Wyatt Magnusson, the feline primogenitor."

G abrielle sat off to one side of the shifters that gathered for the operation to block the orphanage raid. A faint breeze tugged at her hair and kissed her face, and the faint smells wafting from the diner made her question her commitment to waiting where she sat while everyone gathered. Her mind drifted back to the roar of approval when Alistair introduced Wyatt on the impromptu stage. She wanted Vicki close to her in case several of the locals objected to the change in leadership, but she worried for nothing. If anything, having a new Alpha for the town and county energized the people. Even Buddy and his crew cheered, and they seemed to have lost most of the bullying swagger since Wyatt's dominance fight with Thomas Carlyle.

Movement drew Gabrielle's attention, and she saw Wyatt and Karleen approaching her. They didn't make very good progress, because everyone wanted to congratulate Wyatt and introduce themselves. Still, though, Gabrielle fought the urge to smile with pride at how Wyatt handled each and every person who held him up with grace and aplomb. She was far enough in her understanding of him that she thought she saw some underlying nervousness or unease, but that was understandable.

"Hi, Alpha Wyatt," Gabrielle said when he reached her at last, and added a playful smile for flavor.

Wyatt shook his head. "Not you, too."

Gabrielle dropped the playful tone and expression. "It's only right and fair, Wyatt. You're Alpha now, and respect and deference come with the position. So, come to give us a pep talk before the Magi arrive?"

"Nope. I'm going with you. Alistair can handle things here in town until we get back." That was… good. Both the townsfolk in Precious and the rest of Godwin County would appreciate and respect an Alpha who led from the front. "But that's not the sole reason I'm here. We need new betas. One of Jason's crew decided to challenge the new guy, and I ripped his head off in the arena. For all I know, the corpse is still over there. But I want you to be one of my betas. Karleen already accepted."

"That's not how it works, Wyatt." Gabrielle shook her head. "You put out a call for betas and state how many you want, and anyone interested puts their name on a list. Once the sign-up window closes, everyone pairs off in a single-elimination series of dominance fights, and the top however-many become your betas. The good news is that these fights are not to the death unless you mandate that. I have heard of a few shifter groups who do death fights to select betas, but the community at large tends to regard those groups as backward and near-feral."

Wyatt scowled. "What if I don't want it to work that way?"

Gabrielle shrugged. "Too bad. Beta selection is one of the oldest traditions we have. There's a lot of changes the people will put up with—or even welcome—but not changes to how we select betas."

"Well, damn," Wyatt growled. "Fine. We'll deal with it once everyone's healed up after the orphanage op. I wonder why Alistair didn't mention that."

"He wasn't with us when you offered me a beta position," Karleen answered. "He's probably thinking to mention it once everything settles down or trusts Gabrielle to handle it… like she just did."

Wyatt chuckled. "Yeah, okay. Fair point. You going to sign up?"

"Me?" Karleen asked. "You know it. I've never been a beta before… or even a member of a community aside from my parents' pack."

There was a story there. Gabrielle wondered why Karleen wasn't still with her parents' pack, but at the same time, it wasn't uncommon for shifters to move around a bit once they reached their majority. Karleen just took things to an extreme when she left shifter society in general.

"How about you, Gabrielle?" Wyatt asked.

"To be honest, I'm not sure. I never considered it, honestly, since Jace's betas were all his close friends. I'll think about it after the op, and you'll have your answer if you see my name on the list."

Vicki arrived at Wyatt's side just as a disturbance behind them drew their attention, and Karleen and Wyatt both stepped aside as they turned to allow Gabrielle to see whatever it was. 'It' happened to be several large rifts forming about a hundred yards into the field. They looked like out-sized Magi portals.

"Oh, wow," Vicki said. "Grandpa and Grandma pulled out all the stops."

"What?" Wyatt asked. "Why do you say that?"

"Those are assault rifts. Only Magi who have achieved a Grandmaster certification in long-distance teleportation can create them and, sometimes not even then, if the person isn't inherently powerful enough. Assault rifts are large enough and last long enough that a significant force can use them."

The rifts opened, and Magi streamed through them.

"I'd better get over there," Vicki said. "As far as I know, I'm still in command of the 7th Magi Expeditionary Unit, and I'll need to coordinate with whoever the overall commander is."

Wyatt shrugged. "Let's go. I should probably introduce Gabrielle as well."

∾

I MADE a valiant effort to stay at Vicki's side as she wended her way through the crowd of shifters to greet the Magi. It seemed like I encountered someone who had not yet greeted the new Alpha every few feet, and Vicki was already in conversation with a couple of Magi by the time I broke through the crowd of shifters to stand at her side.

"And this is my brother, Wyatt," Vicki said as I arrived. "Wyatt, this is Travis Burke and Shelly Oldaker. The Assembly voted to reinforce the 7th, and while I still command the 7th, I've never commanded a force as large as it is now. Travis and Shelly have considerable experience leading a force this size and larger, and they'll serve as executive officers for lack of a better term."

For a moment, my mind locked at the question of whom I should greet first. Before I could spiral down that rabbit hole, I held out my hand to Shelly for the simple reason that she was closest.

"Hello. Like Vicki said, I'm Wyatt. Welcome to Precious." After shaking hands with both of them, I scanned the force still collecting in front of the assault gates. "How many Magi will we have?"

Shelly answered, "One thousand in total... half in War

Magi with the remainder split evenly between support disciplines. Healers, engineers, teleporters, and so on. It's our standard roster for expeditionary units."

"Say," Travis spoke up, "can you point me toward the local Alpha? We'd like to use Precious as our staging area and set up a temporary encampment."

Vicki giggled as I raised my hand. "Yeah, that's me."

Both Travis and Shelly looked at me like I sprouted a third arm out of my chest and a second head.

"But... you're..." Travis stammered.

Shelly seemed more in control, saying, "Aren't you a Magnusson? Magi can't be turned. How'd you end up as Alpha?"

Gabrielle and Karleen arrived just as I replied, "I was the first Magnusson born in something like eight hundred years with no trace of Magi talents whatsoever. A couple weeks ago—crap... has it really only been a couple weeks? Anyway, I went out hiking, and a rogue cougar shifter attacked me. I killed the cougar, thanks to a shifter-bane Bowie knife my grandfather gave me, but not before it savaged me pretty thoroughly. I passed out thinking I was going to die and woke up in the infirmary here."

Shelly and Travis shared a look. Travis said, "A Magnusson shifter who's brother to the heiress... well, that's certainly fortuitous."

"What's that supposed to mean?" Vicki asked, her expression tightening into a frown.

"Just that relations between shifters and Magi have a tendency to be like the tides," Shelly explained. "It would be good if the two of you end up helping us develop a friendly stability. There are maybe five million shifters and about half that number of Magi with every *other* person on the world being plain, vanilla human. I don't like those numbers. If it ever came down to a fight, I'm not sure we'd win."

Travis looked over my shoulder, and I smiled. "Let me introduce Gabrielle Hassan and Karleen Vesper. Gabrielle is my guide for all things shifter and also the commander of our war party, and Karleen is the North American dire wolf."

Both ladies greeted the two Magi, then Travis said, "Shelly, if you want to get started with planning, I'll get our people started on the camp."

Shelly nodded, and Travis turned to the group milling around the field behind them. He raised his hands and made a gesture I didn't recognize, and three Magi broke off from the group to meet him. Our shifter hearing was keen enough to hear him tell the approaching Magi that the cougar Alpha gave his permission to build the camp in the field.

Gabrielle broke out into a grin at the same time Karleen giggled.

"What?" Shelly asked.

"Travis called him a cougar Alpha," Gabrielle answered.

Vicki was quick to defend him, saying, "Hey, now. It's not his fault. *We* can't determine shifter species by scent; it takes a spell that's something like a two-minute cast."

Shelly eyed the four of us like we tried to lay a con on her. "But you said a rogue cougar attacked you."

"That's right, but when I had my first shift, I wasn't a cougar."

"How... that doesn't make any sense," Shelly protested. "I've never heard of a turned shifter being a species other than the shifter that did the turning."

Before any of us could answer, one of Buddy's crew approached at a jog. He slowed and came to stop in front of us, saying, "Alpha Primogenitor, the county council has arrived. They came to ask Jason McCourtney why Precious put out a call for a thousand combat-experienced shifters, and Alistair sent me to find you while he explained the change in leadership and why there hasn't been a territory-wide announcement."

"Damn," I muttered. "Can they block or impede what we need to do here?"

"No," Gabrielle replied. "The Godwin County Council is an advisory and executive body reporting to the Alpha. They are responsible for enacting and enforcing the Alpha's directives outside of Precious. They'll offer advice if you ask, but ultimately, you're Alpha. The only authority to supersede or countermand you is the North American Shifter Council."

Then, I noticed Shelly. Her pupils looked like black bullseyes on pistol targets. She clenched her hands into tight fists. The rapid-fire staccato of her heartbeat sounded like an automatic rifle. Her breathing came shallow and rapid. And... she was almost two feet farther away than she was prior to the wolf shifter arriving. She froze the moment I looked at her.

Wow... she was full-on fight or flight, and it seemed like she chose 'flight.'

"Shelly?" Vicki asked. "What's wrong?"

For several moments, I wondered if Shelly even knew Vicki spoke. Her eyes remained laser-focused on me. Then, she flicked her eyes to Vicki several times as if she acknowledged her question without wanting to take her eyes off me. When she spoke at last, her jaw trembled so much that it gave her a stutter.

"P-p-p... y-you're a primogenitor? A feline primogenitor?"

"I am."

Now, the faint flush that had colored her skin vanished. "And you were turned?"

"I was."

Shelly's eyes flicked between all of us. "I-I need to go. May I go? Please?"

"Shelly, what's wrong?" Vicki asked. "You're acting like Wyatt's some kind of rabid killer."

As she spoke, Vicki took a couple cautious steps toward Shelly. The moment Vicki partially stood between me and Shelly, Shelly pivoted on her heel and took off for one of the assault rifts. Vicki surged after her, and she was almost to the incoming Magi when Vicki finally caught up with her. But my shifter hearing more than compensated for the distance.

"Shelly... Shelly, stop! You have to tell me what's wrong," Vicki said as she grabbed Shelly's wrist. "He's my *brother*. You can't run off in a fright without telling me what's wrong."

Shelly spun to face Vicki, and even at our distance, I clearly saw the terror in her expression. "Vicki, you don't understand. I have to tell the Assembly. They need to know the feline primogenitor is finally here."

"What are you talking about?" Vicki pressed. "You can't start acting like a terrified field mouse with no warning and then run off to tell the Magi Assembly that my brother is a feline primogenitor without *some kind* of explanation."

I wondered how much Magi knew about shifters. Because so far, none of them acted like they knew we had enhanced senses even as humans, instead of just in our animal forms.

Shelly paused and closed her eyes, and I watched her take a deep, deep breath. Then, she spoke. "Vicki, for all that you've had very good teachers, you're still very young as a Magi. The day the Goths sacked Rome, one of the few recorded Magi with the prophecy talent went into a trance and started talking about a *feline* primogenitor who could be our greatest ally... or our greatest threat. I've answered your question, Vicki. Now, the Assembly has to know."

"I imagine they already do," Vicki replied in a voice almost too soft for me to hear. "Our grandparents know he's a primogenitor."

Shelly stopped her efforts to pull free of Vicki and blinked. The visible symptoms of her fight or flight response faded over the next few seconds. "They know? You're sure they know?"

"Yeah. I coaxed Wyatt to shift when Grandpa and I came to Precious to find him. Look, it's a long story, but Grandpa knows he's a primogenitor. He saw Wyatt in his animal form."

"Alpha, forgive me," the guy from Buddy's crew said, pulling my attention away from Shelly and my sister, "but the county council is waiting, and Alistair implied it was kind of urgent for you to come."

I nodded. I didn't want to leave, but it seemed like Vicki calmed Shelly. I sighed and nodded again. I was *not* looking forward to this, but I suppose it had to happen.

"All right, let's go."

I felt much better about the meeting when Gabrielle and Karleen joined me, one on either side. I just hoped none of them challenged me to a dominance fight.

20

I followed Buddy's guy as we walked back to the administration building, and it occurred to me that I should probably stop referring to him as "Buddy's guy." That he had been one of the guys sitting at Buddy's table the day of my first shift was all I knew about him.

"There are probably a dozen better ways to phrase this, so please forgive me. May I know your name?"

He smiled. "Don Sykes, and you did okay."

"Thank you, Don," I replied.

A flock of birds flying over the town drew my attention, and I wondered how many were members of the community, if any. That fundamental shift in perspective still worked its way through my mind. Both that I now lived in a world where people could take the shape of either animal or human and that I now governed a community of those people. I still felt a little unsettled about it all.

. . .

"ALPHA WYATT?" Don's question drew me out of my thoughts, and I saw that he held open the door to the administration building for me.

I wondered how long we stood there with me lost in my thoughts, and I chuckled. "Sorry, Don. I was focused on my thoughts. Thank you."

The same young man sat behind the reception desk, and now he smiled when he saw me enter. That was such an improvement over the cowed fear the day Thomas Carlyle came to town.

"Hello, Alpha Wyatt," the young man chirped though a smile that threatened to unzip his head. "Alistair and the county council are waiting for you in the hall."

I returned his smile with one of my own and a "Thank you" before I walked down the hall that led to the room where I smartassed my way into my first dominance fight. The double doors leading into the room hadn't changed, and I took a deep breath before opening one.

The room looked much as it had during my previous visit. Rows of wooden benches with padded seats made up the gallery. A decorative wooden balustrade with a swinging gate separated the gallery from the working area. A massive round table occupied the center of the working area, and people I didn't know once again filled most of the table's chairs. Alistair leaned against the balustrade, but he stood upright when he heard the door open.

"Ah, there you are," Alistair said. "Thank you for coming. Alpha Wyatt, may I present the shifter council of Godwin County?"

He went around the table naming each person, but so many thoughts and concerns jumbled my head that I didn't assimilate the information. The members of the county council ranged in apparent age from just a few years older than me to venerably on par with Alistair or my grandfather.

Most of their expressions led me to believe the person was neutral toward me, but I saw a couple frowns, too.

"Hi, I'm Wyatt Magnusson," I said once Alistair completed the introductions. "I want to be very clear that I didn't want the position of Alpha, but if I have to have it, I will do the job to the best of my ability. So, what brings you to Precious today?"

A man who looked to be one the upper end of middle age filled the silence. "We're here to get an explanation as to why Alistair issued a call for shifters with combat experience under your name. You did not consult with us about it."

His confrontational tone did not sit well with me at all, and rather than respond to him directly, I turned to Alistair and asked, "Alistair, do you mind filling me in on the role and authority of the county council? As we all know, I'm a bit new at this."

Alistair's lips quirked in what might have become a smile in less-public settings. "County councils—or regional councils, if a territory crosses county or state lines—exist to carry out the will of the Alpha."

"So, they answer to me instead of the other way around?"

Alistair began with a solemn nod. "It is not uncommon for a new Alpha to replace a whole council."

"Very well." I returned my focus to the confrontational shifter. "Please consider this your one—and only—warning. Just because I am new—both as a shifter and Alpha—do not make the mistake of thinking me weak. Earlier today, one of Jason McCourtney's betas challenged me for the position of Alpha, and I ended the fight by ripping his head from his shoulders. For all I know, the carcass is drawing flies and scavengers in the arena even yet. If you are unwilling or unable to treat me with the respect due any sapient creature, I invite you to walk out that door right now and vacate your position to save me the time and bother of throwing you out. Do you understand?"

He didn't respond immediately, and I held my eyes on his. The silence extended past the point of being awkward, and I reached the point where I no longer cared.

"Okay. Time's up. You're relieved, effective immediately. Alistair, please post a county-wide notice of the council vacancy and include a call for applicants."

Alistair nodded once and said, "I'll have the announcements made as soon as we leave the meeting."

The man still sat in the seat. He glared at me, a silent refusal to comply. Silence reigned as the other councilmembers waited to see how I'd handle the situation. I supposed the normal recourse was to have one of my betas evict the insubordinate bastard… but I didn't *have* betas yet.

"Alistair," I said, "what's the normal response to an insubordinate council-member refusing to vacate his or her position?"

"The Alpha over the council often sends one of the betas or the head enforcer to forcibly remove the person."

I made a show of heaving a sigh. "Well, never let it be said I have other people handle what I'm unwilling to do myself."

A few, short strides brought me to the back of the man's chair. The chair's feet gave a horrid screech as I pulled it back from the table by sheer strength to the accompaniment of startled exclamations from its occupant. Grasping his collar with my left hand, I pushed my right down between him and the chair to grasp the back of his belt. I set myself as if deadlifting, and the little effort required to pull the man to his feet took me by surprise. Now came the time to explore just how much endurance my new shifter muscles possessed.

The former councilmember waved his arms and locked his knees in a vain attempt to keep me from removing him, all the while bombarding us with vile imprecations and rapid-fire profanity. Gabrielle and Karleen rushed to the double doors and hauled them open just in time for us pass through them. The man's vehemence grew the closer we came to the main doors of the administration building, and he persisted in his attempts to grab me by the back of my head.

As we cleared the hallway and entered the reception area, I found the young man staring at us, total bewilderment dominating his expression. I didn't want to remove either hand from the former councilmember, so I made eye contact with the receptionist and said, "Door, please."

The young man shot to his feet and almost sprinted across the room to throw the doors open wide. Each of them sported a closure mechanism at the top, but Karleen dashed around us to grab one door and pointed to the receptionist to hold the other.

In the last five feet before the threshold, I increased my pace almost to a jog, and when my foot touched the step-plate of the doorframe, I put all my strength into a massive heave. The man flew over the sidewalk and cleared half the parking lane before gravity brought him back to Earth, and none too gently at that. But with his shifter healing, any injuries might last an hour… at most.

The man jumped to his feet and spun to face us. He took one step toward the administration building, and I said, "If you're intent on walking through this door again, you'd better bring a challenge with you. You're costing me time I don't have and patience I can't afford to lose."

At the word 'challenge,' he deflated. He still looked rather irate but didn't take another step.

I held his gaze for a few more moments, saying, "Don't be in town when we leave this building."

Karleen and the receptionist closed the doors behind me when I turned and headed back to the town hall.

. . .

HEARING the background noise of conversation through a door and fifteen feet down the hall still amazed me, and I wondered how long it would take me to accept my enhanced shifter senses. Still, the town hall doors were thick enough that I only knew that people were talking, and the moment I applied pressure to push open the door, the conversation died a quick and brutal death.

I stopped just inside the balustrade gate that separated the meeting space from the gallery and met each person's eyes in turn, asking, "Anyone else? I don't have a lot of time, and I'd much rather fire and toss out all the insubordinate bastards in one go of it." The room was so silent that I almost expected to hear crickets chirping, like in those old Western movies. "Okay, then. Moving right along. The short of it is that we discovered that one group is behind the recent increase in child abductions across human, shifters, and Magi, and this group is planning to raid the Millicent Guthrie Home the day after tomorrow. We are working with the Magi Assembly to stop this, which led to the general call for combat-experienced volunteers. That's the situation in a nutshell. If you feel the need to hear all the nitty gritty details, I'm throwing Alistair under the bus; he is fully up-to-date. Now, if you'll excuse me, I have work to do. I'll call a formal meeting soon to plan the general announcement that I'm the new Alpha. Have a nice day."

Gabrielle and Karleen followed me as I left.

I STEPPED onto the sidewalk and began a deep, calming breath when blunt-force trauma to the back of my head rudely interrupted my budding serenity. Even though I wasn't human anymore, the blow still rung my bell pretty good, and I struggled to catch myself with my hands before I hit the sidewalk.

"You think you can treat me like trash you can just throw out? It's time you had an attitude adjustment," a voice said from behind my right and over me. "I'm gonna beat your sorry hide before I decide whether to let you live."

The sound of ripping fabric filled the air, followed by the growl of a massive wolf with a deep ribcage. My assailant screamed. Wood clattered against the concrete sidewalk. Then, a heavy body hit the ground... hard.

At that point, I recovered enough of my wits to roll over and survey the scene. Gabrielle stood in the doorway, her lips pulled back in an almost-animalistic snarl. The remains of clothes and shoes lay in a pile to her left, half inside the administration building and half on the sidewalk. A bloody bat lay a short distance from my feet. My assailant—and yes, he was the idiot I threw out of the building—lay on the sidewalk with his feet closest the doorway. Karleen in her dire wolf form stood on him, her front paws on his pecs and her back paws on his thighs, and she made for his throat with her teeth.

"Karleen, stop!" I said, lifting my hand in an accompanying gesture. The massive wolf turned to look at me. Amber eyes met mine. "Just hold a moment, okay?

She chuffed at me, then turned back to snarl at the man who hit me.

"Gabrielle, what is the appropriate response to something like this?" I asked. "What would another shifter expect an Alpha to do?"

Without missing a beat, she answered, "Kill him. This is the same situation that made you Alpha. An attack that constitutes an undeclared dominance challenge."

Shit. I really did not like the degree to which killing was a part of the shifter culture. I didn't *want* to kill him. But then, I wasn't sure I could afford to leave him alive to try again. After all, he could always upgrade to a shifter-bane weapon like the knife my grandpa gave me.

Standing up took all my concentration, and my head felt like the metal between a blacksmith's hammer and the anvil. But I stood and stayed upright.

"Karleen, move aside, please."

She looked at me like she wanted to double-check I was sure, and I nodded. She backed away but maintained her readiness. As soon as Karleen was off of him, the man surged to his feet and lunged at me. I met his lunge with a full-force punch to his gut, and the air in his lungs hit me in the face. Damn... would've been nice if he'd used mouthwash before trying to kill me.

I used his moment of impairment to step behind him and snapped his neck before he could rally. He dropped like a puppet with cut strings.

"His body will heal that if you give him enough time," Gabrielle said.

My nod of understanding also carried regret for the entire situation. "I figured it would, but I didn't want a pool of blood on the town sidewalk. Karleen, I'm going to take him to the arena if you'd like to get clothes and catch up to us."

The dire wolf nodded and loped off toward the hotel.

I heaved the insensate form over my shoulder in a fireman's carry and made my way to the arena. Even though it was a long walk, it was the only place that came to mind where a child wasn't likely to happen across the pool of blood that would soon appear. As I trudged—step by step—under the weight of not only the burden draped across my shoulder but also my new society, my mind dwelled on how savage and brutal the shifter world seemed to be. I had killed one man already and won another fight where the people expected the same of me. Did the Magi act like this? There had to be an answer. We were better than this... at least *most* of us were.

Granted, I didn't want to kill this guy. That probably played a significant—yet underlying—role in my thoughts. Perhaps I should've let Karleen rip his throat out. That would've constituted the 'defense of another' justification for homicide to my mind, but I didn't want any child to encounter still yet more blood. I didn't grow up experiencing this savagery as a matter of course. Why should they?

It seemed as though I blinked and we stood in the arena. I realized that I didn't specifically remember the journey as Karleen arrived at a jog in her human form. I laid the guy down on the surface of sawdust and dirt, and I watched a finger twitch intermittently. He stared up at me. His jaw worked like he wanted to speak, but no words came. His spine probably wasn't healed enough yet. I turned to Gabrielle.

"Are you absolutely *sure* I have to do this? There's no other way?"

Gabrielle nodded. Her voice carried tones of resignation and compassion. "Yes, Wyatt, you have to do this, and no, there is no other way."

Physical nausea assaulted me as I knelt and rolled the guy onto his side. The fingers of his hand began twitching feverishly. In my mind, I reached out to the growly voice and asked for one paw with claws. Gabrielle gasped at the sight of my right arm shifting into my Smilodon paw from the elbow down. I flexed the muscles of my paw to extend the claw from what would've been my index finger on my hand, and I leaned closer, using that razor-sharp natural weapon to open the man's throat from artery to artery across the front of his neck. Arterial spray colored the arena floor in a pool of red. In less than a minute, it was over.

"Gabrielle, call Doc, please. I want these remains in the infirmary morgue ASAP."

Without another word or even waiting for anyone else, I turned and left the arena. I understood now why Karleen isolated herself from the shifter world, and I wished I could join her there.

21

Gabrielle watched Wyatt leave the arena while she withdrew her phone from her hip pocket and made the call Wyatt requested. Even had she not possessed the enhanced senses of a shifter, Wyatt's change in demeanor was almost glaring. In the corner of her eye, she watched Karleen look from Wyatt's retreating form to her and back again; the dire wolf shifter looked like she wanted to say something, but Gabrielle was too busy with the phone call to Doc. As soon as Gabrielle ended the call, though, she spoke.

"I'm not sure Wyatt will survive shifter society," Karleen said, falling into step beside Gabrielle as they walked out of the arena.

Gabrielle wanted to deny her statement, but... she couldn't. "Did you give a second thought at all about that guy needing to die for what he did?"

Karleen scoffed. "He would have bled out on the sidewalk if Wyatt hadn't stopped me."

"Does that make us better or worse people?"

Karleen shrugged as she shook her head. "I'm not sure I'm one to judge. I grew up inside our society and culture the same as you. I withdrew, yes, because I'm too strong for any dominance fights with me to be fair. People still talk about how Wyatt dealt with Thomas Carlyle, and from my experiences, that is the norm for primogenitors. I don't know if our hide is tougher or thicker or what, but 'normal' shifter teeth and claws have a difficult time getting through it. And before you ask, no; bullets still punch through, just not as bad. And they hurt... *a lot*."

Both Gabrielle and Karleen nodded a greeting to Doc as they passed him pulling a gurney toward the arena, and Gabrielle asked, "How did you come to get shot?"

"Oh," Karleen began, sighing out the word, "it was during my young and dumb years when I first withdrew from shifter society. I wanted to try a year or two as a wolf to see what it was like, but I didn't take a few things into account."

"Really?" Gabrielle asked, frowning her confusion. "Like what?"

"Elk hunters, for one."

Understanding clicked, and Gabrielle nodded her agreement. "Yeah, I can see that. What happened?"

"I was hungry and angling after a calf that frolicked a little too close to the tree-line and too far away from its parent herd. I was downwind of it and had no idea there was a hunting blind about four hundred yards away, which was also downwind of both me *and* the elk herd. I guess they decided to try for a wolf trophy to go with their elk. They hit me with an angled shot across the base of my ribcage. I loped off into the woods as best I could, and my shifter healing pushed the bullet out and closed the wound."

"How did you get away?" Gabrielle asked. "Professional hunters—even if they are just human—can be damned good trackers."

Karleen chuckled. "I knew of a rock shelf that had tree limbs shading one corner and ran for it like I did the hundred-meter dash. I arrived far enough ahead of them that I had time to shift and climb into the tree using a branch that hung low over the rock shelf. I laid on a branch for the better part of an hour while they tried to find where the wolf left the shelf, and let me tell you... tree bark is not kind to sensitive female bits. Not at all. Sap isn't that great, either."

Gabrielle bit down her laugh and turned it into a coughing snort. "No, I don't imagine it would be."

"It's okay to laugh. After all, it is kind of funny now, all these years later. Needless to say, though, I'm *very* careful about hunting in wolf form during any of the major hunting seasons for humans."

"I shouldn't laugh at your misfortune," Gabrielle said, "but yeah, the thought is kind of funny in a 'thank goodness it didn't happen to me' way."

Karleen laughed her agreement. "I know... right?"

They fell into a companionable silence for a short distance until Karleen asked, "So, what are we going to do about Wyatt?"

Gabrielle sighed. "I don't know. Our culture and society is what it is to me. I mean... it feels odd—cognitive dissonance kind of odd—that I pretty much had to tell him to kill that guy. It's probably part of the transition from human to shifter, and I'm kinda glad he's not someone who relishes killing his opponents. But still... he has to find some way to reconcile his human morals with his shifter identity. I suppose Wyatt could have just sent the guy out of the territory; it's not like he could ever present a realistic threat to Wyatt."

"Oh, sure... he might not have presented a threat to *Wyatt*, but suppose he gathered his own pack and returned for war? That's not without precedent in our society."

Gabrielle nodded, taking a deep breath and exhaling it as a puff between her lips. "Yeah, there is that to consider, too."

Karleen shrugged. "I'm not sure we can do anything more than be the best friends we can be. I'd like to be more, but right now probably isn't the best time to advance that goal."

They fell into another silence as they stepped onto Main Street's sidewalk and turned toward the mustering area. Ahead of them, Wyatt trudged his way toward the same destination. Even at a distance, his posture advertised his mood for any who cared to notice. Gabrielle ached to have some way of helping Wyatt through his troubles, but it wasn't her place to determine the proper course for Wyatt. Only he—and he alone—could do that.

MY MOOD HAD NOT IMPROVED by the time I arrived at the edge of the area where shifters and Magi alike gathered for the defense of the Millicent Guthrie Home. I knew I telegraphed my foul frame of mind with every movement and expression, but I simply could not find it within me to put on a happy face, as the song said. The more I learned of shifter society, the more I questioned my gratitude over surviving the cougar.

"Ah, there you are, Wyatt," Alistair's voice drew my attention, and I saw my grandpa's old friend moving through the crowd toward me. "I explained the crisis to the county council in as much detail as I felt appropriate. We haven't ruled out the presence of shifters in these abduction teams, so I felt the situation warranted a certain level of operational security."

"Thank you, Alistair. I appreciate you handling that for me."

"Forgive me, my boy, but your expression is a veritable storm cloud. May I ask what changed between when you left us and now?"

I blinked. "You don't know? The young guy at the reception desk didn't tell you?"

"Tell me what?"

Well, damn. I guess I had to relive it sooner than I anticipated. "The council-member I evicted was waiting with a baseball bat when I left the administration building and clocked me pretty good across the back of my head. Karleen was all set to rip out his throat right there on the sidewalk, but I staved that off in favor of handling it at the arena. I didn't want blood right there in plain view."

"Good for you, lad," Alistair said, clapping me on my shoulder. "I know joining our world has been a shock to your system, but I'm glad to see you're coming around to doing things the shifter way."

I didn't know whether to shout at him or simply walk away.

"Yeah," I replied, and my voice sounded flat and dead even on the inside. "I suppose you're right."

"Miss Vicki is looking for you and Gabrielle," Alistair went on. "Something about intelligence reports from the initial survey of the orphanage, I think. I'll head back to my office and mind the store here."

I nodded my agreement. "Thank you, Alistair."

Alistair clapped me on the shoulder once more before he ambled off toward the administration building. I watched for a heartbeat or two, then turned and began a search for my sister. I soon found her in what appeared to be a command pavilion situated between the shifters and the Magi. She stood at a table, switching between papers that covered her immediate vicinity of the tabletop. She looked up at my approach and smiled.

"Hiya, brother mine!" Then, she realized my mood through the subtle, immeasurable means of twins the world over, and she froze, her expression becoming one of concern.

It was only a matter of time before she discarded the paper in her hand and rushed to swarm me in one of her deepest hugs, shrouding me in her unyielding and unequivocal love. She thought those were the best medicine for whatever ailed me, and by and large, she was right. Just not today.

I shook my head. "We can discuss it later, sis. Alistair said you were looking for me?"

Vicki searched my expression with her eyes, and I could tell she questioned whether to comply with my request. Even though she eventually nodded her agreement, I knew it was grudging at best.

"Have you seen Gabrielle?" she asked. "She needs to hear what I have, as the leader of the shifter war party, and you know how I hate to repeat myself."

"She's on the way," I replied, just as Gabrielle and Karleen arrived on either side of me.

Gabrielle went straight to the table. "What do you have for us?"

"Preliminary intel reports on the Millicent Guthrie Home," Vicki answered, gesturing across the papers before her like the hostess of a game show. "Our people on-site say the facility appears to be inhabited and operating normally. They spoke with staff there under the guise of writing a biography of Millicent Guthrie, focusing on her humanitarian work, and went on a tour of the facility."

I blinked. Something seemed... off... about that somehow. "Wait. The staff just welcomed your people with open arms? Without any identification or credentials?"

"Oh, but you're wrong, brother dear," Vicki replied, throwing me her most earnest expression. "My investigators showed them identification and a very thorough backlist of critically acclaimed biographies."

I gaped; I couldn't help myself. "Your intel people are actual biographers?"

Vicki's entire demeanor changed from 'innocent, pure-souled prom queen' to 'unrepentantly mischievous imp' in the blink of an eye. "Of course not, Wyatt. They're Master-certified in Illusion."

Well… now, I felt like an idiot. It made such perfect sense. Rather than dig my proverbial hole any deeper, I merely nodded my understanding.

Vicki winked, communicating she knew very well the thoughts crossing my mind, but we were like that. When we hit our stride, we could finish each other's sentences without missing a beat.

"All this looks like it hangs together," Gabrielle remarked as she returned the last report to the tabletop. "None of it gives me the feeling of being too perfect. Unless you or your people have any objections, I think we're good to go."

Travis and Shelly arrived at the table then, coming from a cluster of workspaces farther back in the pavilion. Shelly still looked a little wild around the eyes anytime she regarded me, but she made no mention of her earlier reaction.

Vicki turned to them, saying, "Are you both current on the intel reports?"

"We are," Shelly answered.

"Thoughts?"

Travis answered, "We've discussed it and examined it from every angle we can come up with, and there's no reason we shouldn't move ahead with our plans."

"Very well, then," Vicki responded. She took a half-step to retrieve a rolled-up paper from a nearby table behind her and moved it to our table, unrolling it to reveal a map of the facility grounds. "Let's get to planning."

∼

HECTOR OLMSTADT STOOD and regarded the world beyond the window in his office. Two knocks on the door heralded the arrival of Tammy Beckett, the person in charge of their... hospitality.

"Well?" Hector grunted.

Tammy answered with an almost predatory grin as she slipped into one of the plush armchairs Hector kept for office guests. "I think they bought it. They certainly gave no indication they detected the charm I wore. Of course, I wear it inside my clothes, like we all do, and made every effort to act like I saw whatever illusions they tried to spin."

"Okay, then. If they found the NAS at the steel mill, they should believe we will attempt a raid on this facility two days from now. Start sending the kids out through the tunnel to the truck stop and get them on their way. I'll call in our reinforcements that are already waiting there and alert everyone that we need to shift operations to... oh... the Gamma-Eight sites. Were we able to get hold of any of that special ammunition we've heard rumors about?"

Tammy shook her head. "No. Everyone I've contacted just laughed at me for believing old tales."

"So be it," Hector remarked with a shrug. "If we can't be surgical with quality, we'll just overwhelm them with quantity."

As she stood to leave, Tammy gave one last predatory smile. "Do you think those freaks have any idea what they're walking into?"

"I sincerely hope not, or we'll be on the receiving end of the ambush."

Hector started working on the tasks to finalize their ambush as Tammy left his office. No... he most certainly did not want their guests to have sniffed out the ruse. No matter where you looked across all recorded history of ambushes, it rarely went well for the attacker when the supposed victim *chose* to spring the trap. Tammy was the last person to report an evaluation of their act, earlier that day, and everyone believed the freaks posing as biographers swallowed the spiel like the main course at a five-star restaurant.

Sending out the notifications took only a matter of minutes, and once that was finished, Hector leaned back in his seat and closed his eyes. Then, he began the arduous process of mentally gaming out every scenario he could think of. This part of the op was as reflexive as breathing to him, and it was the only way he'd ever found to reduce any complications delivered by the ages-old foe of preparation: the dreaded Murphy.

22

Vicki and Gabrielle gestured to the map unrolled on the table as they briefed the team leads.

"We will arrive about a mile out from the facility," Vicki said, "and move out as units. The goal is to make contact with the facility's staff and inform them they are the target of an impending raid for their children. Our hope is that they welcome us into the facility so we can fortify it and prepare a defense, but if they refuse, we'll set up in the forest just beyond their property line."

"What about whoever owns the property bordering the facility?" a cougar shifter team leader asked. "We'll be trespassing."

Gabrielle gave him a flat look. "We're shifters, and most of us are hunters on top of that. If you get caught in the woods, I'll send you back to school with the young."

"Yeah, I get that," the cougar persisted, "but I'll have two Magi with my team. What if they're not up on their woodcraft?"

Gabrielle turned to Vicki and raised an eyebrow in silent question.

Vicki shrugged. "Pass the word to bring any Magi who embarrass you to me, as long as you understand that we'll bring any shifters who embarrass us to Gabrielle... or Wyatt."

More than one shifter sent a cautious glance toward the new Alpha. His own thoughts consumed him, however, to the point that he didn't notice.

Gabrielle and Vicki resumed the briefing, discussing their defense plan if they succeeded in gaining permission to set up inside the facility, as well as their readiness plan if they had to withdraw to the property line. The entire process took upwards of two hours, and the entire time, Wyatt stood off to one side, his mind clearly not on the briefing. Once they'd worked through the plans and the questions afterward, Gabrielle and Vicki sent the shifters and Magi on their way to form up for departure. Gabrielle and Vicki had one last necessary conversation.

"Wyatt?" Gabrielle's voice jerked me out of my thoughts.

I knew I didn't hide my surprise that only Gabrielle, my sister, and I now stood in the command pavilion. "So... I missed the briefing?"

"You did," Gabrielle agreed.

Vicki chimed in, "All two hours of it."

Well, shit. That wasn't good. I needed to get my head right if I was going on this op. I couldn't afford to be oblivious like that on what would essentially be a battlefield.

"Sorry. I suppose everyone else noticed?"

"There wasn't really any hiding it," Vicki replied. "Well, I suppose we could've thrown a couch cover over you, but then everyone would've wondered why you wore a bad ghost costume."

Gabrielle stepped closer, and her hand twitched like she

wanted to reach out to me. "Do you want to talk about whatever it is?"

Seriously? She didn't *know* what was on my mind?

"We don't have time for any of that," I countered.

"We'll make time for it," Gabrielle rebutted. "You need to be able to focus on what we're doing."

I nodded my agreement. "I know, and I can. Which team am I in?"

Vicki looked like she wanted to say more, but I didn't miss Gabrielle touching her arm. "You're with the same team you were for the steel mill. It's just expanded."

"Okay. I'll go find them."

I turned and left the pavilion before they could press me further, especially my sister.

GABRIELLE HELD up her hand to stay Vicki's question after Wyatt left the pavilion. She stepped to the door and watched him leave, trying to gauge the distance until they'd be able to converse without him hearing. When she felt safe to speak, she returned to Vicki and drew Wyatt's sister further into the pavilion.

"What's the deal with Wyatt?" Vicki asked, complying with Gabrielle's gestures to speak softly.

"He killed someone today for something that doesn't warrant death in human society but does in shifter society. I don't think he's handling it well."

Vicki looked over her shoulder toward the direction Wyatt took upon leaving the pavilion. When she turned back to Gabrielle, she asked, "Seriously? If he's that deep in his own head, he has no business being on this op. He could get someone killed or get killed himself."

"I know, but do *you* want to have that conversation with him?"

"I'm not afraid of my brother, Gabrielle," Vicki shot back. "I remember when we both went through potty training."

Gabrielle fought back a snort of laughter. It *was* rather difficult to put someone on a pedestal when you went through potty training with them. Wait... she frowned her confusion as she asked, "You actually remember that stage of your life? I didn't think people remembered that."

"Maybe most people don't, but my earliest memories are from a time before I could walk. I don't know if all Magi are like me, but yeah. Believe me... I would very much appreciate not remembering what it felt like to need my diaper changed, but such is my life, I guess. Do you want me to talk to him?"

Gabrielle took a deep breath and exhaled it as a slow, heavy sigh. "I don't know. I'm not sure what he'd say about me telling you. And on top of that, suppose we talked him out of going and something bad happened he could've stopped by being there?"

"We can't play that game," Vicki countered. "As the top-level commanders of this mission, we have to evaluate the situation with objectivity. Do we have any evidence that he's a critical mission asset to this op? Do we have proof that we will fail to protect the orphanage if he isn't there?"

"No."

Vicki gestured her agreement with the answer. "If something bad happens that Wyatt could've stopped and he takes an attitude about being benched, we just have to tell him he should've had his head right if he wanted to go on the op."

"Okay. Let's not put it off." Gabrielle said. "He's going to hate being left behind."

Gabrielle turned and led Vicki out of the command pavilion, heading off in search of Wyatt.

. . .

THE SEARCH PROVED TO BE... interesting. Everyone admitted seeing him within the last few minutes, but no one seemed to know where he *was*.

Gabrielle and Vicki stood in the middle of a milling mass of shifters and Magi. A few of the shifters were already in their animal forms. Both ladies stood with their fists resting on their hips, feeling very put upon over not finding Wyatt, when a hush washed over the group like a tidal wave coming into shore. Those standing between the ladies and the town parted at a stately pace like the Red Sea before Moses, revealing the source of the hush. The world's only known living Smilodon trotted up to the group and headed straight for Gabrielle and his Magi sister. When Wyatt reached them, he meowed a greeting and sat on his haunches.

Vicki's resolve melted first. She took the few steps necessary to bring her to her brother's side and said, "I'm sorry, Wyatt, but I would love to pet you."

Wyatt leaned toward her slightly and lifted his head. When he stood on his four paws, his front shoulders were somewhere between his sister's waist and the bottom of her ribcage, so even with Wyatt sitting, it wasn't like she had to bend down.

Gabrielle watched her co-leader sliding her hand along Wyatt's neck, shoulders, and spine, and for a moment, she allowed herself to feel a bit betrayed. Vicki was supposed to be telling Wyatt that he couldn't go on the op, but here she was, petting him like a proud pet owner. Part of Gabrielle wanted to say Vicki's conduct was undignified, but she also felt a little envious. She liked the feel of his fur, too.

"Are you ready for this?" Gabrielle asked.

The massive cat bobbed his head in a clear, affirmative nod.

"You have your head right?"

Another nod.

Gabrielle fought the urge to sigh. Fine... so be it. She'd have a quiet word with Wyatt's team leader, but apparently, neither she nor his sister wanted to stand up to him while he was being adorable.

"Okay. I'll trust you this time. As soon as Agents Hauser and Burke arrive, we'll head out."

~

HAUSER SCOWLED at the stylized American flag broach made from polished stones that rested in the palm of her hand. She glanced at Burke and found her equally disbelieving before she returned her attention to Vicki and asked, "So, you're telling me this little thing will protect me from getting shot?"

"Yep, and do the job so much better than your vests. Unlike a vest, if you get shot wearing this, you won't even feel it," Vicki answered, giving the agent her best prom queen smile. "It will protect you from a few other things, too. We don't *think* we'll face anything like the extreme heat of lava, extreme cold of liquid nitrogen, corrosive acid, or poison gas, but it never hurts to be prepared. Naturally, I'll want those back at the end of this; we're very careful about who has imbued items like them."

Agent Hauser looked from Vicki to her fellow agent. Burke said, "I don't know that I want to trust my life to a brooch without proof first."

"Well, we can't exactly shoot you here," Vicki countered. "I wish you'd brought this up before we left Precious."

Burke transferred her glare from Hauser to Vicki. "You didn't *mention* these back in Precious."

Vicki's eyes went almost comically wide. "I didn't? Oh, dearie me... I must be having early-onset senior moments."

Hauser barked a laugh before she could stop herself, and Burke didn't seem to appreciate that at all.

"Besides," Vicki continued, returning to her serious expression, "it's not like your vests are all that reliable. Armor-piercing ammunition or a bullet that comes in on an angle away from the chest- or back-plates will still get you. These brooches will protect you from all of that and more, too. Swords, knives, explosions… the list goes on and on."

"If these charms are so good," Burke asked, "how do you Magi wage your wars?"

Vicki beamed. "That's simple. We don't. There hasn't been a war among the Magi families since the fall of the Roman Empire. In fact, it was the last Magi war that actually caused the fall of Constantinople, the city most humans know today as Istanbul."

Burke gaped. "Seriously? Everyone on the planet has wars."

"We don't, Agent Burke," Vicki countered, her expression and demeanor solemn. "When we have wars, every combatant is a nuclear power in his or her own right. Re-arranging local geography—like… say… causing Mount Vesuvius to erupt—is tame compared to the full extent of our capabilities."

Both Burke *and* Hauser paled.

"Yeah," Vicki continued. "I've read the journals of the depraved madman who did that. Trust me, agents; *no one* wants to see the Magi make war."

Hauser and Burke both pinned the offered broaches to the left shoulder of their shirts without further comment.

A SHORT TIME LATER, Hauser and Burke led Gabrielle and Vicki up the steps of the Millicent Guthrie House. It seemed so odd to nestle a sprawling mansion and its associated grounds in a quiet valley of rolling foothills that fed into the Cascade Mountains, but from all accounts, the mining heiress loved the area more than anywhere else she'd ever lived.

Hauser pressed the doorbell's button a couple times and knocked on the door as well. She wasn't looking forward to having this conversation, especially since she wasn't in a position to reveal much of their evidence about the imminent raid. She expected the discussion to resemble an uphill battle.

The door opened on silent hinges, revealing a pleasant woman in a navy-blue pantsuit.

"Good day, and welcome to the Millicent Guthrie House," she said. "I'm Tammy Beckett, and I'm responsible for hospitality and media relations. How can I help you?"

Hauser presented her identification folio, prompting Burke to do the same. "Hello, Tammy. I'm Special Agent Winnifred Hauser, and these are my associates, Special Agent Burke, Gabrielle Hassan, and Victoria Magnusson. We would like to speak with your executive director and head of security as soon as possible please."

Gabrielle heard the woman's heart rate erupt at the sight of the official identification, and the color drained from Tammy's face almost as quickly.

"I… I'm sorry, Agents," Tammy stammered. "I'm afraid the executive director and head of security are off-site at the moment, attending a conference."

"Then, I'll accept their designees, if you please. This is an urgent matter."

BOOM!

A shotgun blast erupted from a window overlooking the entrance.

~

Tammy locked the deadbolt and dropped the bar across the door as she crouched against the wall.

Hector came running, decked out in full battle rattle. "What the hell happened?"

"How should I know? One of your damn fool eager beavers upstairs blasted away with a shotgun! They're federal agents, Hector! You never said *anything* about the Feds being involved!"

Hector froze. "The Feds?"

"Yes, damn you. I saw the identification and badges myself, and I'm wearing one of your precious charms, so they weren't fake."

"Oh, shit..." Hector growled as he reached for his radio. "I have to stop—"

Before Hector even touched his mic to key it, the radio erupted. "Engage! Engage! Weapons free!"

The entire property erupted in gunfire. Even over the din of several dozen firearms, a ferocious roar unlike anything they'd ever heard shook them out of their heated conversation. Hector and Tammy looked at each other. Their eyes met. Their expressions mirrored one another. Sheer, unadulterated terror.

The forest surrounding the Millicent Guthrie Home consisted of mostly conifers with a few deciduous trees as well. Hundreds of new and interesting scents pulled at my attention as I trotted beside my team leader, and I wondered how wolves coped with having an even better sense of smell. The forest floor under my paws felt rather nice, too.

We were close to the entrance by that point, and there was a clear line of sight to the orphanage's front door. Motion caught my eye, and I watched a window on the second floor of the house edge upward. I saw a flash before I heard the boom of a shotgun. Gabrielle screamed and collapsed.

Sod-covered plywood slats erupted out of the ground all around the house, and people in tactical gear stormed into the light, their weapons at the ready.

Icy claws of fear gripped my heart as I realized we had walked right into a trap. Then, my eyes returned to the stoop. Burke knelt over Gabrielle as Hauser turned from side to side, sidearm in hand. Vicki stood tall, her staff in hand and held high as a shimmering dome winked into existence over them. My eyes went to Gabrielle, her expression contorted in a rictus of pain. Icy fear sublimated into fiery rage, and I filled the valley with my roar.

I erupted from the tree line already moving at a full sprint, and I wasn't alone. A dire wolf fell in beside me, and hundreds of shifters followed us. Cougars. Wolves. Bears. Lions. Tigers. Eagles. Hawks. Falcons. Our force contained almost every species of predator shifter known to exist.

I reared up to shred the closest enemy, my claws extended to slice his chest to ribbons. Except they didn't. My claws stuck in his vest. I pulled him down with me, but the vest had to be a stab vest or something like it. I couldn't rip through it. In fact, my claws were stuck in it. More enemies stacked up to my right, charging up out of the ground, and I snarled at them, even as I shook my paw in a futile attempt to dislodge my first victim.

Hmmm... perhaps angular momentum would succeed where gravity failed.

I dropped my right side into a roll and put every ounce of strength I had into lifting the man stuck in my claws. I brought my foreleg up and over, aiming the man for the leading ranks of his own people. At the apex of his screaming flight, I retracted my claws. Thankfully, the two movements combined to free my claws, and the man struck his comrades square in their chests. The collision turned into a pile-up.

BOOM!

The shotgun on the second floor blasted again, peppering my side and the ground to my right. I completed my roll and stood. I looked up at the window and roared my defiance. I couldn't see much through the glass with the sun above creating glare, but the opening was wide enough that I saw a hand work the shotgun's pump action.

Hoping Vicki's dome wasn't just a light show, I made a charging leap toward it. I wished I could cheer when my paws touched solidity, and I used it as a springboard to pivot and leap at the offending window. The crash of shattering glass accompanied by terrified screams heralded my arrival on the second floor. I left paw prints and claw marks in the wall as I used it as a springboard, too, to arrest my forward motion, then pivoted to pounce on the wielder of the shotgun. I rode him to the floor in my pounce, and the sheer weight atop my paws crushed his shoulders when he hit the floor. A quick swipe of a claw opened his throat and painted my chest and neck in arterial spray, but I didn't care.

The door was closed, and I wasn't about to shift just to manipulate a doorknob. I pushed off the soon-to-be corpse beneath me and struck the door in a bounding leap. The door broke free of the framing, and both it and I fell into the hallway beyond. My perch wasn't level, though, and I thought I heard a strangled scream beneath the door. I hopped like I was testing a trampoline, eliciting more sounds of distress.

Moving off the door, I swept the wreckage away to reveal my next victim. The person beneath the door wore gear like the man with the shotgun, and as she struggled to sit up, blood gushed out of her broken nose. I started to kill her, just as I had the man, but I remembered that Vicki liked prisoners. She opened her eyes just then and screamed at the sight of me, her hands scrabbling at the holster on her hip. I let her draw the pistol and batted it away with my paw.

The woman darted a glance to my left and rolled away from me, covering her head with her arms. I turned to look and took a shotgun blast square in my side before I saw my attacker. The pain was *intense*, and I roared my pain and rage. Blood dripped from my torso and ran down my left legs.

A man with a shotgun stood a few yards down the hall, and I charged him as best I could. The man worked the shotgun's pump action and looked down in horror when the breach locked open. He fumbled with a pouch at his belt and pulled a single shotgun shell, then slapped it home.

Before he could chamber the shell, I lunged up just enough to clamp my jaws around his forearm, and I felt bones break between my teeth. The man forgot all about his shotgun, crying out in pain as I put my paw against his waist. I pushed with my paw as I clenched my jaw and jerked my head toward my right shoulder will all my might. Savage cracks and pops rippled up the arm all the way to the shoulder, and with a savage tear and eruption of blood, I ripped the man's arm from his torso.

The man collapsed to the floor and fell silent as his eyes rolled back in his head. I opened my jaws wide and shook the arm free of my mouth. I turned my attention back to the woman and found her gaping at me in terror. I didn't want her running off before we could interrogate her, but neither did I like my options for ensuring she stayed around. I didn't exactly have shackles or handcuffs in my fur. I gave a resigned chuff and ambled back over to her, where I pushed my right forepaw under her ankle and placed my left forepaw on top of her knee.

She must have realized what was about to happen,

because she lifted her hands in a 'stop' gesture as she begged, "No... please! I won't—"

Her words cut off, replaced by an agonized scream as pushed down with my left paw and snapped something in her knee. I removed my paws as gently as I could, then limped off in search of the next enemy.

~

WHEN SOMETHING massive crashed through an upstairs window, Hector looked at Tammy and shook his head. The so-called ambush was not going well at all, especially if they really were Feds outside. He gestured for Tammy to cross the foyer to him. She seemed wary about it, but she hustled in a crouch and knelt at his side.

"I think this is going south faster than a flock of geese in September," Hector whispered. "Let's get out of here. Everyone should be engaged at the front of the building by now. Let's take the tunnel to the truck stop and use one of the emergency vehicles to be somewhere else and fast."

"Wha-what about everyone else?"

The sound of what seemed like a door breaking filtered down from the floor above. One of their mercenaries charged up the steps, shotgun in hand. He fired, and another ferocious roar shook the house.

Hector pointed toward the roar, as he asked, "Do you really want to meet whatever made that?"

Tammy shook her head several times in short, rapid jerks.

"Let's go, then. I'll key the demolition charges on the tunnel after we're through."

23

_____

The silence filling the valley held an eerie quality. Gabrielle waved away one of the Magi with the healing talent. Her shifter healing saw to the injuries caused by the buckshot. All that remained was ruined and bloody clothing. She looked over the remnants of the battlefield—such as it was—and felt a swell of gratitude for her primogenitor Alpha. Wyatt's overreaction and divergence from the plan probably saved them crucial moments of surprise or shock at the attempted ambush; she wasn't sure even a lion or tiger shifter could beat his roar.

Speaking of Wyatt... where was he? No one had seen him since he used Vicki's shield as a springboard to enter the upper floor window. He left a trail of savaged bodies in his wake, but the trail faded deeper in the house.

Gabrielle's eyes returned to Wyatt's sister where she sat off to one side with a number of other Magi. Each of the Magi—Vicki included—held a sixteen-ounce bottle of orange juice in one hand and a handful of cookies in the other. Apparently, extended use of their talents under stress presented symptoms like hypoglycemia in Magi. She saw

Vicki break out in a goofy grin mere moments before a cold nose nudged her elbow. Her reflex to flinch and yelp completed the actions before she could exert control, and she turned to see a sabertooth cat looking up at her.

"There you are," Gabrielle said. "We were getting a little worried. Are you hurt?"

Wyatt shook his massive head.

Gabrielle leaned to the side and took in the blood-matted fur. "Are you sure?"

Wyatt nodded, then he made an obvious point of looking at the artifacts of her previous wounds.

"Yes, I know. It hurt like a bastard, but I'm fine now. You didn't stop to think about shifter healing before you charged in, did you?"

Wyatt dropped his eyes to the ground and shook his head like an embarrassed schoolchild.

Gabrielle ruffled the fur on his head, and she didn't have to reach far. Even with Wyatt hanging his head, it was still about level with the bottom of her hips. "It's okay. You probably saved us from being completely surprised by the ambush. I don't think they were prepared for a charging Smilodon. When we get back to Precious, the first thing we're doing is washing that blood off your fur. I don't understand it, but it will be there every time you shift until you do wash it off. We might as well take care of it sooner rather than later." Then, she giggled. "Don't worry; I'm sure Vicki will find us some pet-friendly shampoo."

The silent look Wyatt gave her spoke volumes.

"Come on," Gabrielle said, fighting valiantly to restrain her humor. "Vicki was worried about you."

Gabrielle staggered when Wyatt nudged her with his shoulder as he passed on his way to see Vicki.

Vicki finished her cookies and orange juice by the time

Wyatt reached her. He looked her over and made a happy chuff when he didn't find any injuries.

"Yes, I'm fine," Vicki agreed. "I was just a little woozy. Sustained use of our talents under stress can cause symptoms like low blood sugar, and that's why I'm sitting over here with the rest of the cool kids. Some Magi get migraines if they use their talent too much."

Karleen trotted up to them and sat beside Wyatt, then leaned into him. Wyatt turned to look at her, and she returned his curiosity with a playful nip at his nose.

Vicki faced Gabrielle and asked, "So, did we get anything to make this nightmare even slightly successful?"

"We have all these prisoners to interrogate and anything they left in the house," Gabrielle replied, waving her hand in the general direction of the bound survivors. "One of the Magi found a broach just inside the main door that looks like the work of a hedge wizard, but we'll know more once we've had time to investigate everything. We should take Wyatt with us in his animal form when we do interrogate them, though. There's a woman with a bashed nose and savaged knee who's absolutely terrified of him. Keeps babbling about how he ripped off a guy's arm."

Wyatt nodded twice before gesturing to his bloody fur with a sweep of his head.

"Oh, that's the guy who shot you?" Gabrielle asked.

Wyatt nodded.

"I would say that'll teach him, but he bled out before the healers reached him. So, I guess that'll teach the rest of them."

Travis and Shelly arrived, and they both shot nervous glances Wyatt's way before they turned to Vicki.

Travis said, "All the prisoners who can be healed have been. We were going to give the healers a few minutes to catch their breath, but they'd rather do that back at the camp in Precious. So, unless there's something else left to do here, I think we're done."

Vicki nodded and pushed herself to her feet. "Gabrielle, are we ready?"

Gabrielle turned to look at the mansion. "I think we still have intel teams going through the place. Can you leave one Magi capable of teleportation for them?"

"Already arranged," Shelly replied. "One of our people on the intel team is also Master-certified in long-distance tele-portation, and you don't need an assault rift for ten or fifteen people."

Gabrielle's eyes roved over the scene once more, then shrugged. "Do they have a way to call for help if more of these people show up after we leave?"

"They do," Shelly answered.

"Then, I guess we're done here."

GABRIELLE STRETCHED and rolled her shoulders as she stood off to one side of the arrival zone in Precious. No matter where she went—or the method she used to travel—she always felt better when she returned home.

Karleen arrived at her side. Back in her human form, the dire wolf primogenitor stood in a t-shirt, denim cut-off shorts, and sandals.

"Well, that was fun," Karleen remarked as she shook out her hair. "Those hidden mustering areas looked like they prepared to ambush us. I guess they didn't expect a Smilodon who'd lose his shit over you getting shot. What happened to the two Feds?"

Gabrielle winced. "They... well, they weren't ready for Wyatt on the warpath. They fertilized the shrubbery back at the orphanage with their breakfast, almost as soon as the shooting stopped. The last I saw, Hauser seemed okay, but Burke still looked like vomit was imminent."

"Yeah, Wyatt is really something. I mean… we all can tear through humans like tissue paper, but he just makes a mess while he does it."

"You're one to talk," Gabrielle riposted. "I just hope none of those throats you ripped out belonged to people with crucial information."

Karleen at least had the good sense to look sheepish. "Sorry. I'm not used to needing survivors."

Gabrielle shrugged. "There's no point in getting wound up about it. Besides, ripping out those throats may have saved lives. I just didn't want you thinking Wyatt was alone in the contest of carnage. Oh, hey… speaking of Wyatt, I need some help. Do you have a bikini close?"

Karleen's confused expression was adorable, and Gabrielle fought the urge to smile.

"He has blood matted in his fur all down his left flank, and I was going to wash it out," Gabrielle explained. "Want to help?"

"Sure! Do you think Hank has bikinis in stock?"

"He should. That's where I bought mine." Then, a thought occurred to Gabrielle. "Might want to get a pair of flip-flops, too."

Karleen smiled and nodded. "Good catch on the flip-flops. Where should I meet you?"

"It's about time to introduce Wyatt to his new house. Ask Hank for directions to the Alpha's home; we'll be out back."

AFTER ALL THE nods to reassure everyone I was okay despite my left side being covered in dried blood, my neck felt like giving up and letting my head fall off. Gabrielle told me not to shift back until she washed the blood out of my fur, and I trusted her judgment about it. I already felt uncomfortable with how the matted blood pulled at my fur as I moved.

I sat beside Vicki while she worked through reports and waited for Gabrielle to collect me. I didn't know where we'd go to wash off the blood, but I couldn't wait. I just hoped she didn't follow through on her threat to have Vicki get some pet-friendly shampoo.

Gabrielle leaned into the pavilion and waved for me to follow her. I stood and nudged Vicki with my shoulder to say goodbye, then padded outside. I fell into step with Gabrielle on her left side. She still wore the ruined clothes from the raid, but I still wanted to keep my bloody fur away from her until she was ready to help me wash it off.

"So, we're going across town to the Alpha's house," Gabrielle said.

I froze. The Alpha has his own house? I suppose it was better than racking up a huge hotel bill, but wasn't the place full of Jace's stuff?

Gabrielle stopped and laid her hand on my shoulder. "It's okay, Wyatt. First, you're Alpha now, and second, Alistair had Jace's stuff boxed up already so you didn't have to deal with it."

Oh. That was better. I guess having the house meant I could get the stuff from my old apartment out of storage, but the whole situation still felt odd to me.

We resumed our walk, even as my mind swirled over moving into the Alpha's house. What else waited to surprise me?

THE ALPHA'S house was a single-floor ranch house. The walls were a gray stone, and the roof was the new metal slats with curved ribs that had become so popular. These metal slats were green, and after a few moments, I realized I liked it. The green gave the stone house the impression of a freshly thatched roof.

Gabrielle led me around to a gate in the privacy fence beside the detached garage and let me into the backyard. She busied herself with the garden hose while I waited. She ran it out to where I stood and dropped it on the ground.

"Okay," she said. "I'll be right back. Wait for me here?"

I bobbed my head in a nod and sat on my haunches to wait.

One thing I've noticed is that time doesn't mean much when I'm in my animal form, so I wasn't really sure how much time passed when I heard the gate open and close behind me. I turned to look... well, damn. Gabrielle *and* Karleen headed toward me, and they both wore bikinis. Maybe this wouldn't be as bad as I thought.

"I THINK THAT WENT WELL," Karleen said as she stretched out on the chaise lounge in the backyard of the Alpha's home.

Gabrielle lazily turned her head to look at her partner in crime from her own lounge and smiled. "You do, do you?"

Karleen nodded. "Yeah. Now, I will say there are far more interesting and enjoyable ways to spend an afternoon than shampooing a Smilodon. Still, though, I think we made an excellent impression on him. I think we made our intentions clear."

"I'd say so," Gabrielle agreed. "Wyatt didn't seem too interested in leaving to find clothes, did he?"

"I still say he should've just shifted back to human. He could've always found clothes later."

"Sure about that? I mean... that was a lot of cat to shampoo. I'm kinda worn out."

Karleen sighed. "Yeah, you're probably right. You know, I'm sure Wyatt isn't as tired as we are."

Gabrielle snorted a laugh. "Of course not. He just had to stand there."

"Did you see him flinch when we popped the cap on the shampoo bottle? He was so busy looking at us that he never realized we had it."

"I know," Gabrielle replied, then gave over to giggles. "It took all I had not to laugh at how he jumped."

"Did you think to bring sunscreen?"

Gabrielle groaned. She didn't want to move, but at the same time, she didn't want a sunburn. Shifter sunburns were the worst. With shifter healing, sunburns shouldn't be a thing, right? Wrong! Shifter healing kicked in and started repairing the damage even as the sunburn formed; the whole process created a low-grade tingling burn as the UV sun rays and shifter healing fought each other that was right up there with nails on a chalkboard for the torture factor. Almost every shifter experienced one sunburn... and only one. That was sufficient for the shifter to learn a valuable lesson.

"Come on," Gabrielle said as she rolled to a sitting position. "If you're going to be such a killjoy, there's no reason for you to lay around, especially when Wyatt hasn't even formally taken possession of the house yet."

Karleen sighed as she stood. "I suppose you're right. I think I'm going back to the hotel for a good soak in the bath. Besides, you'll thank me when you're not suffering later."

Gabrielle smiled as Karleen fell into step beside her. "A nice soak sounds great right now. Thanks for that idea. Tomorrow, we get to figure out how they were able to build an ambush after Magi scouted them."

Karleen unlatched the gate and gestured for Gabrielle to precede her through it. Then, she pulled the gate closed behind her and made sure it latched. Gabrielle walked with her to the hotel, where they parted ways.

~

WYATT SMILED as he laid out clothes on the bed in his hotel room. If his old colleague knew he'd just spent almost an hour getting shampooed by two gorgeous women in bikinis, the poor soul would drop dead from envy that very instant. Maybe there was something to that pride business after all.

Of course, there is, the growly voice remarked. *I'm rarely wrong.*

You've been silent for quite a while, Wyatt commented. *I thought you might have left me.*

The growly voice conveyed a sense of a disparaging snort. *That's impossible. There is no 'you.' There is just me. Why would I leave me?*

Yeah, that does sound weird. Did you enjoy the bath?

A sense of smug satisfaction filled his mind, and Wyatt fought the urge to grin. It was a shame he felt duty-bound to find Alistair and find out what else waited to surprise him as Alpha. Wait... Gabrielle was a born shifter, and she grew up inside the shifter world. Shouldn't she be able to educate him on being Alpha just as easily as Alistair?

Hmmm... let's think about that. Option A: learn about a new role I didn't want with not just a guy but a guy old enough to be good friends with Grandpa. Option B: learn about it with Gabrielle and possibly Karleen, too. Yeah... only an idiot would choose Option A.

But the first thing I'll ask Gabrielle is why I still smell like pet shampoo after shifting...

Hector leaned back against his seat as he watched the footage from the hidden cameras scattered around their fake orphanage. There was no denying it. The old tales about mages were true. His eyes fell on the monitor that held a freeze-frame from the camera above the main door. The image on the screen depicted a shimmering dome that rebuffed all attacks. He had already watched the footage all the way through until they found the camera, so he knew the young woman collapsed the dome by choice instead of it just fading away or wearing out. He almost clicked 'Play' to watch it through one more time, but there was no need. Watching it again wouldn't miraculously give him the hows and whys of it.

Instead, he sought as many good-quality pictures of faces as he could find. He wanted to know who came for them. The federal agents were a dead end; all of his contacts said they didn't exist. So, who were these other people? More importantly, where did they live? If people paid him top six figures for the correct child, what would they pay him for a supposedly extinct cat or someone who could work magic?

In a way, the loss of the orphanage galled him, even if it had been fake. It was the perfect cover. Kids come and go from orphanages all the time, especially if they run away. Perfect explanation for why the place always seemed to have a different group of kids. No one ever seemed to trip to the fact it was a waystation in a massive child abduction ring.

His phone dinged, notifying him of a new email. He looked at the email and sighed. Their broker had a new order. Yet another request for a blond-haired and blue-eyed boy. Seriously? What did they think this was? Some sort of mail-order catalog for kids? He stopped his grumbling when he reached the line that listed how much the couple offered. Talk about a lot of zeroes. Ugh... fine. He might as well send a note to the teams to keep an eye out for a boy matching the requested description. If they got lucky, though, they'd get *really* lucky. A cool two million. Heh. He'd tell whatever team that found the kid they'd only been paid a million and split it between them. Morale for the troops and a stuffed bank account for him. Win-win all the way around.

As much as he wanted to take time to email the "be on the lookout" notice to his teams, Hector knew he needed the people from the orphanage identified. So, with a bemused sigh, he went back to the monotonous task of freeze-framing video footage.

THREE DAYS after the orphanage assault, Vicki left the boutique with a smile. She didn't mind the shifters; in fact, she rather enjoyed them. Especially when Gabrielle and Karleen came to her asking if she wanted to spell Wyatt's clothing to smell like pet shampoo. But for all that she enjoyed her brother's new society, she was a city girl at heart. She liked her shops, her boutiques, her spa days. She doubted

Karleen or Gabrielle even knew what a spa was. No slight to them, either. When you risked your wardrobe every time you lost your temper, it made sense to shop off the rack.

The sun shone down from a cloudless sky, warming her face, as she considered her next stop. Grandma had been after her to attend one of the Assembly's balls again, something about a cute son of some family or other. She didn't feel like she was in the market for a new suitor at the moment—being far more interested in helping Gabrielle and Karleen catch her brother—but it never hurt to keep Grandma and Grandpa happy.

A man fell in at her side and looped his arm around her. Just as she started to protest his unwarranted familiarity, she heard his rough voice say, "Hello, princess. You've led us on quite the chase."

Something sharp pricked her neck, and the world seemed to go blurry before everything faded to black.

I SAT with Gabrielle and Alistair in the first of what promised to be many "how to be an Alpha" teaching sessions. My mind kept wandering, though. Both Gabrielle and Karleen had been thoroughly unhelpful when I asked them about still smelling pet shampoo, and the scent persisted... even across laundry runs and human showers and baths. The thought occurred to me that, perhaps, I asked the wrong women. The situation had all the hallmarks of my sister.

My cell phone rang, and that was such an odd occurrence that I checked it. Grandma. Why would Grandma being calling me? We talked just the night before, and it was usually a couple days between calls for us. I apologized to Gabrielle and Alistair, then accepted the call.

"Hi, Grandma. What's up?"

"Wyatt, is your sister with you?"

I frowned. "No, I don't think so. I haven't seen her since the Magi tore down their field encampment. Hang on." I turned my attention to Gabrielle. "Is Vicki in town?"

Gabrielle frowned her confusion, the same as me. "No. At least not that I know, anyway. She left with the Magi. You hugged her goodbye, remember?"

"Yeah, that's what I thought," I replied and turned back to the call. "No, Grandma, we haven't seen her. Why?"

"She isn't answering her phone."

I felt my incisors lengthen as I clenched the fist that didn't hold the phone. From Gabrielle's expression, my eyes went feline, too. "What can I do, Grandma?"

"Well, we're not sure yet, dear. We're still piecing every-thing together. I'll call you as soon as we know more."

"Okay, thank you." I ended the call with a thumb tap and gently laid the phone on the table when all I wanted to do was hurl it against the wall and roar my rage that anyone would dare harm my family. And it was my awareness of those impulses that set me back. I had never been a particu-larly angry person, never once lost my cool or gave in to physical displays of anger.

"Are rage problems common?" I asked in a deceptively calm voice.

"They can be," Alistair answered. "Do you want to talk about it?"

"Vicki's missing."

Alistair moved his eyes from me to Gabrielle and then to the tabletop. "If it's foul play, I'm not certain which would be worse for the perpetrators... that Connor finds them first or you do."

"I didn't use to be like this," I protested. "I didn't use to settle matters with my teeth and claws."

Alistair gave him a grandfatherly smile. "Lad, until

recently, you didn't *have* claws. Any shifter is a gestalt of both sides of who they are. The multi-faceted human on one side and the raw, primal animal on the other. The more dominant the shifter, the stronger... no, 'stronger' is the wrong word. I've known many non-dominant shifters who were as strong as any dominant. The more dominant the shifter, the more forceful the animal can be. The more willing to get in someone's face and mix it up to resolve differences. And you're not just a dominant alpha shifter; you're a primogenitor. We don't fully understand primogenitors because there are so few of them that we know of, but those we do know of are in classes by themselves."

A knock heralded Karleen's arrival. She sauntered around the room and sat on my right. "So, what have I missed?"

"Vicki's missing," Gabrielle answered.

Karleen swiveled to face me. "Who do we kill?"

She didn't miss a beat, and she didn't bat an eye at the thought, either.

"We don't know much yet," I explained, "just that she's missing. Grandma said she'll keep me in the loop."

Karleen shook her head. "No, Wyatt, you don't get it. In all the wars we've ever had, it's always been understood that no one touches our family. Combatant family members are one thing, but... well... okay. I suppose you could argue that Vicki is a combatant, but be that as it may, the one thing someone can do to get the attention of *a lot* of pissed off shifters is to attack one's family. All you have to do is acknowledge Vicki as your sister in the greater community, and half the Shifter Nation will stand up and ask who dies. If this *was* foul play, whoever did it doesn't know about the supernatural world; otherwise, they'd understand just what kind of hell they brought on themselves."

"Supernatural world?" I asked. "I thought it was just Magi and shifters."

Karleen snorted a laugh. "Goodness, no. They must be easing you into it. Think about every myth and legend you've ever heard of, and chances are, there's something real at the root of it. Vampires and other forms of undead. Fae. Hedge wizards. Witches. As diverse as vanilla humanity is, so is the supernatural world."

"Vicki said something about hedge wizards back at the orphanage. What's the difference between hedge wizards, witches, and Magi?"

"The same difference as there is between a shade-tree mechanic and someone who went to school for it. Yes, family members train Magi for the most part, at least at the social level your family is at, but Magi have actual schools and universities that study the nature of their talents and how they do what they do. If Vicki hadn't been a Magnusson and Merlin's literal great-great-granddaughter, she would've gone to one of those when she first manifested her talents."

The thought that Grandma might have known *the* Merlin pulled me away from the precipice of rage, and I felt a half-smile curl my lips.

"That thought," Karleen said. "What is it?"

"Vicki is Merlin's great-great-granddaughter. I can't help but think it would be so cool to have known him. The stories Grandma could tell." I looked up just in time to see everyone else share a look. "Okay… so, what was that?"

"Wyatt…" Alistair began, looking for all the world like he tried to think of a way to tell me I had terminal cancer. "Merlin may not be dead. The rumors of his death have always been just that… rumors. The one location certain scholars *knew* was his grave isn't a grave. If he isn't dead and if he learns of this? It will be bad. No, not bad. Apocalyptic."

"Seriously?" I asked, not quite believing the risk could be so great.

Alistair nodded. "Ask your grandmother sometime."

Silence reigned for several moments.

"I don't think we'll make much progress right now," Alistair said at last. "Gabrielle, Karleen... why don't you take our new Alpha out for a run or something? It might help him clear his head."

"But Grandma said she'd call..."

Gabrielle gave me a soft smile. "We have ways of carrying cell phones. Don't worry; if we go for a run, you won't miss her."

VICKI RETURNED to awareness at a snail's pace. Her head felt like it was packed in wool or cotton or some other material meant to smother her thoughts. Something wasn't right. She wasn't sure *what* wasn't right, but she knew it was important, whatever it was. If she could put her thoughts in order, that might help.

Water dripped somewhere close by, and each drop struck something metal. It was a steady *ping... ping... ping...* that brought a metronome to mind. But why was it there at all? The maintenance staff would never let a leak... oh, wait. She wasn't home. She... well, she didn't know precisely *where* she was. The last she remembered, she stood on a sidewalk in the city. She was taking a shopping and spa day for herself.

Her eyes shot wide as she realized what was wrong. She couldn't feel her talent... at least not at its normal intensity. Now that she was back to her full awareness—at least mental awareness—she realized she wore a collar of some sort, too. Was the collar keeping her from accessing her talent? Was that it?

Well, one thing a time. She lay on the floor of a dingy storage-like room. A single bulb quasi-lit the room, and exposed piping ran along one corner. One of the pipes leaked, the source of the dripping water. It didn't look like her abductors disturbed any of her clothes or jewelry, which was good for her on multiple levels. Firstly, they didn't take her for a bit of 'fun.' Secondly, she still wore the emergency bracelet. It looked like a charm bracelet any college-age young woman might wear, and her grandmother drilled into her that she should never remove it, not even for a bath. Her grandmother wove the effects into the bracelet itself, and Vicki could activate any or all of them by breaking off individual 'charms.' Why would they put an anti-magic collar on her but leave the bracelet? Huh... maybe they didn't *know* what the bracelet could do.

She pushed herself to her feet and started a slow examination of her surroundings, turning in place as she did so. She looked for cameras, but it wouldn't hurt to know what she shared her space with, all the same. She spent upwards of ten minutes examining every part of the space she could see. Nothing leapt out at her as a camera—obvious or suspected —but that wasn't necessarily a guarantee. The thought of activating the bracelet galled her. If she could just call her staff, she could damn well rescue herself, thank you very much.

Might as well try...

She closed her eyes, took several deep breaths, and touched the place in her mind where the connection to her staff *should* have been. It felt like a faint whisper at a party. Like she was just on the cusp of the conversation, but not truly close enough to hear. After several moments of no success, she stopped, afraid she might hurt herself somehow. Fine. What did the bracelet have that might help?

The obvious answer was the All-Seeing Eye charm. It was the Magi equivalent of a red SOS flare on the scale of a massive thermonuclear blast. *Every* Magi in North America would know she needed help if she activated that. Not quite her first choice.

Her eyes landed on the flame charms. She really should've paid more attention to the bracelet. One of the flame charms looked like a campfire. The other looked like an open flame. The campfire was a protection against fire or extreme heat; if she activated that one, she couldn't be burned for something like an hour. The open flame charm would burn through whatever she placed it against after activation.

She could always activate the campfire charm and then use the flame charm to burn through the collar. But... imbued items sometimes went *BOOM* if something damaged them sufficiently to destroy them. If only she could see it... Vicki dithered for several moments while she examined her surroundings for anything she could use as a mirror. Nothing.

Fine. Nothing ventured, nothing gained.

She knelt, closed her eyes, and whispered a prayer. Then, she broke the campfire charm free from the bracelet. Less than a heartbeat later, a red aura suffused her entire form. She broke the flame charm free from the bracelet and bent forward so that she was on her hands—well, one hand—and knees. She slapped the already-hot flame charm against the collar and put that hand flat on the floor. After all, if the charm melted the metal, she wanted gravity to pull it away from her, heat protection or no. It was one thing to trust the magic. It was something else entirely to be stupid about it.

Mere moments later, the sound of sizzling metal reached her ears. She wanted to know what was happening, but she didn't dare touch the collar to find out.

SPLAT! A drop of molten metal struck the concrete between her hands, and she fought the urge to cheer. Both her natural impatience and concern that the flame charm might just melt a hole through the collar without completely severing it prompted her to lift her hands and grasp the collar under each ear. Then, she pulled. And pulled. And pulled some more. At long last, after what felt like hours of effort to no avail (but was really little more than a few minutes), the weakened metal of the collar broke free of itself.

Sparks erupted from the collar as it died, and the sole light overhead flickered in time with the sparks. Vicki lifted the remains away from her neck and tossed it away just in time for it to erupt in a massive fan of lightning that shorted out the electrical system and plunged her room into darkness.

But Vicki didn't care. Oh, no. She did not care one whit that she now knelt in total darkness. Access to her talents was back… and just as strong as it ever was.

She held out her right hand and touched the part of her mind that housed the connection to her staff, and it answered. In the wink of an eye, she held a battle-staff passed down across centuries and generations. Not even *Merlin* knew the origin of the staff, at least not according to his journals. It was a dark and almost evil thing, made for one purpose and one purpose only: unbridled warfare and the mass slaughter of one's enemies. It wasn't *quite* sapient, but something lurked within the strands of power woven into wood smoothed and oiled by countless hands across countless years. And there had been far too little carnage lately for its liking.

Vicki used the staff to steady herself as she stood. Her first reflex was to conjure a ball of light, but no one should ever follow the *first* reflex. The ball of light would illuminate her surroundings, sure. But if the collar shorted out the electricity across the entire building, that ball of light would also advertise her location to anyone with working eyes. Instead, Vicki sifted through her memories for a spell that would grant her dark-sight; it was no good for color differentiation at all, but with it, she could see in total darkness without giving away her position.

She drew on her talent and recited the spell and watched it take hold in a series of gradients until she stood in a world of black and white. Well, maybe not black and white, per se. Black and not-black? Just as she acclimatized herself to the strange vision presented by dark-sight, light appeared under the door. Keys jangled as someone unlocked it.

25

M y cell phone blared the alert klaxon of a popular TV show I watched in my teens. It was the ringtone I set for Grandma's and Grandpa's contacts until we brought Vicki home safe. A few of the people at nearby tables shot looks my way, and I made eye contact with one soul who looked particularly belligerent and mouthed, "Bring it."

He chose to go back to his meal. Odd, that.

By then, I thumbed the accept slider to take the call and held the phone to my ear. "Yes, Grandma?"

"We have her," she said, and I felt like jumping to my feet and cheering. "Well, at least we have her location. She used her charm bracelet, Wyatt."

I blinked. Her charm bracelet? "Uhh... Grandma, I don't understand why that's significant."

"Oh, dearie me, of course not. The charm bracelet is something I developed across many years. Your father hated to wear one. It's a series of useful effects embedded in a bracelet, and you activate them by breaking off the appropriate charm. I also built the bracelet to inform me and your grandfather when it's used, plus location, health status, and other things like that. Her adrenaline is up, but her pain response is off, so she's relatively okay for the moment. She used the heat charms, both the protection *and* the damage."

"I want to be with the team that goes to get her," I said, almost growling it out.

"You darling boy, I'm so glad you said that. She's at an abandoned mining facility. We can tell roughly where she is; she's not inside the mine. But there's some kind of teleportation block in place. We can't just bop over there and grab her. We also can't tell anything about the place. We have no way of telling you whether you're walking into five guys or five hundred."

Now, I did growl. "I have a war party just waiting for me to say 'go.' Three hundred shifters ought to be sufficient for whatever we find."

At the mention of 'three hundred shifters,' Gabrielle stood from the table and stepped across to the table where Buddy and his crew sat. She leaned close and whispered for a moment, then returned. Buddy nodded and dropped some bills on the table before he and his crew left the diner.

"Yes, I'd say so, dear. We'll send Magi with you, too, of course… but I doubt they will keep up with you. Two legs are never a match for four."

I nodded, even though Grandma couldn't see it. "I promise we might leave some for them, Grandma, but they shouldn't dawdle."

"Of course not, dear. When do you want the Magi?"

"If I had Vicki's location," I replied, "I'd already be on my way."

Grandma chuckled. "Your grandfather and I have always loved how the two of you hang together. Even with such a fundamental change to your life, Wyatt, or perhaps I should say *especially* with such a fundamental change. Arabella is creating the portal now; she can raise an assault rift. Now, do be careful, Wyatt. I don't know what we'd do if something happened to you, too."

"I will, Grandma, and I'll have Vicki home soon."

We ended the call, and I looked up to see the street outside the diner filled with shifters. Several shifters inside the diner stood as if waiting as well.

The belligerent guy said, "The call went out for a war party to rescue your sister, Alpha."

I looked over the faces of everyone standing and smiled as I nodded. "Thank you all. As soon as the Magi arrive, we'll head out. Let's get our fur on."

WE HAD enough time to go to our homes to leave our clothes and shift. Then, we all regrouped on Main Street. The expression of utter shock when a woman who looked to be in her mid-30s led a group of fifty Magi through a portal was priceless. I guessed she'd never seen a street full of wolves, bears, various breeds of large cats, and a few predator breeds of birds in a column five abreast and a hundred deep. Fortunately, the person who stepped around her was Shelly from the orphanage operation.

"Ah, there you are, Wyatt," Shelly said, walking right up to me. "Is this everyone?"

I bobbed my massive head in a nod.

Shelly turned. "Arabella, we're ready here. Are you ready to raise the assault rift?"

The thirty-something woman jerked a quick nod. "I just need a couple moments."

Just then, a car turned onto Main Street behind the Magi. The driver stopped, honked his horn, and leaned out the window to shout something about clearing the street. I stood and padded over to the edge of the Magi where I could see the driver, and his heated expression vanished at the sight of me. I snarled at him and waved my left forepaw in a shooing gesture. He bobbed a quick nod and almost peeled out after throwing the car in reverse. By the time I returned to my position in the center of the front rank, Arabella began the incantation to create the assault rift.

As Arabella chanted, a circular section of reality as wide as Main Street began swirling like a kaleidoscopic, two-dimensional whirlpool. The swirling increased in rate and intensity over the course of the incantation, and just as Arabella's voice reached its crescendo, the whirlpool bent outward toward us before it snapped back and bowed out away from us. In a flash of kaleidoscopic light and crackling energy, the whirlpool became an assault rift, an archway that spanned Main Street and became a gateway to another place.

I started to move, but Shelly lifted her hand. She said, "The abandoned mine is in the southern Cascades. We haven't been able to determine what sensors or alarms they may have, and this is as close as we could raise a rift... about two miles out."

I nodded my understanding and waved my paw in an 'out of our way' gesture. The Magi quickly complied, especially those who were at the fake orphanage, and I lunged into a distance-devouring lope.

THE DOOR EASED open on silent hinges, and Vicki readied herself. As soon as she saw enough of the guy coming to check on her, she whispered the lightning-fast incantation of the charm spell. The guy stopped and weaved on his feet for a moment, then brought his hands to his face... flashlight and all. When he pulled his hands away, he turned to look directly at her and started to speak.

Vicki held up her hand in a gesture to stop him and

crossed the short distance to stand close. "Only speak at a whisper. Where are we?"

"An abandoned mine in the southern Cascades, Mistress. It's the Gamma-Eight site for this region."

"Gamma-Eight? Explain that."

"We have a whole host of sites. Alpha is the primary list, and they run up through Epsilon. Then, under each letter, there are ten groups of sites. So... Gamma-Eight."

Well, damn. Neither her Magi nor the shifter intel people had even a hint these people were so organized. If they hadn't abducted her, the Magi and shifters probably would never have learned about all this.

"Are we in the actual mine?" Vicki asked.

"No, Mistress. The mine collapsed decades ago. We use the buildings surrounding the old entrance."

"How many people do you have here?"

The guy scratched his chin. "Uhh... something like eight hundred, I think? But most of them are kids. Someone attacked the orphanage and ruined our ambush, and Hector had all the kids from all the regional sites in the surrounding states moved here."

"Define 'most.'"

"Uhh... five to six hundred? Maybe? I know we bring in trucks full of food every week, just to feed them. Can't sell malnourished kids for as much as well-fed ones, ya know?"

Just then, another voice carried over in a shout. "Well, Red? What's the deal? Is she still out?"

"Do you smoke?" Vicki whispered.

The guy—Red, apparently—nodded.

"Shout back that I'm still unconscious and you're going to get a smoke."

"Yeah, she's still out, Frank," Red shouted back. "I'm grabbing a smoke."

Vicki gestured deeper into the room. "Get inside and lay down."

Red did as she bade, but fear dominated his expression. "Are you going to kill me, Mistress?"

"I probably should, but no." Then, Vicki recited the incantation for a sleep spell, and Red's head lolled to one side. As Vicki retrieved his keys, Red started snoring softly. Vicki turned off the guy's flashlight and slipped out of the storage room, locking it behind her.

Six hundred kids? How am I supposed to rescue them and *myself? I need help. Damn. I should've checked Red for a cell phone, but this far out, there probably isn't service anyhow.*

Still, she couldn't pass up the chance. She turned and slipped back into the room, closing the door behind her. She didn't really like the idea of searching the guy for a cell phone, but breaking the sleep spell to ask him might break the charm spell, too.

He didn't make it easy on her, either. In the spell-induced sleep, he was little more than dead weight, and he wasn't small. Vicki finally found a cell phone in a pocket of his vest, and it was locked with a key code. It was one of the models with a fingerprint reader, so she took a gamble and pressed his right index finger against it. Thank goodness, it unlocked.

The first thing she did was set all sounds and tones to silent. No chirping cell phone to give her away, oh no. Huh... the signal meter indicated one bar. Was that enough? It would have to be. She opened the text app and created a new group message, putting in both her grandfather's and her grandmother's cell numbers. She lifted her head to focus on the sounds around her, but she didn't hear anyone moving close. She returned her focus to the phone and tapped out her message.

Hey, it's Vicki. Stole a cell phone. At an abandoned mine.

Southern Cascades. Six hundred kids. Two hundred bad guys. Need help to rescue the kids.

The wait gnawed at her soul. Was there enough signal to get her text out? Were they even watching their phones? While she waited, she turned off the screen lock setting, so even if the screen shut off, it wouldn't lock on her. That took swiping Red's finger again, but no biggie.

A notification popped up just as she finished—New Text Message Received—and she had to keep from cheering. The message came from Grandma.

Oh, dear girl. So glad you're okay. Wyatt's on the way with five hundred shifters. Less than two miles out. Magi follow. Protect the kids. Luv you.

Vicki looked away from the phone and fought the urge to cry. Bawling like a baby over her brother coming to get her wasn't very heroine-like, but everything just became so much easier. All she had to do was find the kids and keep any of these people from taking them, while waiting for Wyatt and the Magi. She could do that. She might have been the heiress to the Magnusson dynasty, but that didn't mean she was ready to face down *two hundred* baddies. Grandpa or Grandma could do it, no problem, but she wasn't to that level yet.

Vicki returned her attention to the phone and tapped out a quick message:

Luv you, too, Grandma. I'll fort up with the kids.

She slipped the purloined cell phone into her hip pocket and lifted her staff in a solid grip. Then, she slipped out of the storage room, re-locked it, and went off in search of the kids.

IT WASN'T NIGHT YET. She saw that as soon as she reached an exterior wall of her building. Whoever built her storage room just put it inside a hollowed-out cave. Hmmm... did that mean it was something like a cellar for food? Vicki moved to a window and searched the surrounding area with her eyes. The mining complex sat in the end of a small box canyon that butted up against the base of a mountain. Cliffs ranging from a mere thirty feet high to over a hundred ringed the complex, with the entrance of the collapsed mine at the very back of the canyon. None of the ramshackle buildings that she could see *looked* like a place to hold six hundred children. She worried about bumbling into a bunkhouse with the baddies, instead of the bunkhouse with the kiddos. That would not go well.

A charmed roving sentry told her where the children were, and she divested him of his weapons, phone, and radio before sending him off into the forest at a dead sprint. He'd sprint until the charm expired... or he died, whichever came first. That was the important thing about charm spells. You couldn't order a charmed person to kill themselves, but you *could* order them to do something with a high probability of death. Hence, 'sprint until you drop' versus 'take your knife and slit your throat.' Subtle difference, perhaps, but very crucial.

She arrived at the building that held the children in short order. One guard paced in front of the door, an automatic rifle hanging across his torso from a speed sling. A quick charm spell revealed that he was the only person assigned to guard the children for the next four hours, so Vicki had him walk around behind the building and lay down in the grass. Then, a sleep spell.

She stopped and leaned against the corner of the building as she surveyed the area. She'd been using magic a lot in the last hour or so, and she felt it. If she kept up at her current rate, hypoglycemia was not too far off. But she couldn't stop. Not yet. She needed to hold this building until Wyatt and his war party secured the complex. These kids were going home today if she had anything to say about it.

Okay. She'd rested long enough. She didn't see anyone, so she slipped around the corner and moved to the door. It was locked. Of course it was. She went back to the sleeping guard and pawed through his pockets until she found a keyring, then went back and unlocked the door. Slipping inside, she found several dozen children looking at her. She quickly gestured for them to be quiet and smiled.

"I'm here to take you home," Vicki said, "but we have to be quiet until my friends arrive. Okay?"

Before she had time to do anything else, a girl who looked around twelve or thirteen pushed her way through the crowd and ran to Vicki, throwing her arms around Vicki in a tight hug. Just when Vicki started feeling a little awkward, the girl released her and took a step back; she grinned and pointed to Vicki's staff.

"You're like me," she whispered.

Vicki blinked. "Like you?"

The girl nodded. "Momma and Daddy said they'd help me pick my staff when I was older."

Vicki fought to keep her expression neutral. How many of these other children were Magi, too? It was one thing to *know* these people took Magi children; it was something else entirely to get hugged by one in the holding facility.

Another child—this one a boy of no more than six or so—arrived at Vicki's side and tugged on her pant leg. Vicki turned away from the Magi child, and the little boy motioned for her to lean close.

When she did, the boy whispered, "What about Daisy?"

"Daisy?" Vicki asked.

The boy nodded. "One of the bad guys took her a little while ago."

Of course. It had all been a little too easy. But she wasn't going to leave without knowing Daisy's fate at least. She'd prefer to take Daisy with her, naturally, but if Daisy was already gone, that might not be immediately possible.

"Okay. I'll go look for her, but since I won't be here to protect you, I'm going to lock the building so no one can get in or out. Can you two pass the word to wait for me?"

The Magi girl nodded, and the boy quickly followed suit.

"All right. Everyone be good, and we'll see about getting you home today. I'll be back as soon as I can. Oh… and if you hear a huge roar here in a little bit, don't be afraid; he's one of the good guys."

That said, Vicki slipped back outside. The incantation to secure the building was not easy, and it would take a considerable chunk of her remaining power. But she wasn't going to leave the children defenseless while she looked for Daisy. She rushed the incantation a little bit, but it took hold, staggering her. She held out her hand to the building and leaned against it for a few moments until she felt steady enough to move. Then, she turned and scanned the compound.

"Right, then," she whispered. "Where would I take a little girl if I was an evil bastard abducting children for money?"

One of the buildings had the look of a mess hall about it, and she felt she could at least peek in a window. She set off, keeping to the buildings and the growing shadows of the late afternoon. She chose avoidance over engagement as she crossed the compound and saw several people; she didn't have the reserves to put everyone she encountered to sleep.

Vicki soon saw people gathering in a central courtyard-like space, and a rough-looking fellow held a small girl by the arm. Dammit. All she could do was to delay them until the cavalry arrived.

Vicki stepped away from the building and strode toward the collection of people with intent. No one noticed her right away, as the imminent confrontation between two men—the one holding the child and another one—kept everyone's focus. She reached earshot of the conversation, still without any kind of challenge.

"Karl, let her go," the other man said. "We don't mess with the merchandise, even if they were not children."

The guy holding the little girl—Karl, apparently—snarled. "I've had it with this punishment duty, Hector. You order us all into the backwoods ass-end of nowhere after *you* botched the ambush at the orphanage, and you have the gall to tell me I can't enjoy myself? Go to hell, and take the rest of the high-and-mighty jackasses around here with you."

That was too good of an opening to pass up. Vicki stepped through the last cluster of people that loosely ringed the confrontation and said, "You first."

Vicki whispered an incantation as she focused on Karl, and it was all she could do to remain impassive when the incantation robbed her of what little strength she had left. Karl, though, didn't fare so well; he collapsed, dead before his head struck the grass. Vicki waved her left hand at the little girl, motioning for the child to come to her, and the little girl almost knocked Vicki flat when they collided.

Hector turned to face her, and Vicki realized she now held everyone else's undivided attention.

"How did you get free?" Hector asked, his tone almost making it a rhetorical question.

Vicki shook her head. "That doesn't matter. If we make a deal right here and now for the children and I to leave peacefully, the day will end a lot better for you."

Chuckles and outright laughter circled through the assembled onlookers, as Hector himself betrayed amusement, saying, "Is that so? Has it occurred to you yet just how outnumbered you are?"

Vicki adopted what she hoped was a cocksure smirk. "Are you truly *sure* about that?"

Hector threw his arms wide. "Little lady, everyone you see here answers to me. If we're so outnumbered, where are your people?"

Before anyone could say or do anything else, motion in the corner of her eye attracted Vicki's attention. A massive shape of tawny fur and curved incisors burst out of the tree line at the top of the thirty-foot cliff and leaped. The first Smilodon to walk the Earth in thousands of years kicked up a cloud when he landed, and his roar rattled windowpanes and the bones of everyone who heard it. Wolves, bears, a few lions, and even a tiger—all led by a black jaguar and a dire wolf—charged into the yard, surrounding Hector's men in a snarling wall that thirsted for their blood.

Vicki watched Hector's bravado vanish, as he stared at her brother in sheer terror. She gave the man her best happy cheerleader smile as she said, "Too late, Hector. You really should've made the deal. Come on, Sweetheart; we don't need to see what happens next."

Vicki hefted the little girl into her arms and turned, walking back toward the building where the other children waited. The shifters were kind enough to wait until they were out of sight, and soon, the screams of the dying and sounds of rending flesh echoed across the compound.

26

The Magi created temporary shelters for the children in Precious and brought in healers to assess their health and wellness. Magi, shifters, and Hauser's branch of its agency worked overtime and then some to identify all the children as well as their families. It was a Herculean effort that would take days to complete, but not even one person in the cast of hundreds already involved begrudged the loss of sleep.

Vicki insisted on seeing the children returned to their families before going home. She called her grandparents to let them know she was back in Precious with Wyatt and his people and that she'd be home once all the children were safe at their homes. Her grandfather grumbled a bit, but her grandmother cheered her on and said she'd have Vicki's favorite pie waiting for her when she stepped through the door.

~

THE SECOND DAY Precious hosted the children, Hauser and Burke tracked down Wyatt. They found him sitting with Vicki, Gabrielle, Karleen, and Alistair in the diner, and they looked both apologetic and determined at the same time.

"Wyatt," Hauser said, "do you have time to take a call?"

Wyatt shrugged. "That depends. If it's a telemarketer, no. I'm on my first break in six hours of interviewing children to help find where they belong."

"It's the deputy director in charge of my branch," Hauser replied.

"Oh," Wyatt remarked, much of the fire gone from his tone. "I suppose I probably should."

Hauser handed him her phone, and Wyatt said, "Wyatt Magnusson."

"Hello, young man. I'll trust Special Agent Hauser introduced me and get right into it. Both the Shifter Council and the Magi Assembly tell me you were the one in charge at the sharp end of the spear. Is there anyone or anything you want to hand off to Uncle Sam?"

"We're still sifting through everything we found at the old mine, sir," Wyatt explained. "I imagine the entire operation is sufficiently large that, yes, we would greatly appreciate the assistance of the United States government in rolling up all their teams. At present, though, we don't have a clear enough picture to lay a stack of evidence on your desk."

"Makes sense," the deputy director replied. "What about the people responsible?"

Wyatt fought the urge to shudder as his own memories of the slaughter rushed to the forefront of his mind. "No, sir; not at the moment. We handled it."

"Fair enough. I appreciate your time, and I'll leave Special Agents Hauser and Burke as your official liaisons at least until this ghastly operation has been thoroughly broken. I hope you don't need them, but it never hurts to have a couple federal Special Agents to smooth the way."

"Thank you, sir," Wyatt said. "I can tell you they've represented your agency well."

"If you don't mind, I'll see that statement makes it to their personnel files. That will reflect well on them when we consider them for future positions of authority."

Wyatt smiled. "I don't mind at all, sir, and I'm happy to write up a formal statement once we're at the end of this."

"I'll hold you to that, lad. Well, I've taken up enough of your time. Unless you have anything else for me?"

"No, sir, and thank you again."

The call clicked off before Wyatt could thumb the 'end call' button, and he returned the phone to Hauser. Both Hauser and Burke looked a little awed that Wyatt gave them the endorsement he did for no more than they had been involved, but they nodded their thanks and left the diner.

A WEEK LATER...

I leaned against the railing of the back deck, looking out over my grandparents' sculpted and landscaped grounds. A peculiar calm always descended on me whenever I visited the home where I grew up, and I savored my keen senses as I took in all the little scents carried on the breeze from the gardens. I knew without a doubt that I would always be welcome here, and yet, I felt like I belonged in Precious more.

My thoughts drifted back to a conversation I had sat in on between my grandparents and Vicki. The charms we found at the orphanage and the collar Vicki had worn were definitely made by a hedge wizard. Despite the Magi's preference of looking down on the 'lesser practitioners,' the hedge wizards and witches of the world, they were not totally inept, and no matter what the Magi might prefer, magic was magic. If a person was gifted with it, the person could learn to use it, regardless of *what* they learned. Grandpa had been very clear that the Assembly sought the source of those charms and the collar, but it might be some time before any information surfaced.

Motion to my right drew my attention, and I saw Miles stop an arm's length away and lean against the railing with his back to the gardens. I had known Miles my whole life, even though I never really understood his role... general handyman or some such, I had always guessed. He stood equal in stature to my grandfather, and he wore a well-maintained snow-white beard that touched his sternum. A worn khaki Fedora rested atop his head, and I could not remember ever seeing him without it. When he spoke, his voice hovered toward the deeper end of the spectrum, but not quite as deep as the likes of James Earl Jones. I finally recognized the look in his gray—or possibly hazel—eyes; Miles had survived his share of carnage and then some.

"It's a fine thing having the Young Miss back," Miles said, his voice carrying hints of an accent I couldn't quite identify. "Ye do your family proud, Young Master."

"Me?" I asked, taken off guard. "I'm not the Magi; Vicki is." Then, the bottom dropped out of my stomach. Did Miles even *know* about Magi?

"Lad, do ye think I spent the last thirty years pruning hedges and weeding flowerbeds around here to watch yet another Magi come into her power? As dear a lass as she is, your sister isn't the special one in the family. That'd be you... Primogenitor. A destiny awaits ye, lad; never be afraid to stand up for what you *know* is right."

I gaped. Mind blown. How did he know? Had he overheard my grandparents talking? Then, recognition of his accent clicked in my head. Gaelic... maybe even Celtic?

"Your name isn't Miles, is it?" I asked.

The old gardener shrugged. "It's as good a name as any other. Fits in rather well around here, too."

He pushed himself off the railing and sauntered away. He stopped at the top of the short steps that led down to the garden and turned back to me. An impish smirk curled his lips, and I couldn't believe how much he looked like Vicki in that moment.

"I will tell you this much, lad," he said. "The Lady o' the Lake is a damn good kisser."

WHAT'S NEXT?

Have you read "Lone Wolf," Karleen's origin story?

If not, sign up for my newsletter to get it:
https://kfplink.com/tps

∽

"Roc," Book 2 of the Primogenitor Saga, is available for pre-order now.

Visit the book's page to choose your vendor:
https://kfplink.com/roc

RATE THIS BOOK

Did you enjoy this story? If you did, please consider leaving a review.

Reviews are the lifeblood of visibility for independent authors, especially on the eBook retailers. The more reviews a book has, the more visible it will be on the retailers' sites.

I appreciate all reviews…good, bad, or indifferent.

AUTHOR'S NOTE

6 FEBRUARY 2021

First and foremost, thank you for reading…both the novel and these notes! I hope you enjoyed *Smilodon*!

This is my eighth novel, with many more to come, and I'm currently working on the second books of the Primogenitor Saga.

This was a fun story to tell. It was bouncing around in my mind for about a year before I settled down to write it. Circumstances reached the point that I couldn't concentrate on what I thought I needed to write, and I took that as a sign.

I have at least a one-sentence summary for something like 130 books across 14 series. Most of them are Fantasy in one form or another, but there are a few Science Fiction (well, Space Opera, really… but what's a label between friends?) as well. Knowing how my mind works, there will be more.

This is also my first "wide" novel, in that the eBook is not exclusive to Amazon. These stories are my primary source of income, and eBooks are the predominant share of that. One of the few things that both side of the US government can agree on right now is that something has to be done about

Big Tech (i.e. Amazon, Apple, Facebook, & Google), and I cannot help but think of the fate of Ma Bell (https://kfplink.com/MaBell), which is why I decided to take my catalog "wide."

The Histories of Drakmoor eBooks will remain exclusive to Amazon to fulfill a promise I made to my readers at the start of the COVID-19 Pandemic, here in the USA and back in 2020). But all new series will be available almost anywhere eBooks are sold.

If you're still reading this, thanks for the dedication…or perhaps the curiosity. :) As I said above, I hope you enjoyed reading *Smilodon*. Thank you.

ACKNOWLEDGMENTS

There's an old saying: it takes a village to raise a child. I don't know if that's true or not, but it certainly seems true where publishing a novel is concerned. You would not be reading this were it not for contributions from several people.

Did you like the cover? Dolton Richards (doltonrichards.com) is an awesome artist, and what strikes me as hilarious in its irony is that I've known of him *for years*. He's a friend of two of my closest friends.

No story should reach the public without passing through the scrutiny of a quality editor or editors, and TF Poist is one of the best.

I also want to thank J. M. Martin for proofreading the manuscript and providing one last set of eyes.

I'm sure there are many who will see this next paragraph and think, "Goodness, he's acknowledging his parents and grandparents *again?*" My greatest regret is that I cannot hand my grandfather, Bob Miller, a paperback copy of my novels. So, yes… the Acknowledgements page of *every* book I publish will have the paragraph that follows. Consider yourselves forewarned.

Without my grandparents, Bob & Janice Miller, I honestly don't know where I'd be today; my grandfather taught me to read and love reading, and my grandmother taught me to develop and exercise my imagination. This novel (not to mention my life in general) certainly would not have happened without my parents, Vernon & Judy Kerns.

THE NOVELS OF ROBERT M. KERNS

For a complete and accurate listing of all publications, both currently available and forthcoming, please visit Knightsfall Press.

Knightsfall Press - Books

https://knightsfall.press/books

SO...WHO'S THE AUTHOR?

Robert M. Kerns (or Rob if you ever meet him in person) is a geek, and he claims that label proudly. Most of his geekiness revolves around Information Technology (IT), having over fifteen years in the industry; within IT, he especially prefers Servers and Networks, and he often makes the claim that his residence has a better data infrastructure than some businesses.

Beyond IT, Rob enjoys Science Fiction and Fantasy of (almost) all stripes. He is a voracious reader, with his favorite books too numerous to list.

Rob has been writing for over 20 years, and *Awakening* is his debut novel.

facebook.com/RobertMKerns

amazon.com/author/robertmkerns

bookbub.com/authors/robert-m-kerns

Made in the USA
Middletown, DE
09 September 2021

47861048R00177